OFFICE MATE

BY KATIE ASHLEY

Love & hugs,
Katie
Ashley

CHAPTER ONE

Isabel

There are some days that are destined to change your life. Ones when you're old and grey, you'll look back on as the day when everything became different—the day when your ship finally came in. If you're a Type A extreme planner like me, you're lucky enough to know when and where fate is going to smile on you. Therefore, you're able to prepare for the enormity of the moment. You've thought out every scenario and have a plan of action for each and every possibility to ensure you make the most of your day.

The day of my own personal life changer had arrived. Everything I'd been working for professionally converged on this moment. The years spent slaving over textbooks and writing countless essays while getting my undergrad and MBA, the sixteen-hour work days after landing my job, the weekends spent in the office away from family and friends—it all came down to this promotion, the day I, at just twenty-nine, would be elevated to a vice president in investment banking at the Callahan Corporation.

Sorry, I had to add that part. It probably sounds pretentious, or like I'm bragging. Trust me, I hate when people do that—like, it's a serious pet peeve. It's just I've been through a hell of a lot to get where I am. I was the first member of my family to graduate college, let alone get a graduate degree. As a kid who grew up on free lunches and thrift store clothes, the odds were stacked against me from the start. A lot was made harder simply because I possessed a vagina.

I'll be forever grateful to the women before me who shattered the corporate glass ceiling. The thing is, even in 2018, the shards from that glass can still cut you. Women have to work harder to get where they are, and for someone like me who didn't come from a prestigious family with connections, I had to do even more.

Back home in my small, backwoods town of Dawsonville, Georgia, my family wasn't part of society. If you want a small glimpse into my childhood, watch *Sweet Home Alabama*. While my father didn't do the Civil War reenactments, I did grow up in a double-wide trailer, and my mom did shove me into every imaginable pageant to pad my scholarship fund to get me the hell out of town. She wanted me to have all the opportunities in life she hadn't. It's why when I was eight, she went to battle with the administration at my elementary school to allow me to skip a grade. Little girls who lived in trailers weren't always the first ones on the list for special testing and advancement. I was grateful I'd inherited her intelligence and tenacity, along with her auburn hair and blue eyes. The junk-in-the-trunk booty she'd graced me with wasn't exactly on my preferred trait list, but such was life.

Thinking of my mom caused a wave of homesickness to wash over me. She was a thousand miles and what seemed like a lifetime away. When I was just twenty years old, I'd traded the Peach State for the Big Apple. After transferring to Columbia, I'd finished my undergrad before entering the accelerated MBA program. While my dad had harbored hopes I might come back to Georgia and find work in Atlanta, I'd taken a job with the company where I'd interned: the Callahan Corporation. I made it home for Sunday dinner at least once a month, even though my parents and sister teasingly called me a Yankee.

Speaking of work, I eyed my phone. It was five minutes until my alarm went off. In spite of my scheduled wake-up time not having come yet, I'd already been awake for an hour. Staring up at the ceiling, I'd gone over in my mind exactly what I planned to say when the job was formally offered to me, my own version of an Academy Award acceptance speech. I wanted to appear humble, yet at the same time highlight the reasons I'd been chosen. Remember how I said I hate bragging? Anyway, I'd even gone so far as to practice it in front of the mirror the previous night to analyze not just my word choices but also my facial expressions.

It's probably right about now you're thinking I'm a wee bit of a perfectionist. The phrase "control freak" might be flashing like neon in your mind, and trust me, I get it. In fact, I embrace my perfectionist side. Without that essential yet equally annoying quality, I wouldn't be where I am today.

With a pep in my step I didn't usually possess in the mornings, I threw back the covers and hopped out of bed. My dog, Dani, popped one eye open and gave me a disapproving look for disturbing her sleep. Once I got into the bathroom, I flipped on my iHome. Instead of an upbeat pop tune or a hardcore rap beat filling the room, it was the latest stock market updates from Bloomberg Radio. Perfectionist, remember? I liked to get a feel for the markets first thing.

After showering, I took extra time on my hair and makeup. Most days, I went for a look that was natural but still utilized all the tools in my arsenal, including eyeliner, mascara, and lipstick. Since I was knocking on thirty's door, I couldn't quite get away with what I had in my early twenties.

Once I was satisfied with my makeup, I tied my long hair into a trendy twist at the base of my neck. I snickered at the thought that I could pull off a sexy librarian look. Of course, I'd tossed my glasses years ago after getting Lasik.

Now that I was finished in the bathroom, I headed back into my bedroom to get dressed. I slipped into a cream-colored silk shirt and a navy pinstripe skirt that hit just at my knee, and then I slid on my matching suit jacket. As I straightened the lapels, I nodded at my reflection in the mirror.

I threw a glance at Dani over my shoulder. "Whatcha think, girl? Does Mommy look like a vice president?" Dani's response came in the form of a yawn. "I'll take that as a yes," I replied as I walked over to the bed. "You have fun today at doggy daycare."

Yes, I'm not ashamed to admit I send my dog to daycare. It was the only way a dog as large as Dani could stay sane in the city and not devour my furniture. Thankfully for me and for Dani, they had pick-up and drop-off service.

When I opened my bedroom door, a wave of confetti blasted me in the face. "Happy Promotion Day!" my roommate and best friend, Mila, cried out enthusiastically. Her dog, Drogo, barked in congratulations, which instantly got Dani going. Drogo and Dani were littermates Mila and I had adopted through the rescue where we volunteered—well, it was more like Mila did the hands-on work while I helped out financially. While my job came with many blessings, the one curse was that it didn't leave me a lot of free time.

"Pft," I muttered as I was momentarily blinded by the multicolored bomb that coated my eyelashes and mouth. As soon as I could see and breathe again, I grinned at Mila. "Oh my God, you are too much."

"But you love me anyway," she countered.

"More than you could ever know," I replied before reaching out to hug her. After squeezing her tight, I pulled away to eye her curiously. "What in the world are you doing up this early?"

As the chief makeup artist at the Palace Theater on Broadway, Mila's late nights meant she was always still snoozing when I left for work. From the outside, most people would wonder how an investment banker and a makeup artist were best friends. I'd met Mila when I first came to New York to attend Columbia. While we had attended different schools in the daytime, we'd waited tables in the same restaurant at night.

Though we didn't share similar professions, our hearts were on the same wavelength. We had both traded small-town life for the big city. We both had a soft spot for animals, and we both enjoyed the same movies and television. Two years before when I'd finally felt financially stable enough to buy a decent apartment in the Financial District, Mila had been going through a nasty divorce and needed a place to live. Once she moved in, she never moved out, even though it was a longer commute for her over to Times Square.

With her brown eyes sparkling, Mila replied, "I knew today was a big day, so I decided to get up early."

"Aw, you really are too much, and I thank you." After spinning around, I asked, "How do I look?"

"Like Corporate Barbie."

I snorted. "Seriously?"

Mila nodded. "Totally. Slap you in a box and little girls everywhere would be inspired to be all they can be."

"Isn't that the Army's slogan?"

She waved her hand dismissively. "Whatever. It still works."

"Do I really look that much different than I usually do?"

Eyeing me thoughtfully, Mila replied, "I think it's the severity of the twist that sets everything off. You're more of a ponytail girl."

"If I'd known you were up, I would have asked you to do it."

"Yeah, but then I would have given you some kind of ethereal flair with some side braiding like Daenerys Targaryen."

One thing Mila and I had in common was our adoration for *Game of Thrones*. Although our schedules never worked out to watch it together, we always met for lunch on Mondays to chat about the show.

I drew in a deep breath while debating whether to wipe my already sweaty palms on my skirt. "I will be channeling my inner Daenerys today for sure."

Placing her hands on my shoulders, Mila smiled. "You've got this in the bag, girl. No need to unleash the dragons."

With a laugh, I replied, "Okay, I'll remember that."

"Want me to meet you for a celebratory lunch today?"

"I would love that."

"I'll make sure I'm ready to roll by noon."

"Sounds good. I'll text you when I'm about to leave."

"Mad Dog so we can toast with our favorite margaritas?"

Tapping my chin thoughtfully, I replied, "You think a vice president can get away with one margarita on her lunch break?"

"Hell yeah she can," Mila replied with a grin.

I returned her smile. "Then Mad Dog and Beans it is."

Mila dropped her hands from my shoulders. "Now go get 'em, tiger!"

"Yes, ma'am," I replied with a salute.

"As you head off to take the corporate world by storm, I'm going back to bed."

I grinned as I pulled on my coat. "I don't blame you. Thanks for getting up for me."

She yawned. "It was nothing."

After throwing the strap of my leather laptop bag across my shoulder, I picked up my keys and purse. "See you later." Craning my neck, I called, "Bye, Dani!" This time she woofed in acknowledgement.

With a quick wave to Mila, I headed out the door. I'd chose to live in the Financial District so I could be close to work, and I couldn't have been happier with my decision. Being just four blocks from the office really came in handy with my crazy late-night working hours.

"Good morning, Lloyd," I said to the elderly doorman who had become a friend over the last two years.

"Good morning, Sass," he replied with his usual smile. He'd given me the nickname shortly after I moved in, a subtle nod to my "Southern sassiness", as he called it. "Today is the day, huh?"

"Excuse me?"

He winked. "Mila was telling me about your promotion when she came out earlier to get coffee."

Leave it to Mila to pre-spill the beans to Lloyd. "Well, I haven't officially gotten the promotion yet, but it looks very promising."

"I'm sure you've got it in the bag."

"Thanks, Lloyd. I appreciate that."

"You'll have to tell me all about it tomorrow."

"I promise."

I then started hustling down the street. I can imagine what you're thinking right about now—wasn't I counting my chickens before they hatched by celebrating a job that wasn't officially mine? Okay, so maybe you weren't going for a chicken-specific analogy. That was a favorite of my mom's, and considering I grew up with chickens littering the yard, it wasn't too farfetched.

Anyway, here's why I had reason to put the cart before the horse (another one of my mom's analogies): one of the vice presidents had just retired, and while it usually took quite a few years to get promoted from associate to vice president, I had shown the most productivity and growth, so it was pretty much a given I would take the open position. For the last week, my boss had been preparing me to receive the news of a promotion.

As a creature of habit, I stopped for an overpriced latte at one of the food trucks outside the building. While I could have just waited five minutes and gotten a free coffee inside, I liked to hit the ground running once I stepped into my office.

Just as I rushed forward to head into the building, a wall of muscled flesh plowed into me. The momentum sent the cup of steaming hot espresso and steamed milk crashing against my chest, and the scorching liquid sloshed out, cascading over my blouse and seeping through the light fabric to burn my skin. "FUCK!" I screamed as the fiery trail singed my skin.

"Oh my God, I'm so sorry," a deep male voice boomed above me.

When I jerked my head up to glare at him, the raging inferno of second- or third-degree burns on my boobs were momentarily forgotten in light of the sheer perfection that met my eyes. An Armani-wearing Adonis stood before me, and with his towering height, bulging muscles, and chiseled features, he appeared to have just taken flight off Mt. Olympus—a true god among men.

He certainly was a sight for sore eyes. You didn't get a lot of panty-melting investment bankers on my floor, and if you found an impossibly built hottie with a panty-dropping smile, he was often unfortunately interested in dropping briefs rather than panties—hence the age-old adage about all the good ones being gay.

The reprieve from my pain was short-lived. When I came back to reality, huffing and puffing in agony, the Adonis said, "I didn't even see you."

"While I might be slightly vertically challenged, how in the hell could you possibly miss me?" I demanded, fanning my stinging chest.

"My head was somewhere else."

"Like up your ass?"

He had the gall to chuckle. "Yeah, pretty much."

With the pain subsiding slightly, I surveyed the aesthetic damage to my blouse. Brown, blotchy stains streaked down my top, causing me to groan. "Shit, I'm a wreck."

"Here, let me help." He reached for the crisp white handkerchief in his suit pocket, but instead of handing it to me for cleanup duty, he proceeded to reach out and run his hands all over my chest. While my traitorous nipples had the audacity to harden at the attention, red flashed before my eyes, causing my right fist to ball at my side.

The next thing I knew I was executing an epic right hook to his gorgeous face. As my knuckle connected with his nose, the dream of my perfect day was shattered.

CHAPTER TWO

Thorn

My breath came in rushed pants as my feet pounded along the pavement. The brutally cold February air burned my lungs, making it hard to take a deep breath. It was quite a difference from the desert heat I'd grown accustomed to during the last year of my deployment, not to mention the urban scenery currently surrounding me. As I sprinted down the pre-dawn Manhattan sidewalks, the city that allegedly never slept slowly came alive.

After my alarm had woken me at six, I'd lumbered out of bed. Although I'd been stateside for three weeks, my body still clung to Afghanistan time, which was eight hours ahead of New York.

I hoped like hell that I could shake my wonky sleep patterns soon. Flicking the light on in the closet, I bypassed my comfort clothes, AKA my cammies. Instead, I donned my Under Armour winterized running gear. While I could've been racking up my miles on the treadmill in my home gym, I preferred being outside. It was another throwback to my time in the Army, and it made me feel a little less displaced. If I were honest, it was more of a necessity than a preference. The more daylight hours I spent inside, the more restless I became.

An ache reverberated through my chest, but this time it wasn't from the elements. Rather, it was from the pain of losing the thing that defined me. From the time I was a kid, there was nothing else in the world I wanted to be other than a solider. I'd mastered a salute before I was out of diapers, and I'd relished watching war movies and playing *Call of Duty*. While some kids were scared straight by the threat of military school, I couldn't wait to enroll at West Point. More than anything, I wanted to follow in my father's footsteps.

But now, all of that was over.

Glancing over my shoulder, I shouted, "I know you're back there. Quit being a pansy ass and catch up."

My Secret Service agent, Ty, hustled up to my side. "You've got to stop this, Thorn. You know you're not supposed to go out in public without me," he huffed due to a combination of exertion and indignation.

I shot him a look. "Do you honestly think some disenfranchised voter who hates my dad's policies is going to be waiting to take me out on my six a.m. jog?"

Ty grunted. "You never know. Stranger things have happened."

"Bullshit."

I seemed to be getting a lot of mileage out of that word lately; I'd said the exact same thing to my father after he was elected president and I was issued a Secret Service agent upon my return to the States. I could understand the young children of presidents having agents, and I was even happy to hear my college-aged sister, Caroline, would have armed supervision to prevent some douchebag taking advantage of her, but the president's adult children? It was a little ridiculous, not to mention completely demeaning for someone like me. Considering I'd spent my adult life protecting others, there was no way in hell I was going to agree to having my every move shadowed.

It was bad enough I'd had to leave my military career as a result of my father's presidency, but now I was being emasculated even further. While I might've been forced to leave my post and my fellow service men and women, I'd put my foot down on who was going to be protecting me. I wasn't going to accept some hotshot who had been through the minimal twenty-eight-week Secret Service training program in Georgia and D.C. No, I wanted a seasoned military man. When it came down to it, I hadn't just demanded a military man who had fought in combat and knew what a soldier experienced mentally and physically.

I'd demanded Ty.

Ty Frasier was a half-Brit, half-Scot who had grown up in London's East End, or as he loved to refer to it, the dodgy part. Not only had he been a member of the Rifles regiment in the British Army, he'd trained and worked for the elite Blackstone Security Agency in London. For the past couple of years, Ty had been the personal body-guard for my younger brother, Barrett. Their working relationship had actually started as a personal one—they'd become friends when Ty had first moved to New York from London. That relationship was why I imagined Barrett being pissed at me requesting Ty, but surprisingly, he'd given me the green light.

"Would you just get off my dick and let me do my job?" Ty questioned.

"Fine. I'll try," I grumbled.

"Thank you."

We ran the rest of the five miles in silence. That was another thing I admired about Ty: his integrity. Even though he was a family friend and could have taken advantage of that to screw off, he always had his head in the game, not to mention he took great offense when he wasn't able to do his job as thoroughly as he preferred. While I focused on the run, I knew his senses were on high alert for any danger that might pop up. If—God forbid—some nut-job actually tried to hurt me, there wasn't a doubt in my mind that Ty would give his life for mine.

For that very reason, I really needed to stop being a prick about him protecting me. Truthfully, I needed to stop being a prick to basi-cally everyone. I still felt so much anger and resentment about being forced to give up my military career. You would've thought after what I'd seen in life coupled with my age, I would be better equipped to handle my emotions, but I wasn't. I seemed hell-bent on the childish mentality of making everyone around me as miserable as I was.

As I neared my apartment building, my right leg, which had been aching for the last two miles, began screaming in agony. At what must've been my anguished expression, Ty asked, "War wound giving you trouble?"

I nodded. Five months before, a convoy I was leading had come under enemy fire before a set of roadside bombs exploded all around us. Bastards took out two of my men while I ended up with a leg full of shrapnel. The head surgeon at Landstuhl in Germany told me if one of the pieces had hit just an inch higher, it would have gotten my femoral artery and I would have bled to death. While a solider stares down the Grim Reaper every day he or she is in battle, it was sobering to hear just how close I'd come, not to mention how precariously close it had come to taking off my dick.

Thankfully, the wounds had healed quickly, and I was allowed back in the field a week later, but my stay in Afghanistan was short-lived. Two months later, my dad was elected president. While I was home for the inauguration, Dad had taken me aside. Six weeks had passed since then, and the day was still so fresh in my mind.

"I'm glad to have you home, son."

I'd returned his smile. "It's good being home. Of course, I'm also anxious to get back to the field and finish out this deployment."

Dad's expression had saddened. "Since I was elected, the Department of Defense has made me aware of security concerns. Their latest intel is very troubling."

I'd furrowed my brows at him. "Is my unit facing increasing danger?"

He'd nodded. "But not because of any growing factions."

"I don't think I understand."

"They're in danger because of you."

"Me?"

"You're the president's son, Thorn, a trophy to be won and exploited for political gain. As we speak, forces are working double time to locate you." Dad had shaken his head. "I can't afford the risk."

"But I took an oath to serve and protect this country, not to mention to lead my men and women. I'm sorry, but I refuse to back down just because my life is in slightly more danger than it was before you became president."

"It's simply unprecedented to have a sitting president's child in combat."

"What about Prince Harry? He was able to secretly lead his unit on combat missions when he was in service," I challenged.

"Harry was third in line to the throne, and he wasn't the prime minister's son."

"He still would have been 'a prize to be won', as you called it."

"Don't you see? It's not just about you. Our enemies will do whatever it takes to get to you. They couldn't care less about the collateral damage that stands in their way."

It was those words that had changed everything for me. When it came to my own life, I was willing to let the chips fall where they may, but I would never, ever bring undue risk to my men and women. "So that's it? I just walk away and never go back?"

Dad had given me an apologetic smile. "I'm so very sorry, son. I never imagined it would come to this. We will arrange for you to go back and speak with your unit."

I'd thrown my hands up in frustration. "And then what? I mean, what the fuck am I supposed to do with my life?"

"You're Ivy-League educated, intelligent, and highly capable. We'll find you a job within the company until you decide what it is you want to do."

The company he was referring to was the Callahan Corporation, a financial conglomerate that had been started by my grandfather, James Thornton Callahan. Dad, or James Thornton Callahan II, had worked there full-time until he'd won his first senatorial race. After that, he'd worked as a consultant when the senate wasn't in session. It had been expected that I, James Thornton Callahan III, AKA Thorn, would work there as well—at least it had been until I'd expressed interest in a military career.

When I hadn't appeared convinced, Dad had said, "It won't be forever, Thorn. I'm only guaranteed the next four years."

Four years might as well have been forty. I couldn't see four months into a future that didn't involve the military, not to mention not being able to recall any officers who had come back from the civilian life.

"Thorn?"

Ty's voice brought me out of my thoughts and back to the present. Our run had ended outside the entrance to the Park Avenue apartment building where I'd been living the last three weeks. Although my parents considered Virginia home, they'd kept the apartment since I was a kid. With its marble floors, crystal chandeliers, and oil paintings, it was a little highbrow for my taste, and my first on my t-do list once I got settled into my job was to find an apartment in the Financial District.

Turning my attention to Ty, I asked, "What did you say?"

Using his forearm, he swiped the sweat from his brow. "I just asked what time you're leaving for the office."

"I want to get there by eight-thirty."

He tilted his head in thought. I knew he was calculating the time the route would take. "We should leave here at eight to ensure we can stop for coffee and breakfast."

"Sounds good to me."

I nodded a hello at the doorman before we headed inside the palatial lobby. When Ty walked ahead of me to check out the elevator, I rolled my eyes—like anyone sketchy was going to get past the intense security. After he slid in his keycard, the elevator took us up to the eleventh floor and the doors opened up to the apartment. Yes, we had the entire floor, and yeah, I guess you could consider me an elite asshole.

Motioning to the foyer, Ty said, "I'll be waiting out here by seven-thirty just in case you try to give me the slip again."

Chuckling, I glanced over my shoulder at him. "Don't worry, I'll play nice today."

Although he didn't look convinced, he managed to nod. "Good. See you in an hour."

As I trudged toward my bedroom to get ready, anxiety blanketed me at the idea of going to the office. While no one had expected me to get off the plane from Kabul and head straight into the corporate world, I'd somehow managed to put off taking my next step in life. For the last three weeks, I'd kept up my morning runs and gym trips along with acclimating back to civilian life.

My version of acclimating had concerned my parents, Ty, and Barrett. I guess they interpreted me barely leaving the apartment, binging on Netflix, and sleeping during the day as "unhealthy". Finally, my loved ones had had enough of what they saw as potentially destructive behavior. You would have thought I was thirteen, not thirty. When

I went down to D.C. to have dinner with them last week, a sort of intervention had taken place. To put my parents' minds at ease, I had agreed to start working. Now I was having second thoughts about fulfilling that promise.

When I was in uniform, everything made sense. There wasn't a single issue or task put in front of me that I didn't feel I could handle. I'd been in the military world for twelve years, and I wasn't entirely sure I could assimilate again, not to mention relating to civilians. That disarming fact would make it impossible to interact with investors, which were pretty essential to investment banking.

Yeah, I was feeling like a complete and total pussy, a ball-less wonder. I'd been in combat, for fuck's sake, yet there I was practically pissing myself at the idea of putting on a suit and sitting down at a desk. Besides worrying about being unable to interact with the investors, I was also scared out of my mind that I wouldn't be able to do my job.

After years in the desert, what the hell did I really know about investment banking? Sure, I'd earned a double major in business and finance before entering the Army's officer program, and in the downtime between deployments, I'd earned my MBA predominantly online while spending a few months working at the Callahan Corporation, but all that felt like a lifetime ago.

In the end, I knew I had to conceal my fear. I had to appear cool, calm, and collected. While I might have been falling apart on the inside, I would slide on a mask the same way I would put on my suit.

True to his word, Ty was waiting for me in the foyer. I'm not sure why I expected anything less from him. After an elevator trip down-stairs, a car was waiting outside to take us to the office.

"I'm not sure about this," I muttered as I slid across the leather seats.

"About what?"

"The car."

"I'm sorry we couldn't get a Humvee on short notice," Ty quipped.

"Har-fucking-har. It's not about the type of ride—it's the ride itself. I'd prefer the subway."

Ty grimaced. "Do you know what a logistical nightmare that will be?"

With a grunt, I replied, "Fine. I'll keep playing Posh Spice with the car."

"Don't knock my Spice Girls. I love them," Ty mused with a grin.

"You would."

"Where to, sir?" the driver asked as Ty walked around to get in the front seat.

"Some fried deliciousness from Trend Diner."

The driver nodded, and once Ty buckled his seat belt, we pulled out into traffic. I fielded a few emails and texts on the drive. While I might've been a slug for the first two weeks of being back, I had at least spent the last week getting reacquainted with the ins and outs of my new job as best I could. I'd even had several working lunches with Ted Beaton, the guy I would be replacing.

Even though it had been years since I'd eaten there, Trend was just like I'd remembered it—small and cozy. After the hostess led us to a booth, Ty winked at me. "That chick was totally drooling over you."

"She was not."

"Yeah, man, she was."

Glancing back over my shoulder, I caught the blue-eyed woman's gaze. When she winked at me, I startled and quickly stared down my menu. Since returning to American soil, I'd been so immersed in my own self-loathing that I'd been ignoring my baser urges—namely, the morning salute from my cock. Ignoring him meant ignoring any female attention.

Ty chuckled at my response. "I can't believe how blind you are. Everywhere we go, there's always a chick eye-fucking you."

Furrowing my brows, I took a thoughtful sip of my coffee. "I guess with everything going on the last few months, I haven't really thought about dating."

Ty shook his head. "Forget dating—you need to get laid."

I snorted. "I think you're confusing me with Barrett. I don't do the random hookup scene."

"Why not?"

With a shrug, I replied, "Good question. I don't really know why. I guess I'm just some leftover relic from the past when monogamy was cool."

"There's nothing wrong with monogamy. I've tried it a few times myself."

"Tried it? Did it not stick?"

He nodded. "I don't have a lot of time for dating, so I guess I look at hookups as a hazard of my trade."

Curiosity got the better of me. "When was your last one?"

"A month ago." At what must've been my questioning look, a slow, lascivious smile curved on his lips. "The new White House assistant social secretary."

"The tall redhead?"

"Yep."

"Nice one. I've always had a thing for redheads, especially ones whose drapes match the carpeting."

Ty waggled his brows. "Well, this one was completely smooth down there, so I couldn't tell."

"I got ya."

"How long has it been for you?"

"Since before I shipped out nine months ago, back when Marcella and I were still together." Yeah, it was more like back when I was an idiot and thought Marcella Romano, the daughter of the Italian ambassador, was the one. Sure, she wanted to get married as much as I did, but as it turned out, not for the same reasons. While my reasons for matrimony were love, commitment, and companionship, hers

19

were more about landing a rich American husband and being on Page Six.

"Jesus, she was such a bitch," Ty murmured around the mouth of his coffee cup.

He was right about that one. Instead of a Dear John letter, Marcella had given me the boot during one of our Skype video calls. Her excuse was my deployment just being too hard on her, but then she also managed to find consolation with a Greek shipping tycoon just a few weeks after our breakup.

"Well, if that was the last piece of ass you got then you're way overdue."

"I wish it were that easy."

"It can be. Go get the hostess's number. When the two of you get off work, you work on getting each other off."

"Tempting, but I better pass."

With a grunt of frustration, Ty stared down at the menu. "If you say so."

After we finished eating, we had about ten minutes to get to the office. When Ty motioned to the car that was waiting by the curb, I groaned. "You know, I could walk."

"The car will get us there faster."

"No shit," I mumbled.

"I see what you're doing."

"And what is that?"

"Stalling."

Damn. He was good. "I don't know what you're talking about," I mumbled as we headed out the door.

Ty chuckled. "I know it's been a while for you, but your poker face could use some work."

"Whatever."

Before I could get into the car, Ty grabbed my arm. "You know, Thorn, it's okay to be anxious about today. You've had a mind-fuck with what's happened in the last six weeks. Anyone would be a little shaken up."

Now I was slightly regretting requesting Ty. While I respected his honesty, that was the last thing I wanted to hear. If he could see through me, that meant someone at work could do the same, and that idea unnerved me.

I glanced back at Ty. Any thoughts of biting his head off or making some smartass remark evaporated at the sight of his knowing yet empathetic expression. I remembered once again that he was a military man, and he got me. "Thank you," I replied before I slipped into the car.

He nodded before closing my door. The two-minute drive was silent except for the voices in our heads, and by the time Ty opened the door for me, I had slid my mask firmly back on.

"Listen, when we get into the building, I don't want you on my ass. I don't intend to call any more attention to my presence than absolutely necessary."

"I'll maintain my usual respectful distance," Ty responded diplomatically.

I grunted. "Yeah, we'll see about that."

"Ready?"

Once again wanting to stall, I shook my head. "I'm going to grab a coffee from one of the food trucks."

"Okay."

While Ty continued surmising any potential dangers, I did some surmising of my own. Tilting my head up, I eyed the massive skyscraper. While it shouldn't have, it almost seemed bigger than it had when I was a kid and came to work with my dad.

It loomed above me—my unwanted destiny. To me, it was the

enemy in range. I couldn't help keeping my eye on the target even as I started toward the food truck.

That was a tactical error on my part because the next thing I knew, I was crashing into someone. At a feminine shriek of pain, I tore my gaze from the building. "Oh my God, I'm so sorry," I apologized.

When she jerked her head up to glare at me, I felt a sharp kick to the groin. Holy shit was she beautiful—like, make-a-guy-like-me-speechless kind of beautiful. Although her crystal blue eyes were full of rage directed right at me, I could have spent hours staring into them. They reminded me of the water at Martha's Vineyard. I wanted to kiss her perfect, pouty lips—which were currently pursed in anger—while running my fingers through her auburn hair. Oh yeah, she was also a redhead—in other words, my fantasy woman. From the seething fury she exhibited, I surmised she had the fiery personality to match her hair.

As we stared into each other's eyes, her expression converted to one of disbelief, if not awe, but the moment was short-lived because she suddenly began sucking in harsh breaths like she was in pain.

"I didn't even see you," I lamented.

"While I might be slightly vertically challenged, how in the hell could you possibly miss me?"

She was a spitfire, and I experienced another kick in the pants at the thought of what she would be like in the bedroom. "My head was somewhere else," I replied honestly.

"Like up your ass?"

I chuckled. I couldn't remember the last time anyone had talked to me the way she was. I was used to most people being slightly intimidated by me. "Yeah, pretty much."

She tore her eyes from mine to stare down at her shirt. Groaning, she said, "Shit, I'm a wreck."

A wreck? You're the most beautiful woman I've ever seen. When I eyed the damage I'd singlehandedly inflicted on her blouse, I grimaced and reached for the crisp white handkerchief in my suit pocket. "Here, let me help."

Desperately wanting to right my wrong, I began feverishly working at getting the stains off her shirt. It was only at her sharp intake of breath that I realized my second tactical error. *Oh Jesus.* I was full-on touching her tits. Okay, forget touching them—I was *massaging* them, *caressing* them.

Before I could jerk my hand away and apologize profusely for my oversight in judgment, the woman's fist was connecting with my nose so hard I saw stars. *Holy fucking hell.*

At the sound of scuffling behind me, the woman screamed. Even with my eyes pinched shut, I knew what was happening. "Back off, Ty! I'm fine," I muttered as I brought my hand up to cup my nose.

Blood poured into my palm, and for the moment, I could focus on nothing but the pain. For a tiny thing, she sure packed a hell of a wallop. She would have fit in well in my unit. As I fought to try to make out her blurry image, I heard her call me a pussy before she gathered up her things and scurried off.

When Ty started to go after her, I growled, "I said back the fuck off."

"But she just punched you!"

"Because I was touching her tits."

Ty's mouth opened and closed a few times like he was a fish out of water. "When I said you should get laid, I didn't mean for you to touch some random woman's tits."

I snorted at the absurdity of the situation, which only caused my nose to scream in agony. "FUCK!" I groaned. When the pain subsided slightly, I saw the woman's retreating form pushing through the revolving doors of the building. That was an interesting development. The Callahan Corporation operated on five floors and there were many other financial companies housed on the others, but if she worked in the building, I could probably track her down somehow.

Sweeping his hands to his hips, Ty asked, "You wanna tell me what exactly happened? I mean, I saw you run into the woman, but then your back was to me."

"For the record, I didn't mean to touch her tits. I was trying to clean up her shirt after I caused her to spill her coffee."

"What were you thinking?"

"She was worried about her shirt, so I was just trying to help."

Ty chuckled. "Yeah, you helped yourself to some epic second base action."

"What the fuck ever." I moved the handkerchief away from my face to determine if I was still bleeding. Thankfully, it looked like it was slowing down.

After glancing around, Ty shook his head. "We need to get you inside. It's not going to be long before someone recognizes you."

At the sight of a woman raising her phone in my direction, I grunted, "Too late."

"Let's go." Ty placed his right hand on my elbow and started leading me toward the building. With his free hand, he motioned onlookers away from us. When we got inside the lobby, I exhaled the breath I'd been holding. "Just one more thing," he said.

"What?" I asked, glancing around to see if there were any more cameras trained on us.

Ty flashed me a wicked grin. "How did the tits feel?"

I laughed. "Fucking fantastic."

CHAPTER THREE

REMEMBER how I said I'd worked out every possible scenario of how this day could possibly go? Well, getting burned by my latte and punching a strange man for copping a feel was certainly not one of them. Not even in my worst nightmare could I have prepared for the shit-show I was currently experiencing.

"Fuck," I muttered, shaking my hand out. Now my knuckles were screaming in almost as much agony as my burnt boob skin.

Before I could stop and survey the damage I'd done to the Armani god, another Armani-suited man rushed forward with a determined look etched across his handsome face. *Oh shit.* He wasn't swooping in to help his friend—he was coming for me. When he started to launch himself at me, I screamed and ducked out of the way.

"Back off, Ty! I'm fine," the guy muttered, his hand cupping his nose.

"What kind of pussy needs another dude to fight his battles?" I demanded as I scrambled to pick up my purse and laptop bag.

The Armani god ignored me and turned his attention to his friend. With the two of them were speaking heatedly, I scurried away, ignoring the stares of the onlookers around us. My erratic heartbeat thumped loudly in my ears as I made my way to the elevator on shaky legs. Although it was clearly packed full, I squeezed in between two people just before the door closed. I didn't want to run the risk of the rude stranger and his henchman following me.

As the elevator whooshed upward, I bit down on my lip, desperately fighting the tears that pooled in my eyes. *No. Nope. No way.* I was *not* going to cry over a little spilled latte or a handsy asshole. I was not going to let it ruin my perfect day. This was merely a minor detour. After a few small adjustments, I could be back on track.

The first adjustment would be a change of clothes, at least for my top half. I power walked through the maze of offices and when I arrived outside mine, I saw my secretary, Cheryl, wasn't at her desk. Since the computer was on and her usual cup of coffee was beside the keyboard, I knew she must've just stepped away for a moment.

Once I got inside my office, I dropped my bags and went over to the closet. This was where that part about me being a perfectionist actually came in handy. I always left a suit and several blouses inside, along with a couple of changes of underwear. Over the years, I'd been known to pull a few overnighters after which I would shower and get ready there at the office.

Since I didn't want anyone else seeing me in my wrecked state, I started undressing behind the open closet door. After jerking the hem of my shirt out of my skirt, I whipped it up over my head and tossed it onto the desk. My arms reached around my back to the clasp on my now soaked bra. Once I pulled the bra off, I used my old shirt to wipe the remaining coffee off my red, blotchy skin. I'd have to see if Cheryl had any aloe lying around, not to mention maybe popping some Advil.

Just as I was pulling out a new bra, a knock sounded. "Come on in, Cheryl." Turning my back to the opening door, I said, "I'm glad you're here. I was wondering if you had any aloe in your desk or if there's any in the first aid kit. Some bastard with his head up his ass ran right into me, and my boobs are burned to a crisp."

"Uh, it's not Cheryl," said a cautious male voice…a somewhat familiar male voice.

I whirled around to see the Armani Adonis and his henchman. Both of their eyes widened in shock at the sight of me. Then both of their gazes dropped to my bare breasts. With a squeal, I fumbled for my blouse in the closet. "What the hell are you doing here?" I demanded as I pivoted around, blocking their view of my boobs.

The Adonis cleared his throat. "I'm supposed to meet with an Isabel Flannery this morning. The secretary wasn't outside, so I figured I'd knock."

As I yanked the blouse down to try to cover my breasts, my earring caught on the fabric. When I tugged on the shirt, pain shot through my earlobe, causing me to shriek.

"Um, are you all right?"

I huffed out a frustrated breath. "No, I'm not. It appears my earring is caught in my blouse."

"Can I help?"

Peering over my shoulder at him, I countered, "I seem to recall the last time you helped me, I got felt up."

The henchman had the audacity to chuckle while the Adonis shot him a menacing look. He then turned his attention back to me. "If anyone should be skittish, it's me. After all, I just got punched in the face."

"What did you expect me to do?"

"Obviously, if I'd expected you to punch me, I would have been better prepared."

I rolled my eyes. "Whatever. Just help me."

He crossed the room toward me. With his gaze once again zeroing in on my chest, I crossed my arms over my boobs, which only made my C cups bulge up over my arms. At least my nipples were covered.

"Okay, I'm going to touch you now," he warned.

"Thank you for the heads-up."

At the feel of his fingers just below my ear, I shivered. I didn't like my body reacting to him so viscerally, but it wasn't just his slight touch on my skin that affected me. It was the musky male scent of his cologne. It was his body looming over me, the ripped muscles only slightly obscured beneath the fabric of his shirt and pants. Damn, he had tree-trunk-like thighs I imagined pillowing my ass on as I rode his cock.

Wait, what? Was I seriously having a fantasy about the jackass who had just felt me up and seen me topless? My first order of business after the promotion was official was to sign up for online dating and get laid. Then I wouldn't be having fantasies about random men.

A string snapped, and then I was free. When I glanced up at him, I found he was staring intently at me. At least his gaze was head level and not trying to steal another peek at my boobs.

"Thank you," I murmured.

He gave me a small smile. "You're welcome." We stood there for a moment just staring at each other. Then he cleared his throat. "I should let you get dressed."

Oh, right. I was currently standing topless in front of two strange men. "If you will be so kind as to wait outside, I'll be right with you."

He nodded before turning back to his henchman. Once they closed the door behind them, I exhaled raggedly. If having my boobs burned by coffee and punching a guy were outside my perfectly planned scenarios, you could sure as hell believe having said guy see my breasts was completely and totally not part of the plan.

Even though I was shaking, I somehow got redressed in record speed. I lamented the fact that I didn't have any alcohol in my desk. While it wasn't even nine a.m., I could have used a shot of liquid courage after the shit-show of a morning I'd experienced.

After smoothing my hair down, I opened the door and motioned him inside. "I'm so sorry about that. What is it that you're here to see me about?"

He offered me his hand, and I shook it. "I wanted to introduce myself. I'm the new vice president."

When I jerked away from our handshake, the Adonis gave me a strange look. "I'm sorry—what did you just say?" I demanded.

"I'm the new vice president."

"Yes, that's what I thought you said. It's just I hoped I had heard you wrong, because I can't fathom that being true." A manic laugh escaped my lips. *No, no, NO!* This couldn't be happening. I couldn't possibly not have gotten the promotion. There was no way I had come this close just to have some outside usurper take it from me.

No, it all had to be some terrible nightmare. That was the only logical explanation. Maybe if I pinched myself, I would wake up to find myself back in bed with Dani.

"I understand you're supposed to show me the ropes."

"Who told you that?"

"While that is confidential, I'm to report to Murray Moskowitz this morning."

Red flooded my vision just like it had when he'd groped me with his handkerchief. Last time I'd checked, Murray was the man who was supposed to formally offer me the job, not stab me in the back. Until I heard it from his lips, I wasn't going to believe it was true. It could all be some colossal joke Murray was playing on me—not that he was exactly known for his pranks, but stranger things had happened.

"You're going to have to excuse me for a minute. I need to get something cleared up before we proceed."

The supposed new vice president's mouth dropped open in surprise as I blew past him and out of my office. Without looking back, I stalked down the hallway to the elevators. After I smacked the button, the doors opened, and I hopped on. As I rode one floor up, I tried to keep the fraying strands of my sanity intact. There was no part of this I could have prepared for.

After I got off the elevator, I headed down the hallway. Murray had the corner office to envy, and it boasted amazing views of the city. At first glance, he might have seemed like the epitome of an asshole boss with his gruff exterior of salt and pepper eyebrows and beard, but Murray really was a more of a giant teddy bear than he was a tyrant. He'd been my supervisor for the last three years, and I'd always felt fortunate that he'd taken me under his wing. While I'd been intimidated by him at first, our relationship had evolved into one more like father and daughter.

When she glanced up and saw me, his secretary, Bonnie, didn't even bother buzzing Murray's office. When I blew through the door, Murray didn't look surprised to see me. "Yes, please come right on in, Isabel. I've been expecting you."

I sucked in an anguished breath. "If you were expecting me, then the strange man in my office is the new vice president."

"Yes, he is," Murray replied gravely.

"How is that even possible? You've all but handed me the keys to my new office."

"I know, and I'm sorry. My hands were tied."

"You are the head of the floor, are you not?"

"I received the order at the end of last week. Those at the top even withheld it from me until the very last moment."

I furrowed my brows. "Like, the board?"

"Yes, the board."

I flounced down into one of the plush chairs in front of Murray's desk. "Whose son is he?"

My stomach churned at the somewhat stricken expression on Murray's face. As if it wasn't bad enough that some strange guy had seen my boobs, it was even worse because he was apparently one of the board members' sons.

"He's James Callahan's son."

Holy. Fucking. Shit. I bolted upright in my chair. "James Callahan as in the son of the starter of this company and the current president of the United States?" I choked out.

"That would be the one."

"But if he's the head honcho's son, where's he been all this time? James's other son has been here for years."

"Thorn followed in his father's footsteps and pursued an active military career after he finished at Harvard. After completing officer training school, he served in Iraq and then lead two missions in Afghanistan."

"At least he's an Ivy Leaguer."

"Yes. He graduated seven years ago."

My mouth dropped open in shock. "He hasn't had any business experience in the last seven years?"

"Not unless it was military related."

"Wait, so you're telling me that not only did I lose out on my promotion because of nepotism, I lost out to someone far less qualified?"

"I'm afraid so."

"This is bullshit."

"I would have to agree."

Dragging my bottom lip between my teeth, I once again fought the urge to cry. This time it was out of pure rage. "Why here? Why now?"

Murray raked a hand over his face. "I'm not supposed to share this with anyone, but considering what has happened, I feel you deserve to know."

I leaned forward in my chair and gave him a pointed look. "You know I won't say anything."

Once he had the assurance I wouldn't go blabbing, Murray nodded his head. "Thorn was forced to leave his post and his men not of his own volition, but because of the security concerns that have arisen since his father became president. He has not been a happy camper. Since his return, his family and friends have worried he is floundering. They thought it best for his mental health to find him a job, and what better place than in the family business?"

Wow. That so wasn't the story I was expecting. I couldn't imagine how hard it must've been for him to give up the only life he'd ever known. Part of me felt terrible for punching someone who had been defending my country and freedom over spilled coffee. *Well, to be fair, there was also the unrestrained boob fondling.*

"Believe me when I say my heart goes out to Thorn for what has happened. I'm the granddaughter of a veteran, so I know what it means to live and die for your country, but wouldn't it be easier on Thorn to put him into a more entry-level position? I mean, talk about from the frying pan into the fire."

Murray chuckled. "I'm not sure a man who's led two tours in Afghanistan would feel the same about the corporate world as he does about combat, but I understand what you're getting at."

"I didn't mean any disrespect. I was merely looking out for Thorn's best interest."

"Sure you were," Murray replied with a wink.

I popped out of my seat to hover over Murray's desk. "What do you expect me to do? Bow out gracefully while throwing out the welcome mat for an under-qualified and undeserving colleague? You should know me too well for that. I've gone above and beyond for this company." I jabbed the air in front of him. "I know it, and you know it. There is no one in this department more qualified than I am. I *deserve* this promotion."

Yeah, my current tirade was nothing like I had rehearsed the night before, not to mention my voice had risen into almost shrill territory.

After taking a deep breath, I tried to get a hold on my runaway emotions and get my mouth in check. "I'm sorry," I mumbled before sitting back down.

"There will be other promotions."

With an immature roll of my eyes, I crossed my arms over my chest. "Sure there will be."

"Isabel, someone with your talents *will* see higher advancement in this company."

"Years from now when I have to choose between a career or a family. *This* is my time."

He sighed. "I am sorry. I'm sorry for both the promotion and what I'm about to ask of you next."

Eyeing him suspiciously, I questioned, "What?"

"I need you to help Thorn transition."

"You're joking."

Murray shook his head. "I wish I was, but Thorn is going to need some help at first."

"Unbelievable."

"Surely you believe in the adage that no good deed goes unrewarded."

"No. I was believing more in the idea that hard work and sacrifice actually pay off," I snapped.

Murray's blue eyes narrowed on mine. "After all these years, would you want me to have to put a note in your file?"

Just like back in high school when I'd feared any detentions or office referrals on my permanent record, I had the same feelings about a note in my file. Just when I thought Murray had become a complete pushover where I was concerned, he pulled out the big-gun threats. "No, sir, I wouldn't," I replied diplomatically.

"Thank you. That's the response I wanted to hear." His expression softened. "I want you to be Thorn's right-hand woman on his initial research and presentations. I'll have Kyle and Marta pick up some of the slack from your load so you'll be free to help."

"I appreciate that," I lied. Part of my annoying perfectionist side meant I was ridiculously territorial when it came to my work. I didn't want any other fingers in my pies, especially fingers that were less qualified and less deserving.

Leaning back in his chair, Murray pressed the tips of his fingers together. "Look at it this way, Isabel: because of who he is, Thorn will be promoted quickly. By helping him, you will have gleaned everything you need to know about your future job."

If there was any consolation to be had in the current hell I found myself in, I supposed that was it. "Yes, sir."

Murray's phone buzzed, and then Bonnie's voice came over the intercom. "Mr. Moskowitz, there's a Thorn Callahan to see you."

As my stomach twisted into a few more knots, Murray raised his brows at me. "Are you ready to formally meet Mr. Callahan?"

Formally? No, not really. *Formally* meeting Mr. Callahan meant accepting that my position as vice president had been obliterated. *Everything I've worked for...* I tried not to seethe, as I knew I was better than that. I also tried not to feel incredibly mortified by what all had transpired between Mr. Callahan and me that morning. I doubted Murray needed to know just how *informally* Mr. Callahan and I had been introduced to each other in the last fifteen minutes. *Lord, how on earth is this going to work?*

I exhaled a ragged breath. "Ready as I'll ever be."

Murray bobbed his head. "Send him in."

When I'd imagined what my first day of work would look like, I never in a million years pictured a fabulous set of tits even remotely being involved. If I had, I probably wouldn't have been such a tight-ass about coming into work. For those of you keeping tabs, the guy who hadn't been laid in nine months had just felt up and seen an amazing rack, and that was all before nine o'clock in the morning.

"Holy fucking shit," I muttered as Ms. Flannery stormed past us and out into the hallway.

"My sentiments exactly."

Turning to Ty, I shook my head. "Did that seriously just happen?"

Ty snorted. "Yeah, man, it did."

We both just stared at each other for a moment. You would think two men as seasoned as we were wouldn't have been so shell-shocked by boobs, yet there we were. Maybe it had to do with the fact that the woman who had just flashed me was also the woman I had accidentally felt up not five minutes before. Crazy coincidences like that didn't happen in real life, instead they were regulated to TV shows and movies. In this case, it would have been more of a raunchy R-rated movie than something on the Lifetime network.

Breaking the silence, Ty said, "I gotta know something."

"Yes, they're better than any I remember in a long, long time."

With a wince, Ty replied, "I was afraid of that."

"Why do you say that?"

"Because Ms. Tantalizing Tits is your employee."

Fuck me. Ty was right. In these modern times, nothing good could come from pursuing a relationship with my subordinate. After the morning's events, I was already at a deficit with Ms. Flannery. Add one lingering glance at her boobs or a suggestive comment and I could be strung up by the balls for harassment. Not only could I not afford a lawsuit, the last thing my father's administration needed was for me to become the poster child for skeezy bosses who take advantage of their position and power.

Staggering back, I questioned, "Jesus, how can I possibly work with her?"

"You just have to mentally castrate yourself in her presence. You don't have a dick, and she doesn't have the vagina you want to put your dick in."

I groaned. "Yeah, the visual on that is so not helping."

"Sorry. I was just trying to help."

"Trust me, mentioning anything about Ms. Flannery's vagina is just downright painful."

Ty chuckled. "Well, look at it this way: when she blew out of here, she seemed pretty fucking pissed about the notion that you were the new vice president. If you're lucky, she already has a strong hate for you, so you don't have to worry about any potential relationship."

Right. That was something I hadn't previously stopped to factor in. Upon further reflection, Ms. Flannery had seemed pretty furious when I told her I was the new vice president. I couldn't imagine she would have stormed out to talk to our superior just because she didn't want the man who had seen her tits to be the new boss. No, it was deeper than that.

When I sucked in a harsh breath, Ty asked, "What?"

"I was thinking about what you just said about her reaction. It was a little too extreme for it to just be about me seeing her boobs and feeling her up."

Ty's brows furrowed. "So what is it then?"

"I'm thinking she must've been up for the job."

"Really?"

I nodded. "It would make sense that they would look to promote someone from within instead of an outside hire."

Shaking his head, Ty said, "Man, if that's the case, it's pretty brutal losing out on a promotion to the guy who saw you topless."

"Once she learns who I am, she's going to think it was nothing but nepotism that got me this job." When Ty gave me a knowing look, I rolled my eyes. "While that is not entirely untrue, I had to have the necessary degrees and skills or they would have placed me somewhere else."

I sounded a lot surer of myself than I felt considering my previous state of anxiety about the whole thing.

I sighed. "In the end, it's probably in my favor that she was up for this job. It just makes it easier for her to hate me and for me to be an asshole. When I'm being an asshole, I'm not being a pervert who is trying to seduce her."

Ty's brows popped. "Let me get this straight: your method for distracting yourself from your attraction to Ms. Flannery is to act like a total asshole?"

"Exactly."

"Jesus, you've been in the field too long."

"What's the problem?"

"Here's the thing—there's a fatal flaw in your master plan."

"I'm really a nice guy, so it'll be hard pulling off the asshole part?" I suggested with a smile.

Ty chuckled. "That's not what I was going to say."

"Fine. What is it?"

"I think you're forgetting about the vast number of women who are extremely attracted to assholes." He glanced around before lowering his voice. "Like, it makes them wet."

"You're joking."

"Sadly, I'm not. There's even a genre of romance novels devoted to men who are assholes."

I shook my head. "That's insane." While I wasn't the Casanova Barrett was, I still considered myself somewhat knowledgeable when it came to women. I'd dated my fair share of them, not to mention I had lived with my mother and younger sister. How was it possible that I'd missed that very important tidbit? "Is it the same thing as chicks wanting to fuck a bad boy?"

Ty nodded. "Pretty much."

"Fabulous," I muttered as I swept my hand over my face. As I processed the information, I peered at Ty. "And just how do you know all this? For the life of me, I can't imagine you acting like an asshole in real life. You're far too much of a Brit not to be a gentleman."

"I don't set out to be an asshole, but I'm sure I have my moments." He winked. "I'd bet my exes might have something to say about me in that department."

"I'm pretty sure even the least asshole of all would get a negative review or two from an ex."

"As far as me knowing about the asshole factor, I guess I've just been observant. Also, while you were expounding on the classics, I was reading a few down-and-dirty romance novels."

I grinned at Ty. "Damn, I'm amazed you will admit that."

"There's no shame in it. At the time, I considered it research. Every chick I was going out with had an e-reader, so I figured I might as well know my competition." He shook his head. "Besides learning about the asshole factor, I also realized I was never going to be able to compete with those romance wankers who never fart or leave the toilet seat up, not to mention having ten-inch dicks."

"Wait, your dick isn't ten inches?" I teased.

"Of course not." He then waggled his brows. "It's twelve."

With a shake of my head, I replied, "Dream on, dude."

Ty grinned. "How did we even get onto this topic?"

"I have no fucking clue. What I do know is that my initial attitude toward this job has changed, but that is life both in and out of the military—plans change, and you have to adapt with them. Like Burns said, 'All the best laid schemes of mice and men.'"

Ty blinked at me. "Did you just quote poetry to me?"

I grinned. "Yes, it would seem so."

"I had no idea you were so deep."

"One has a lot of time to read during deployments—as you should well know."

"I didn't do any deep reading while I was on tour, unless you count some Stephen King novels."

"I don't think those fall under the category of the classics."

"Yeah, yeah, be a literary snob."

As I chuckled, I shot a glance at the clock above Ms. Flannery's desk. It was almost nine o'clock. Since it was apparent she wasn't coming back any time soon, it was time I went to check in with Mr. Moskowitz. Motioning to Ty, I said, "Come on."

"Where are we going?" Ty asked as he fell in step behind me.

"I need to see my point of contact. He's the one who will give me the keys to my office. I can't wait any longer to get this show on the road."

Ty didn't question me any further. Instead, he instantly transitioned back into protection mode. After glancing at my phone for directions to Murray's office, I took the elevator upstairs. Once I arrived on his floor, I began making my way through the maze of cubicles and offices. Just like Ty had done a few minutes before, I got myself back in the zone. After everything that had happened that morning, it wasn't as easy as I thought it would be.

When I arrived, I announced myself to Murray's secretary. Although I was sure Ty still entertained the idea of Ms. Flannery inflicting bodily harm on me, I entered the office alone. When I stepped toward the desk, I saw we were not alone. Ms. Flannery's skin was ashen, and after nodding her head at me, she tucked her chin to her chest.

I threw out my hand. "Mr. Moskowitz, it's a pleasure to meet you."

"Likewise, Mr. Callahan. Please call me Murray."

"Yes, sir."

After shaking my hand, Murray furrowed his brows at me as his gaze zeroed in on my nose. "Are you all right?"

"It's nothing, just a little tango with a door," I lied.

Murray didn't seem too convinced, but he then turned to motion to Ms. Flannery. "This is Isabel Flannery."

"Yes, we met earlier."

When Isabel's frantic eyes met mine, I instantly regretted my choice of words, but there weren't a lot of ways I could've responded that couldn't have been construed as potentially perverted. Since I refused to show any fear, I steeled my shoulders. "I stopped by her office to introduce myself before I came up here." I chose to leave out the part about seeing her topless and almost mowing her down.

When it seemed clear I wasn't going to mention anything embarrassing, the tension visibly melted from Isabel's face. While I wanted to put her at ease, I also didn't want her to get comfortable with me. Yes, ladies and gentlemen, it was time to put on my asshole armor.

Narrowing my eyes at Isabel, I said, "From Ms. Flannery's over-the-top antics bordering on a lack of professionalism, I can assume my presence is a bit of a surprise."

With a strangled gasp, her gaze spun from me over to Murray. I could tell she was both infuriated and mortified by my statement. Truth be told, I was more than a little surprised at it myself, not to mention my somewhat icy tone. You would have thought I was dressing down a new recruit rather than speaking about the liaison for my new job.

When I looked at Murray, he tightened his jaw. "Yes, I'm afraid your inception into the company was unexpected not only to Ms. Flannery, but also myself. I only found out at the end of last week," Murray replied tersely.

"Even though it was somewhat last minute overall, I'm sorry you were not properly notified. I'm looking forward to following in my family's footsteps and making my mark here at the Callahan Corporation."

"We're happy to have you on board. No one is more qualified for helping you with your transition than Ms. Flannery."

"While I'm sure she is, I'm not sure how much help I'll be needing. I spent last week in working lunches with Ted. He did a great job of preparing me."

Out of my peripheral vision, I saw Isabel fighting hard to hide her outrage while Murray appeared extremely pissed. Normally, I wouldn't have mentioned consulting with another team to my current team. Notoriously bad for morale, it also had the potential to be dangerous. Considering their reactions, it worked well with my current campaign to be a full-out asshole to Isabel, thus lessening any potential for sexual harassment claims.

"How fortunate for you," Murray replied while Isabel coughed. I could have sworn there was a "bullshit" muttered within it, but I wasn't completely sure. If Murray heard it, he didn't react. Instead, he gave me a tight smile. "I'm sure that was very beneficial. Ted's knowledge is legendary here. However, at the same time, I cannot discredit the invaluable knowledge Ms. Flannery brings."

"If you say so."

Murray rose out of his chair. "Considering how closely the two of you will be working, perhaps it would be best for Ms. Flannery to show you to your office."

While Isabel appeared ready to throttle Murray for his suggestion, she bobbed her head in agreement. "It would be my pleasure."

Oh Jesus. The last thing I needed was to hear the word *pleasure* come from her lips. It conjured up so many illicit images in my mind. *Get a grip, Thorn.* "Thank you, Ms. Flannery."

After picking up a manila envelope from his desk, Murray came over to hand it to me. "Here are the keys to your office and desk. IT will be by at nine-thirty to get your computer codes set up."

"Thanks. I appreciate it."

He nodded at Isabel. "I'll leave you to it."

Isabel wore an expression like she was about to go to an execution rather than show me around. Motioning to the door, I said, "After you."

When I fell in step beside her, the heady smell of her perfume entered my nostrils. Even though I'd already been in close proximity with her, I hadn't noticed it yet. God, it was distracting. It called to me, telling me to bury my nose in her skin. Maybe I could fake a migraine sensitivity so she wouldn't wear it around me anymore.

Once we were alone in the hallway, Isabel cleared her throat. "I would like to apologize for my earlier behavior in my office. You were correct in calling me out for my unprofessionalism."

Holy shit. I wasn't expecting that one at all. Of course, considering Isabel's previous reactions in Murray's office, I couldn't help wondering about how sincere she really was. While words of apology might've been coming from her lips, the expression in her eyes told me she didn't truly mean them.

"Thank you."

"I hope we can put the past behind us and move forward," she suggested.

I had a feeling she was speaking more about me seeing her topless than any actual attitude she'd displayed. "Yes, I'm sure we can."

Isabel seemed pleased by my response, but her positive feeling was soon replaced by unease when she spotted Ty approaching us. "Now that I know who you are, I guess I can assume he is more than just your henchman?"

"Yes, this is Ty Fraser, my Secret Service agent."

When she paled slightly, I imagined she was trying to process the horror of not only the son of the president of the United States seeing her topless, but also a government employee.

Ty extended his hand. "My apologies for almost tackling you this morning. I wasn't aware of what had happened just prior, so I automatically thought he was in danger."

Isabel nodded while shaking his hand. "That's understandable." She glanced between the two of us. "So you're just going to be hanging out here?"

Ty chuckled. "Something like that. Whatever it takes to keep my eyes and ears on him at all times possible."

"I see."

"After a few weeks, you won't even notice I'm here."

"I'm not so sure about that," she murmured.

It was then I realized Isabel was no longer looking at Ty in embarrassment. Now she was looking at him like he was a grade A piece of man-meat. I imagined she was thinking with his good looks and British accent, it would be impossible not to notice him. While I shouldn't have given two shits about what she thought of Ty, a pang of jealousy crisscrossed through my chest.

I cleared my throat. "How about that tour?"

"Am I to assume Ted didn't take you around the office last week?"

"No. Our meetings were done outside of the building."

"I see. Why don't we start with the break room, and then I can show you the offices of some of the analysts and associates on your team?"

"Sounds good."

As we made our way down the hall, conversation seemed to evade us. I couldn't for the life of me think of what to say to her. Finally, I tried to steer the conversation to something business-related. "How long have you been here?"

"I've been full-time for seven years, and I also did my undergrad internship here."

"That's a pretty short amount of time to be up for a vice president position," I mused.

Isabel bristled. "I know you haven't been in the business world in a few years, but with hard work and sacrifice, it is completely feasible to be promoted that quickly when you show leadership qualities and client management skills."

"I stand corrected."

With a sugary-sweet smile, she replied, "I'm sure this won't be the last time that happens."

Before I could make a smartass remark, she threw her arm out to point at one of the offices to the left of me. She then began rattling off names of people and their titles. I knew I would never remember them, but I managed to nod my head and smile.

The tour ended at my office, which happened to be two doors down from Isabel's. After I took the keycard out of the manila envelope, I opened the door and stepped inside. Even though it was a large, spacious office most of the staff would have killed for, it felt stifling to me, perhaps because I wasn't used to four walls surrounding me.

"Whatever you do not find to your liking with the furniture, you are welcome to change. Your secretary can handle the necessary paper-work," Isabel said as she hung back at the door.

I eyed her curiously over my shoulder. "What were you going to change?"

She shifted uncomfortably on her feet. "I'm not a fan of the modern décor like Ted was."

Neither was I, but Ted obviously had been. It was way too stream-lined to me—too cold and sterile. "I'm sure I can make do for the time being."

After appearing somewhat surprised at my declaration, Isabel replied, "Alice has the catalog whenever you're ready to make your choices."

Nodding, I then walked around the side of the desk and sat down in the chair. A slight shudder went through me at how surreal the moment felt. I'd sat at many desks over the years in my career as a solider, but none had felt quite like this. As a sudden choking feeling overcame me, I fought the urge to reach up and loosen my tie.

Isabel motioned to the files on my desk. "There are several important mergers coming up, and we are also courting several new clients. I'll be happy to walk you through them if you'd like."

Using my index finger, I lazily flipped open one of the folders. "That won't be necessary. I'm sure Ted covered all of this."

After pressing her lips together tightly, Isabel then gave a nod of her head. "I understand. I hope it's not too presumptuous of me to remind you that your most pressing matter is next week's presentation with the potential investor for the Tri-State Chiropractic Board's new coccyx massager, The Tailsmen."

My inner teenage boy fought the urge to snicker at the mention of a coccyx massager. When Ted went over the files with me, we'd both chuckled at the absurdity of such a product. However, this was Isabel, and there was no way in hell I was going to reveal that I was thinking of massaging a cock rather than a coccyx.

"Yes, I'm aware of that. How many analysts do we have on the presentation?"

"Two."

"When do we anticipate them being finished?"

"By Thursday at the latest."

I nodded. "Good."

After cutting her eyes around the room, Isabel shifted on her feet. "Since it seems you have everything under control, I'll go back to my office now."

"Yes, dismissed," I replied. My words had the affect I was looking for because Isabel appeared to be silently seething. I would have given a hundred bucks to be privy to what she was thinking about me in her head. I'm pretty sure she was mentally stabbing me while at the same time kicking me in the junk repeatedly.

"Thank you, Mr. Callahan," she bit out before whirling around. Her heels stomped into the carpeting as she made her way out of the office. Of course, her retreat gave me a fantastic view of her ass, which peeked out beneath her suit jacket. Just before she slammed the door, she caught herself.

As soon as I heard the click, I groaned and rubbed my hands over my eyes. I was in so much fucking trouble.

CHAPTER FIVE

Isabel

When my lunch hour rolled around, I practically bolted from my office. While the celebratory aspect of our lunch no longer applied, I desperately wanted to see Mila. There was no one I could unload my troubles on quite like I could her other than my mom and younger sister, and they were thousands of miles away.

As soon as I exited the building, a crack formed in the façade I'd constructed since leaving Murray's office. It had taken everything within me to endure the sad smiles and forlorn expressions from some of my coworkers who had expected my promotion just as much as I had, but I'd held my head high while appearing every bit a steel magnolia. I would not allow anyone to pity me, although I sure as hell felt sorry for myself.

By the time I waltzed into Mad Dog and Beans, my emotions must've been written all over my face because the moment she saw me, Mila's expression fell. "You didn't get the promotion?"

I shook my head as I flopped down in the booth. "No. I didn't."

"But how is that even possible? It was just supposed to be the formality of him offering you the job."

"We were both unaware of an outside hire. Well, Murray found out late last week. I guess he didn't want to completely ruin my weekend by telling me then."

Mila's brows furrowed. "An outside hire?"

"Not a completely outside hire considering he's the president's son —and when I say president, I don't mean the president of the board. I mean the actual president of the United States."

"You're shitting me!"

"I wish."

"What's he like?"

I shuddered at the thought of my first interactions with Thorn. "It was just a nightmare from start to finish that involved him groping me and seeing my boobs."

Mila's eyes bulged. "Excuse me?"

After drawing in a ragged breath, I proceeded to give her all the gory details. If I hadn't been so traumatized, I might've found her varying expressions somewhat comical, but I'd lost my sense of humor somewhere between punching Thorn and hearing Murray confirm I wasn't getting the job I'd been sacrificing my life for.

When I finished, Mila stared at me open-mouthed. Considering she was rarely speechless, it was a little unnerving. "I don't even have words."

"It really is that bad, huh?"

Mila slowly shook her head. "Belle, if you were hoping I had some words of comfort for you, I'm sorry. I mean, the guy who stole your job saw you topless."

"And felt me up," I added.

"Exactly. It had to be pure torture meeting the guy who had snatched your promotion away from you, but to have all those other things happen on top of it?" She reached across the table to take my hand in hers. "The margaritas are on me today."

"I appreciate that, but I better just stick to one. The last thing I need is to go back to the office blitzed and have everyone talking about how I got sloshed to deal with the pain of not getting the promotion."

"Would it really be a bad thing to appear vulnerable?"

Shaking my head, I replied, "In my business, you cannot afford to appear weak, especially if you're a woman."

"If anyone has the figurative balls to pull it off, it's you," Mila acknowledged.

I laughed. "Thank you."

After we gave our meal orders to the waiter, I slouched back against the booth. "The only small hope I have is that because of who he is, Thorn will be promoted soon."

"Like how soon?" Mila asked.

I shrugged. "A year? Eighteen months? However long it takes him to master the vice president job."

"Hmm," she replied. As she swirled her finger around the rim of her margarita glass, Mila appeared suddenly lost in thought.

"What's the 'hmm' for?"

"I was just thinking…"

"A dangerous pastime," I teased, stealing a line from *Beauty and the Beast*.

Mila fell right in step like only a true best friend could. "I know."

"Seriously though, what's up with the lined-brow contemplation?"

"Twelve to eighteen months is a long time to have to deal with the entitled asshole."

"You're telling me."

"Because of who he is, it isn't likely he would get fired even if he was doing a shitty job."

Now it was my turn for the furrowed brow. "What do you mean?"

Mila began running her finger so quickly around the glass I expected to see smoke curling up at any moment. "Even though Thorn can't get fired for sucking at his job, he *could* get transferred to another department or demoted into another position, right?"

"Maybe. I mean, there are many different facets of the Callahan Corporation. It might be that he's not a good fit in mergers and acquisitions, so they try him out in underwriting. I think private equity and venture capital might be a stretch for him."

"Somewhere along there you stopped speaking my language."

"Sorry. Regardless of the terminology, I was agreeing with you."

"Good. I'm glad to hear you're on board with my evil plan."

I snickered. "Your evil plan? Don't tell me you're devising some scheme to sabotage Thorn?"

Mila nodded. "That's exactly what I'm talking about."

My amusement quickly faded. "You can't be serious."

"Oh, I'm serious as a heart attack."

"Mila, have you lost your mind?"

"Come on. You know you've been quietly contemplating some way to get rid of him so you can reclaim your promotion."

Once again, Mila had the uncanny ability to see straight through me. Refusing to meet her eyes, I shifted in my seat. "Maybe."

"Ha! I knew it."

"But those were just my own private little fantasies. I sure as hell wasn't going to do anything to act on them."

"And what would be so wrong if you did? Broadway is notorious for sabotage."

I rolled my eyes. "I'm not some grasping understudy ready to shove Thorn down a flight of stairs to take his part like in *Showgirls*."

Mila held up her hand. "I know you did *not* just make a reference to *Showgirls* in relation to legitimate theater."

With a roll of my eyes, I replied, "Fine. Would you have preferred me to go for the *All About Eve* reference instead?"

Mila nodded. "Much better, although now I'll forever be imagining Thorn as a drag version of Bette Davis."

"He's far too good-looking for that."

"Oh he is?" She waggled her brows suggestively.

"Yes. The usurper is handsome." When it became clear that Mila was privy to the fact that I was holding back about Thorn, I sighed. "Fine. He's drop-dead gorgeous, like model gorgeous."

At my declaration, Mila grabbed her phone off the table. "What are you doing?"

"Research."

"Excuse me?"

She rolled her eyes. "Duh, you know I don't follow politics, so even though Thorn's the president's son, I have no idea what he looks like." She waved the phone at me. "So, I gotta stalk him."

"That's so unnecessary."

"No, it isn't. I need something to wipe away that drag Bette Davis image in my mind." I was about to answer her verbally—because she'd missed my epic eye roll—when she gasped loudly. "Holy shitballs." She briefly glanced at me but then went straight back to her phone. "Good Lord, the man is *fine*."

I reached across the table to grab her phone. Yeah, the guy had been hotter than anything I'd ever seen in a suit, but surely he couldn't look even better in—

"Oh." Before me was Captain Thorn Callahan in his desert BDU pants looking…positively edible. *How is that possible?*

Before I could form any other words, Mila said, "You get to see *that* every day?"

Since I was still discombobulated, I merely managed a nod.

"Damn, that's unfortunate."

"Tell me about it," I muttered.

"It's easy to sabotage some homely dude who looks like Shrek or Gollum, but it's going to be a hell of an epic undertaking to take out a hottie."

"Whoa, wait a minute—I never agreed to any sabotage."

"You don't have to undertake anything violent, just small things to make him look bad and to make people question his ability to carry out the job."

I felt slightly better that Mila wasn't implying I should shove Thorn down an escalator and land him in a full-body cast, but at the same time, I wasn't completely convinced I could actually do what she was suggesting. "I don't know…"

"Belle, you deserve that promotion. You've worked harder to get where you are than anyone I know outside of the theater."

"I do appreciate your belief in my abilities, but I've never been someone who could break the rules in order to advance my career, and I don't think I could start now."

"You are seriously to be commended for your code of conduct all these years. With that said, I'm pretty sure there's nothing in your employee handbook about sabotage. It's something that occurs each and every day, but no one acknowledges it."

"It just seems so underhanded and despicable."

"So is nepotism and cronyism," Mila countered.

"You have a point."

"I'm glad you're starting to see things my way."

After taking a thoughtful gulp of my margarita, I let the tequila coat my stomach and wash away some of my inhibitions. What would it really hurt to pull a few small pranks on Thorn to make him look bad? No, I wasn't talking about pranks like in *The Office* when Jim put Dwight's office supplies in Jell-O or the time he giftwrapped his desk. I was looking more for underhanded deeds than pranks, anything that could highlight how unqualified for the job Thorn truly was. That wouldn't be so bad, would it?

"Is your silence confirmation that you're plotting?" Mila asked.

With a laugh, I replied, "No, that's not it at all."

"But I thought we were on the same page."

"We are. I'm just going to need some time to come up with the subtle nuances to pull this off. There's too much at stake professionally for me to just go off half-cocked, not to mention the guy's dad is the president." I groaned and covered my face with my hands. "You know that fact alone should give me reservation enough to not do anything to him. It's never a good idea to intimidate a guy whose father could answer the question, 'Yeah, you and what army?' with an *actual army*."

Mila shook her head. "When it's all said and done, I highly doubt President Callahan is going to dispatch the Army or the FBI over some issues his son has at work. He seems like a pretty fair and decent guy."

"He is. I mean, that's what always I've heard, and I also met him briefly one day at work. That's why it's all the more puzzling that he has such a dick for a son."

"Sometimes there's just a bad seed in the family."

"I guess so."

"Just promise me you'll keep me in the loop while you're planning."

"I promise. I might even run some ideas by you," I replied.

With a grin, Mila replied, "That would be awesome."

The waiter arrived with our food, and we started making a dent in our heaping plates of chicken burritos and rice. Something about the overload of carbs and tequila started to slightly elevate my mood. I supposed there was something to be said for comfort food.

I had just swiped my mouth with a napkin when Mila said, "There is one thing I want to know."

"And what is that?"

She jabbed her fork at me. "Have you given any thought to just how hot the angry sex could be between the two of you?"

With a roll of my eyes, I replied, "As a matter of fact, I haven't. I think it got lost somewhere between him seeing me topless and him being a giant tool."

"You said yourself he was gorgeous."

"He is, but—call me crazy—I don't automatically get wet for douchebags." Okay, maybe that was a lie. Maybe I had experienced a fleeting fantasy of Thorn on his knees before me, his face buried between my legs. Normally, I wasn't into BDSM elements like making a man submit, but there was something about Thorn that made me want to dominate him both in and out of the office.

Mila tsked at me. "I'm not buying it, Missy. You've thought about it."

Since I knew it was pointless to argue with her, I sighed. "Fine, I've thought about it. Are you happy?"

She grinned. "Yes and no."

"And why is that?"

"Because I'm happy to know I'm right, but at the same time, I'm sad at the possibility of none of your fantasies with Thorn coming true."

"Don't get your panties in a twist over that. I can assure you I don't plan on losing any sleep over never banging Thorn. Any sleeplessness brought on by him will come from me plotting to overthrow him."

Mila held up the remainder of her margarita. "Here's to hostile takeovers."

I clinked my glass against hers. "To hostile takeovers."

Winking, she added, "Both inside and outside the office."

"You always just have to go one step too far, don't you," I grumbled before downing the rest of the fruity concoction.

CHAPTER SIX

Thorn

Jesus. It had been a hell of a day, and it was only noon, but what did I expect when I'd felt and seen a pair of tits before nine a.m.? After Isabel flounced out of my office, I'd spent the rest of the morning working my way through the ins and outs of the coccyx massager, AKA The Tailsman. Slowly, the business knowledge that had been imparted to me during my undergrad and graduate degrees began to come back, and I started to feel a little more confident that I might actually be able to do this job.

I was debating breaking for lunch when my phone buzzed. "Mr. Callahan, your brother is here to see you."

Fabulous. "Send him in."

Normally, I didn't have a problem with Barrett. Even though we were polar opposites in both looks and personality, I still considered him one of my best friends. Sure, we'd tried to kill each other a few times when we were kids, but that was all part of normal childhood sibling rivalry.

No, my irritation came from the fact that I felt he was coming to check up on me.

With an MBA and years of experience at Callahan, Barrett was cock of the walk two floors above me. While I'd followed in our father's military footsteps, a childhood heart defect had kept Barrett from enlisting. For most of his adult life, he'd been known more on Page Six for his partying and womanizing than he had for his business sense. Thankfully, he'd cleaned his act up over the last year.

The door flung open, and Barrett came bounding into my office like an overeager puppy. His blue eyes twinkled with amusement. In a sing-song voice, he asked, "Hey, honey, how's your day?"

I chuckled in spite of myself. "It's going well." At the sight of the shopping bag in his hand, my brows rose in surprise. "Wow, you brought me lunch?"

"Not just any lunch." He waved the bag at me. "This shit is homemade."

I snorted. "Jesus, you really are becoming domesticated."

"What can I say? Addison enjoys taking care of her man's needs above *and* below the waist."

Against all odds, my manwhore of a brother had met the woman he'd never dared to dream of—the one who had tamed his wild ways and hogtied him into monogamy. The deep family secret was that my dad had originally paid Addison to pretend to be Barrett's fiancée to help his chances in the election. Somewhere along the way while helping my dad campaign, they'd fallen in love for real, and the bastard had shocked the hell out of me by getting engaged at Dad's inauguration. I was slated to be the best man at his wedding in June.

"For a self-respecting career woman, I'm surprised Addison would want to be tied up in apron strings," I mused.

With a roll of his eyes, Barrett replied, "It's just some leftover lasagna and salad, Thorn. I hardly think she's being oppressed by the patriarchy by cooking dinner a few nights a week."

"I'm glad to see she can embrace both her domestic and career sides." With a genuine smile, I added, "You're a very lucky man."

A goofy grin lit up Barrett's face. "I am. I seriously am." After wistfully staring into space for a moment, he shook his head. "Anyway, I have a present for you."

"Are you fucking kidding me?"

"Since when are you anti-presents?" Barrett asked as he dipped his head and began riffling through the contents of the shopping bag.

"I'm not. It's just everyone is acting a little over the top about my first day here at the office. Dad called, and Mom sent me a box of Magnolia Bakery cupcakes—"

Barrett jerked his head up. "Dude, don't hold out on me with those cupcakes—you know they're my favorite too."

"Would you focus?"

"Yeah, yeah," he grumbled before rummaging in the bag again. After a few seconds passed, he cried out, "Aha!" He tossed a box on my desk then flopped down in the chair across from me.

Curiosity got the better of me, so I reached forward to pick up the package. I snorted. "Am I really so hard to buy for that you got me a flashlight?"

"That's not a flashlight. It's a *flesh*light."

"Is there a difference?"

Barrett chuckled. "Turn it over."

Pinching the bridge of my nose, I replied, "I seriously do not have time for games."

"Fine. It's a pocket pussy."

"Excuse me?"

"I think you heard me," Barrett replied with a wicked grin.

"Yes, but I was hoping I misunderstood you."

"Come on, Thorn. I know you're an uptight guy, but surely you've used a sex toy before."

"On a member of the opposite sex, yes, but not on myself." Peering at the box more closely, I realized I had seen one of these before—okay, maybe more than one. Sex toys often made their way through camp during a deployment, and I'd seen several versions of the pocket pussy come from wives and girlfriends; I just didn't have any experience with them myself.

Barrett raked a hand through his dark hair. "I've noticed how tense you are lately. I can only imagine that, after your deployment and injury, it's been a while for you. Since I know you're not the kind of man I could arrange a hookup for, I went for the next best choice for tension relief."

"How kind of you," I mused.

"I try." Barrett motioned to the box. "I also threw in a bottle of heated lube in case you were out."

"And here I thought you had changed your sex-crazed ways now that you're engaged."

With a wink, he replied, "Being monogamous just means I just focus all my energy on one woman. Addison will also be benefitting from my shopping trip."

I opened my bottom desk drawer then picked up the fleshlight. "Well, thank you. I appreciate your kindness."

"From what I hear happened this morning, you already have prime spank bank material."

I groaned as I slid the box into the drawer. "Yeah, I'd like to forget about that."

"Why? Ty said she had a fabulous rack."

Fuck yeah she does. In my mind, I could see those perky, round globes just like they were right back in front of me, those pale pink nipples...God, I wanted nothing more than to bury my face in her chest.

"You have the hots for her!" my brother exclaimed.

"I do not."

"Hell yes you do. You just totally zoned out in a sex fantasy."

Shit. I was going to have to make sure to keep my defenses up even when Isabel wasn't around. Apparently, the mere mention of her was enough for someone to notice I was hot and bothered. "She's my employee, Barrett."

"That just makes it even hotter."

Shaking my head, I replied, "A potential hookup or work romance with Ms. Flannery is completely out of the question."

"Why? You're one of the big dogs. It's not like you'd have to answer to anyone if someone found out."

I rolled my eyes. "In this case, it doesn't help that I'm her boss. I might've been out of the country for the past year, but that doesn't mean I'm not aware of the current climate when it comes to sexual harassment."

"Oh come on, Thorn. You're a smooth, good-looking guy—I hardly think you'd have to blackmail her to get her to have a cup of coffee with you."

Shaking my head, I replied, "I'd be walking across an active land-mine. At any moment, it could go off, and the repercussions could damage not only my reputation but Dad's and that of his administration."

He grimaced. "Jesus, I hadn't even thought of it that way."

"Which is why it's a good thing you are happily engaged and not out potentially screwing up Dad's presidency."

Barrett held up his hands in surrender. "Okay, okay, I agree. The last thing you need is a hot hookup with Ms. Flannery."

"I'm glad you could see the light."

Leaning forward in his chair, Barrett eyed me curiously. "What about a friends-to-lovers thing? Since you're not one for random sex sessions, the two of you could have a slow burn."

"Barrett," I growled.

He laughed. "I'm just joking." Rising out of his chair, he motioned to the table in the corner of my office. "I'm starving. What about you?"

"Yeah, I could eat."

"Good. If you like the lasagna, I'll have Addison make you a couple to freeze. She keeps asking me if there's anything she can do for you now that you're back home."

"While I appreciate the sentiment, I'm not completely helpless, especially since Mom hired a cook and housekeeper for me."

Wagging his brows, Barrett asked, "Either of them young and pert?"

I snorted. "Not quite."

"Bummer. I should have figured she wouldn't willingly hire you some hotties to fornicate with. She wants you marrying a nice girl and popping out some grandbabies."

"Why does she need that from me when you're about to fulfill the fantasy for her?"

"The marriage fantasy, yes, but not the grandbabies. Per Addison's request, we're going to be waiting a few years for any rugrats."

"I still can't imagine you with a diaper bag slung over your shoulder or pushing a stroller."

"Wonders never cease, huh?"

CHAPTER SEVEN

Isabel

TWO WEEKS LATER

Twenty thousand one hundred and sixty minutes—that's exactly how long I'd been enduring Thorn's presence. I'd started keeping track of the time in those increments after I'd made it through the first week, and I tended to sing it to the tune of *Seasons of Love* from *Rent*. Yes, relating to life in show tunes was the hazard of having a roommate who worked on Broadway.

I'm sure you're hoping that after the initial shock wore off about Thorn getting my promotion, I abandoned any ideas of sabotaging him, that I took the high road and rose above any petty, underhanded dealings. You'd be proud to know that at first, I did. I went back to lunch after work determined not to let him get to me. I went so far as to put on meditation music in my office.

But then everything got shot to hell when I watched Thorn waltz out of the office at six o'clock while I remained slaving over projects. Here's a little side note about investment banking: the hours are pure hell. They're even more torturous when you're first starting out. It's why we have something unofficially known as the sleeping room. It's actually an empty office that has space for you to catch a quick power nap when you're pulling twelve to fifteen-hour days.

After I saw Thorn leaving, I scrambled out of my chair and hustled over to the door. As I caught sight of his retreating form, my fists clenched at my sides. Although it was highly doubtful he had actually cleared his workload enough to leave early, it was the last thing he needed to do. He should have been checking in on his associates and analysts. It was the type of thing that caused resentment among coworkers, especially when they had to pick up the slack.

In that moment, I decided I just couldn't let it go. I'd gone above and beyond to both welcome him and make things easier for him, and how had my good deeds been repaid? With utter contempt and absolute assholery. It was then that I embraced the idea that if sabotage was meant to happen, it would.

Not long after, it did.

I'd just consumed a quick, homemade lunch at my desk when I realized I had some paperwork that urgently needed Thorn's John Hancock. With a groan, I peeled myself out of my chair and picked up the manila folder. When I got to his office, I found his secretary wasn't at her desk, which was somewhat surprising since it wasn't her lunch hour.

After I peeked in the open door of Thorn's office, I found the room empty. Instead of waiting on him, I decided to just leave the folder and shoot him a quick email about it. Crossing the room, I walked around the desk. After depositing the folder, I happened to glance over at his computer screen where he had an Excel document open.

Interesting. I would have thought he'd lock his computer before stepping out of the office. I mean, anyone could come by and tamper with a document, which meant an entire morning's worth of work could be lost—and yes, by anyone, I meant myself.

I threw a quick glance over my shoulder. When the coast was clear, I hunched over the keyboard. After highlighting a huge block of figures, I hit undo before quickly saving it. It would take the IT department most of the afternoon to find Thorn's lost work.

With an evil laugh cackling in my head, I snatched the folder off the desk and headed to the door. When I poked my head out, neither Thorn nor his secretary was in sight. Exhaling a relieved breath, I made my way back to my office. Once I was safely back behind my desk, I fired off a quick email to Thorn requesting for him to sign the documents.

I didn't have to wait long to hear back from him. Wherever he was, he was answering messages via his phone.

Come to my office in five minutes.

Okay, I typed back.

It was safe to say that the next five minutes were the longest five minutes I could remember. It was impossible to get any work done. I'd like to say that as the time ticked by, I began to feel a little remorse for what I'd done, but sadly, I didn't.

Once the time was up, I grabbed the folder and headed out of my office. I was almost to Thorn's door when I heard him shout, "No, no, NO! No fucking way!"

Apparently, he had just discovered my handiwork. I glanced over at Alice, who was now back at her desk. "Is he okay?"

"I'm not sure. He told me to send you in when you arrived."

I nodded before pushing my way inside. He stood in front of the computer with his hands wrapped around the back of his head. "Mr. Callahan?"

He whirled around and pinned me with a panicked stare. "Is there a problem?" I questioned.

"My fucking work is wiped."

"Excuse me?"

He rolled his eyes. "The files I was working on this morning—half the information is now missing."

"I'm sure it's just an oversight." I walked over to him. "Did you open up the last saved version of the file?"

"Of course I opened up the last saved version," he replied in an exasperated tone. "It's not fucking there."

Bending over, I feigned peering at the screen. I mean, I knew it wasn't there, and it was going to take an act of the IT gods to get it back. "How much do you think is gone?" Righting myself, I looked at him. "You'll need to see if IT can recover it, but unless you have autosave that's also backed up to the server—"

"Fuck!" he shouted, the veins in his neck bulging.

"Would you like me to call them for you?" I offered, thinking it was the least I could do given his present state of hysterics.

He scowled at me. I was sure he thought I was coddling him, and men like Thorn refused to be coddled, even in times of emotional distress. "No. I'm fully capable of calling them myself."

"Yes, I'm sure you are." I held out the folder. "If you'll just sign these, I'll get out of your hair and let you take care of this."

Thorn snatched a pen out of his suit pocket before jerking the folder from my hands. He made quick work of scribbling his name, and when he finished, he thrust them back at me.

Giving him my most sympathetic smile, I said, "Let me know if there's anything else I can do to help."

He gritted his teeth before biting out, "Thank you, Ms. Flannery."

I nodded then started out of the office, not daring to look back. I was too afraid the part of my conscience that was still working would be horrified by what I'd done.

After I got back to my office, I threw myself into my work. The afternoon hours flew by, and suddenly it was time for dinner. With the end in sight, I pushed on and finally finished shortly before eight.

As I started to leave, a food runner hustled past me. When I glanced back at him, I saw him stop in front of Thorn's office. Since the lights were still on and he was ordering in, I had a feeling he was going to pull his first corporate all-nighter, and let's face it: it was way past time for Thorn to actually put in the hours required by his work. Once again, my pesky conscience reared its head, but I quickly let the devil on my shoulder override it.

The next few days passed without any incidents. The IT gods worked their magic and managed to get Thorn's work back, but he did end up losing a day and a half of work time, which he had to make up by burning the midnight oil.

When I told Mila what I'd done, she high-fived me, and I wasn't sure what it said about our friendship that she was praising me for underhanded behavior. Of course, it had been her idea in the first place. I supposed I didn't have the moral fiber I'd thought I did since I'd been so easily swayed over to the dark side.

On Wednesday, things took an unexpected turn. Just before lunch, I went to Thorn's office to inform him of a call I'd just received. With his head buried in his computer, he didn't bother looking up at me. "Yes, Ms. Flannery?"

"Mr. Gregson just called to say he took an earlier flight and will be arriving this afternoon."

Thorn grimaced as he raked his hand through his hair. Ronald Gregson was the prime investor we were courting for The Tailsmen Coccyx Massager. "Of course he would pull one of the oldest tricks in the book—the sneak attack."

"In spite of that, I assured him we would be ready for the presentation this afternoon."

"Good."

"Have you had a chance to review the information the analysts prepared?"

With a shake of his head, Thorn replied, "No, but I'm sure it's fine."

My mouth dropped open. "You're joking, right?"

"No, Ms. Flannery, I'm not. I'm pretty sure the analysts are capable of completing reports clean enough for the investor's eyes."

Pretty sure? He was *pretty sure* the reports were clean. I wondered if he would have gone on a combat mission if he were *pretty sure* the intelligence was right.

"With all due respect—"

He held up his hand to silence me. "Instead of berating me, would you make yourself useful and go set up the conference room?"

I bit down on my lip to keep from screaming at him, and it took a lot of my willpower not to reach over and choke him. I couldn't believe how flippant he was being. There was no room for error when it came to client presentations. "Yes, Mr. Callahan," I replied through gritted teeth.

After marching out of his office, I went straight to the conference room, and it didn't take long to ensure the laptop was hooked up to the projector. Although I could have walked away then, the perfectionist in me wouldn't allow it. Thorn might not have cared about going over the files, but I did.

I was halfway through the first set when one of my office buddies, Justine, poked her head in. "Here you are. I've been looking all over for you."

"Sorry. The bastard boss ordered me here to set up for this afternoon's surprise presentation."

"I should have figured as much. Anyway, it's a gorgeous day so Tracey and I are going to grab a sandwich from the food trucks. Wanna come?" Justine asked.

"Nah, I better hang back and finish this up."

"But it's not your job to set up for presentations."

"I know."

Justine rolled her eyes. "I wish I had your commitment."

I laughed. "It's probably more my mania you wished you had than my dedication."

"Can I bring you something back?"

"Yeah—club on wheat with no mayo."

She nodded. "Got it."

"Thanks."

"No problem."

Once I'd run through the first file, I opened the next. This one was full of research backing up how much the coccyx massager was needed. I clicked on one of the links and seconds later a giant, throbbing cock appeared on the screen in front of me. "Holy shit!" I cried as moaning noises filled the room.

From what I could deduce, the analyst had accidentally typed "cockx" instead of "coccyx". Normally, one typo wouldn't be a huge deal, but in this case, it took you to a triple-X porn site featuring giant dicks. God, what a nightmare it would have been if I hadn't caught it and the investor saw a giant cock.

Hello, light-bulb moment.

I'd said I wouldn't actively seek ways to sabotage Thorn, and here was a prime example of something just falling into my lap. If I left in the typo, it would serve Thorn right to be embarrassed in front of Gregson for not doing his work. No one would ever know I'd caught the mistake and had the opportunity to change it. I would just sit back and act as horrified as everyone else. Sure, it would hurt the clients if they didn't get the funding they needed, but that wouldn't be on my shoulders. It would be on Thorn's.

Once again, I let the evil side of me override the good.

CHAPTER EIGHT

Thorn

I'd like to say the more time that went by in my job, the better acclimated I became, but that wouldn't be accurate. Regardless of how long I spent evaluating figures and reading files, it never seemed to click. Even when I tried looking at it from a strategy standpoint, it didn't work. In the end, my frustration led me to half-assing things. No one else seemed to notice it except Isabel. Of course, each time she called me out, I realized how much more she belonged in the position than I did.

With today's meeting, I had the chance to turn things around. Sure, I had blown off proofreading the analysts' files, but in my defense, these were Ivy League grads hungry for advancement. They weren't going to screw up.

When the front desk alerted me that Ronald Gregson had arrived, I walked down to the elevators to meet him. As he stepped out of the elevator car, I threw out my hand. "Mr. Gregson, I'm Thorn Callahan. It's a pleasure meeting you."

He smiled. "Nice to meet you as well. Please call me Ron."

"Sure thing, Ron. Did you have a nice flight?"

"I did. Thankfully, it was smooth skies the entire way here."

"You're based in Utah, correct?" It was part of my job to become personally familiar with the investors, and that part I could do easily. "How's the weather in Salt Lake?"

"Snowing like mad even though it's almost April."

I chuckled. "I don't envy you on that one. Of course, it's such a beautiful part of the country."

"Have you visited before?"

"We did some camping there when I was a teenager."

Mr. Gregson appeared somewhat surprised by my response. I guess he didn't imagine a white-collar guy like myself would enjoy roughing it. "You like to camp?"

"I do. It's been my life for the past decade in my military career."

Mentioning my military service might have been a little over the top, but I was willing to pull out all the stops to ensure my client got the funding they needed.

Mr. Gregson gave an appreciative nod. "Thank you for your service."

I smiled. "And thank you for recognizing it."

When we got to the conference room, Isabel was waiting for us along with two of the analysts who had been working on the project. After introducing everyone, I motioned for Ron to have a seat. With a deep breath, I began walking him through the presentation.

It was all smooth sailing until I got to the portion on the scientific research involving the coccyx bone—though I suppose I should say *boner*, because that was what suddenly filled the screen before me. My world slowed down to a crawl.

Shaking my head, I tried jolting myself out of the nightmare I suddenly found myself in. How was it possible that there was a giant dick on the screen? Considering the coccyx bone was in your butt, I could have fathomed a bare ass, but a dick? That was totally out of the realm of normalcy, not to mention the groans of pleasure echoing off the walls of the room.

My gaze spun from the screen over to Mr. Gregson. His eyes bulged in horror while his mouth opened and closed like a fish out of water. Of all the clients to assault with the supersized image of a cock, the nice, somewhat uptight Mormon from Utah was the worst one it could have possibly happened to.

I quickly fumbled for the mouse to click off the offending website. When the screen was finally clear, I exhaled a ragged breath. "Mr. Gregson, I'm so terribly sorry," I croaked.

"What was the meaning of that terribly offensive image?" he demanded, his face blood red.

"I'm so sorry. I would imagine it just comes down to a mix-up."

"A mix-up? Do you normally experience mix-ups that involve pornography?"

"No, sir, we don't."

Mr. Gregson grabbed the handkerchief out of his suit pocket. After dabbing his face, he rose out of his chair. "I don't need to see any more."

FUCK. "I'm sure the rest of the presentation is fine, and this was just a minor oversight."

Ron narrowed his eyes at me. "Can you assure me there is nothing else so offensive?"

Since I hadn't gone through the files to check them, I couldn't. Glancing at the analysts, I said, "Can you two?"

With sheepish expressions, they shook their heads. I momentarily closed my eyes in defeat. I also wanted to avoid looking at Isabel. I was sure she was seething because I hadn't taken the time to check the files like she'd told me to. "Mr. Gregson, while I cannot assure you of the rest of the presentation's content, I can assure you this is a product worthy of your investment." When he started to gather up his things, desperation rocketed through my body, and I held up my hand to stop him. "I'll be happy to run through it without the slides for you."

Mr. Gregson stared curiously at me. "You want to try to sell me on a multimillion-dollar investment by just *telling* me about it?"

"I'd like to try—well, that and I'd like to draw it out for you."

"While everything within me says to walk out of here, my curiosity is piqued by how you can possibly pull this off."

Inwardly, I did a little victory dance while at the same time panic pricked its way up my spine. While I might've sounded confident to Mr. Gregson, I was falling apart on the inside. I motioned to his chair. "Please have a seat."

After flipping on the lights, I armed myself with a few Expo markers before taking my stance in front of the white board. I put on my game face and started going through everything I knew about the coccyx massager. When I finished, my mouth was dry, and the white board was a mess of multicolored marker ink.

Silence hung heavy in the room. While it seemed like everything had finally clicked into place for me, I wasn't sure if it had even made sense in the heat of the moment. After capping the marker in my hand, I placed it in my pocket. "So, what do you think?"

Mr. Gregson cleared his throat. "That was very impressive, Mr. Callahan. I'm not sure I've seen a presentation like that since the early days before technology took over."

"I thank you for the compliment. Does The Tailsmen have your support?"

Across the table from me, Isabel leaned forward, anxiously waiting to hear the verdict.

"While I certainly don't appreciate what happened here earlier, I can't help but be impressed with the rest of your presentation."

"Once again, you have my sincerest apologies as well as my word that anything else that comes to you will be triple-checked to ensure there is nothing inappropriate within it." I narrowed my eyes at the analysts. "I will also be handling the repercussions on our end by changing up the team when we move forward."

Ron nodded his head. "I will hold you to that."

I held out my hand. "Do we have a deal?"

"There are some specifics I'd like to fine-tune in pricing and distribution before I sign on the dotted line."

"I'll be happy to redraw those figures for you and then go back to the Tailsmen people."

"Good. Then we have a deal."

Holy fucking shit. I'd pulled it off. As he shook my hand, I tried not to show my utter and complete disbelief that we actually had his support. "We're happy you're on board."

After taking down some of Gregson's concerns and running some numbers, we came to an agreement to go back to the Tailsmen people with.

"It's been nice meeting with you. I'll head back to the hotel to await the updated information." When I started toward the door with Ron, I glanced over my shoulder at Isabel. She wore an expression both of disgust and disbelief. I got the impression she wasn't too thrilled that Ron had given me a second chance. She would have probably preferred I go down in flames because of my carelessness, and the truth was, that's probably what I deserved.

CHAPTER NINE
Isabel

ONE WEEK LATER

Apparently, the universe hated me. It was the only explanation I could come up for on how Thorn had managed to save the presentation. When I'd executed my evil plan, I hadn't known Ron was a devout Mormon. I happened upon that little tidbit shortly before the meeting started when one of the analysts brought in decaffeinated coffee. It was then I realized just how much worse a giant, throbbing cock on the screen was going to be. Cue me as Hannibal from the old 80s TV show *The A Team* saying, "I love it when a plan comes together."

Even so, all my hopes were dashed when Thorn somehow managed to pull a Hail Mary with a few Expo markers and a whiteboard. As much as I hated to admit it, I was just as impressed as Gregson with how Thorn explained fairly detailed and intricate information without a digital presentation. He knew the material, and that in itself both ticked me off and impressed me. *Damn him.* And, of course, he salvaged the deal, although the rumor mill started saying he had been called into Murray's office for a dressing down.

Today found us doing some last-minute tweaking in preparation for our dinner meeting with George Halliwell. Although it was just a typical business dinner, Thorn appeared exceptionally tense. He kept popping his neck and jerking his hand through his hair. I hated when he did the hair jerk because it made his sandy blond hair look all tousled and sexy like he'd been rolling around in the sheets during a sexathon.

Yes, I utterly despised myself for thinking that.

We'd just hit a tedious part of reviewing the files on the computer when Thorn leaned his head back and pinched the bridge of his nose. "If I'm going to get through the rest of this, I'm going to need some strong coffee." He stared pointedly at me.

Oh. Hell. No. He was *not* suggesting I get his coffee.

In a sugary-sweet tone, I replied, "I believe I showed you where the break room is last week, but if you've forgotten, it's down the hall and then take two lefts."

"I want an espresso from Starbucks."

"Then you're going to need to take the elevator and go down the block."

"How much plainer do I need to make this, Ms. Flannery? I want a Venti espresso from Starbucks, and you're going to get it for me."

"Well, Mr. Callahan, there are a lot of things I want that I don't get. That's just life. Furthermore, I know you're still new to the workforce, but being a coffee runner is not part of my job description. You have an assistant, AKA a secretary for that, not to mention a Secret Service agent who is outside thumbing through *Cosmo*."

His blue eyes narrowed at me. "I never said it was part of your job. However, I do believe it is part of your job description not to be insubordinate to your superior."

If I had been a cartoon character, this was the moment imaginary steam would have billowed from my ears at Thorn's audacity. At that moment, I had two choices—my own version of Robert Frost's *The Road Not Taken*. Fearing for my job, I could bow to Thorn's will and get his damn coffee, or I could throw caution to the wind and put Mr. Trust Fund Baby in his place. By now, you should know me well enough to know which one I chose. It also didn't help that I'd caught the end of *Nine to Five*, one of my all-time favorites, on HBO when I got in from work the night before. Facing down my own version of Franklin Hart, I was going to make Violet, Doralee, and Judy proud.

I jabbed his chest with my index finger. "Look, soldier boy, I know you're used to barking orders and having your men and women scramble to obey them, but we're not in Afghanistan anymore, Toto.

Now I'm going to walk out of here and tell your secretary you're about to piss yourself for an espresso."

While I fully expected Thorn to be enraged by my declaration, I didn't expect the amused smirk that twisted on his face. "Alice isn't here."

"Excuse me?"

"She took a half day to go to the dentist."

Damn Alice and her teeth. Now my ass really was on the line. "Fine. I will go get your precious espresso, but don't doubt for one minute that I'll be filing a grievance via the proper channels," I hissed.

Thorn had the audacity to grin. "You make sure you do that."

MOTHERFUCKER. After I whirled around, I started stalking out of his office.

"Oh, Ms. Flannery?" he called.

I fought the urge to reply, *Yes, Satan?* Instead, I slowly pivoted around. "Yes, Mr. Callahan?"

"I would offer you some cash, but I'm sure you'll want a receipt to corroborate your story."

Smug bastard. Of course I wanted a receipt, and of course I planned to put it with my grievance. I hated that he had the ability to read my mind; it made it hard to maintain any ground with him. Well, *sometimes* he could read my mind—obviously, if he were fully psychic, he would have busted me for the underhanded shit I'd been doing to him.

I gave a nod of my head before turning back around and sprinting out the door. After I stopped by my office for my purse, I hopped on the elevator. When I jabbed the button for the lobby, the woman behind me snickered.

"Tough day, huh?"

"You could say that."

"Trust me, I've been there."

The commiseration was nice, but at the same time, I inwardly groaned at my behavior. I mean, when had I sunk so low as to act like a petulant toddler by taking my frustrations out on an elevator button? That was somewhat of a rhetorical question since I knew exactly why I was acting the way I was. It was all because the devil incarnate had usurped me at my job and was hell-bent on driving me batshit crazy.

While it pained me to admit it, I really, really wanted to hurt Thorn Callahan, and that in itself was unnerving because I normally wasn't a violent person. Back home in Georgia, I was constantly stopping my car to help wayward turtles in the middle of the road. I'd even been known to put spiders outside rather than squishing them.

Ugh, the man was driving me absolutely insane, and it had only been three weeks. How was I possibly going to make it a year to eighteen months with him? As I pushed through the doors of the Starbucks, I found myself actually contemplating the thought of changing companies, but I really didn't want to go that route. It wasn't that I couldn't have found another job, but more about the fact that I loved the Callahan Corporation, which had been home to me for so many years.

After I placed my order for Satan's precious espresso, I started shuffling around in the bottom of my purse for my debit card, and I finally found it hiding under a bottle of dog laxatives. After I handed the card to the barista, my gaze once again fell inside my purse, more specifically on the bottle.

You see, it wasn't normal for me to have dog laxatives rolling around in the bottom of my purse. Dani was known to suffer from constipation from time to time, which the vet assured me was part of living the city dog life. I hadn't meant to bring them with me that day. When I was raking stuff off the kitchen counter and into my purse, I thought I'd swept up a bottle of Midol.

At that moment, a truly devious idea entered my mind. It was so heinous that I actually sucked in an agonized breath upon realizing I'd actually thought it. I even went so far as to glance left and right to make sure no one was staring at me in fear. I don't know why I thought someone could suddenly have the ability to read my mind, but if they did, I would be in big trouble.

I could almost imagine the expressions of horror on their faces, as well as the dialogue that might take place.

"That seemingly normal-looking chick right there? She's debating putting dog laxatives in her boss's coffee."

"Damn, that's cold."

"Forget cold—it's downright psychotic. If she keeps gobbling up the cuckoo puffs, she'll be rocking a straight-jacket down in Bellevue."

"I dunno, bosses can be epic pricks. He probably deserves a lengthy ride on the porcelain chariot."

"Espresso for Isabel." I jumped out of my thoughts at the sound of my name being called.

"Uh, yeah, that's me. Thank you." After tucking my head to my chest, I refused to look at anyone else as I made my way out of the store.

During the trek back to the building, the good and evil sides of my mind were entrenched in raging warfare. I was front and center in my own potential Shakespearian tragedy. To laxative or not laxative—that was the question. My true motive wasn't just about payback for Thorn being such a dick; it was more about the fact that he had stolen my job.

In the midst of it all, I once again thought back to the previous night when I was watching *Nine to Five*. More precisely, I thought about the scene where after a mix-up with some boxes, Violet accidentally spikes her boss's coffee with rat poison. Thankfully, a malfunctioning office chair leads him to fall and hit his head before he can drink the coffee, which also leads to hilarity ensuing in the office.

But this was real life we were talking about. I wasn't sure what the professional ramifications would be for lacing your boss's coffee with dog laxatives. There had been no mention of anything like that in my business ethics courses in either my undergraduate or graduate studies. I had a feeling if anything like that had ever taken place, it wouldn't be documented…well, maybe in court records.

For my own self-preservation, I knew it was important to remember I wasn't trying to kill Thorn. Although there were times I wanted to physically hurt him, I would have never done anything to truly harm him. In the end, I was probably doing him a favor. Everyone could benefit from a good bowel cleaning out from time to time. At that moment, I could've cued the *He's so full of shit* argument as well.

I also knew from personal experience that nothing too horrendous was going to happen to him. Just how did I know this? For starters, it was nothing but natural ingredients like olive and fish oil, pumpkin, and yogurt. Secondly, I had used it on Dani, and nothing bad had happened to her—that is if you didn't consider an epic colon blow bad.

I'd gotten halfway up the block when I suddenly ducked into a Duane Reade. What was I doing in a pharmacy? I'd watched enough episodes of crime TV to know if anything was discovered about the coffee being tampered with, they could pull the security tapes at Starbucks and at work. The last thing I needed was to be on video going into a bathroom with Thorn's coffee.

Keeping my head low, I hurried to the back of the store where the restrooms were. Thankfully, when I got inside, I found myself alone. After locking myself into one of the stalls, I set the coffee down on the back of the toilet. Surprise filled me when I found my hands were shaking slightly.

After screwing open a capsule, my hand hovered over the cup as I felt my professional life hover over a figurative cliff. Assuring myself there was no way possible to detect dog laxatives in a human blood test, I flicked my wrist, and it was done. Since the human digestive system is different than a canine's, I emptied another capsule for good measure.

"You're so going to hell for this," I muttered as I swished the espresso around to stir the contents. I recapped the cup before flushing the remaining capsules down the toilet, and then I wrapped the bottle in toilet paper before pushing it to the bottom of the stall's trash pile.

As I walked the remaining distance back to the office, it felt like I was carrying a bomb rather than a cup of coffee. When I got back up on our floor, I drew in a breath to prepare to face Thorn.

I gave a quick knock on the door before he called for me to enter. When he saw it was me, he rolled his eyes. "Jesus, did you go to the Starbucks ten blocks from here?"

"No, I went to the one just down the street," I replied as I handed him the espresso.

"Well, it took you fucking forever. I might as well have ordered an iced coffee." When he took a sip, I leaned forward on my toes. I didn't dare blink or breathe. After Thorn swallowed, he glanced at me. "It's good," he pronounced.

I exhaled the breath I'd been holding in one long wheeze. "I'm glad to hear that." Actually, I was glad to hear there wasn't any bitter taste from the laxatives.

I thought I saw a momentary flicker of regret in his eyes, but it quickly passed.

"I suppose you're waiting on a thank you?"

Aaaand just like that, any regret I might have had went straight out the window. He deserved every moment of the impending porcelain scourge.

I plastered a sweet smile on my face. "I wouldn't dare expect you to be grateful for someone going above and beyond to do you a favor."

The corners of his lips quirked. "Thank you, Ms. Flannery."

Okay, I wasn't expecting that response. "You're welcome."

When I stood there for a moment, he motioned to the paperwork before us. "Would you like to get back to work so we can be prepared to leave for dinner on time?"

In the blink of an eye, Thorn waved his asshole wand and the bastard reappeared. Even so, I remained professional. "There's nothing I would love to do more."

After Thorn nodded his head, I turned on my heels and tried not to stomp out of the room. *I hope you shit yourself senseless.*

After I left Thorn's office in a huff, I'd like to say I coolly and calmly sat back and waited for the laxatives to work their magic and exact my revenge, but by now, I'm sure you know there's nothing cool and calm about me in stressful situations.

By the time I got back to my office, I was in full panic mode. I couldn't focus on any of the files before me. I kept pacing around the room, nibbling on my nails. Finally, I realized I needed a voice of a reason and comfort. Since it didn't feel safe to talk in the office, I grabbed my phone before heading out of the building.

Once I got outside, I walked as far down the block as I could, as if the closer I stayed to the building, the easier it might be for someone to listen in on my call. Oh yeah, I was completely out there.

After I dialed Mila, I anxiously waited for her to pick up. When she finally answered, I sighed with relief. "Hey, it's me."

"Hey, you. I'm not used to phone calls in the middle of the day."

I was sure she was somewhat surprised as we usually only texted during work. "Yeah, I felt like it was easier to call you than text."

"Where are you?"

"Um, on a street corner outside my building."

"Please tell me you haven't gone full-on *Pretty Woman* and started working street corners to find a man," Mila teased.

I rolled my eyes. "No. That's not it at all."

"Then what the hell is going on?"

"I did something terrible."

"I'm pretty sure you couldn't have done anything worse than Thorn flashing a dick at a Mormon."

"No. It's infinitely worse."

"Okay, Belle. I'm not going to lie—your voice is scaring me a little. Why don't you take a few deep breaths?" After following Mila's instructions, I felt a little less crazy. "Now tell me what's wrong."

"So Thorn was being this big dick about not being able to get through the files he needed to before tonight's dinner meeting without some coffee, but he didn't want coffee from the break room. He demanded I go to Starbucks for him since his secretary was out at the dentist and even though I should have said no—"

"I'm going to need you to get to the point."

I sucked in a ragged breath. "I put some of Dani's dog laxatives in Thorn's coffee," I whispered.

"Wait, what? I didn't hear that last part."

Silently, I cursed New York drivers for their honking horns and screeching tires that drowned out my confession. "I said I put some of Dani's dog laxatives in Thorn's coffee," I repeated a little louder.

The next sound I heard was Mila's hysterical laughter. When she finally caught her breath, she panted, "Oh my God, you didn't!"

"Yes. Yes, I did."

"Holy shit, Belle. That is epic—like, I didn't know you had something so devious inside of you."

I pinched my eyes shut in dismay. "Me either."

"I seriously have tears running down my face right now."

"I'm glad you think it's so funny," I lamented.

"Don't you find it fucking hilarious?"

"Right now I'm in such a paranoid, freak-out state that I'm debating confessing to him in case he needs to get his stomach pumped.

Mila snorted. "You gave him dog laxatives, not antifreeze."

"What if he's allergic to one of the ingredients and has a fatal reaction? I'm pretty sure you don't come back from killing your boss in the corporate world. Do you think it would be a lesser conviction like manslaughter?"

"First of all, if it's the same ones I give Drogo, it has like pumpkin, mineral oil, and some psyllium—nothing life-threatening, so there's no way you're going to be charged with manslaughter or anything like that."

"What if he has a pumpkin allergy and goes into anaphylactic shock?"

I could almost hear Mila's eye roll through the phone. "Uh, I'm not sure I've ever heard of anyone with gourd-specific allergies."

"Maybe I should Google it. Then I can be on the lookout for any symptoms."

"If that would make you feel better and/or quit acting like a paranoid freak, go for it."

"I can't help who I am," I protested.

"Belle, I'm pretty sure the worst thing that's going to happen to Thorn is an epic dump."

"You think so?"

"Well, you and I can vouch for it since we've both seen the insanity that came out of our dogs when we gave it to them."

I wrinkled my nose as I remembered my last experience with the laxatives. "I guess you're right."

"I know I'm right. Now get a hold of yourself and get back to work. For the love of God and everything that is holy, do NOT go confessing anything to Thorn."

"Okay, I won't."

"You promise? Even if he streaks past your office to hit the john?"

"He has a bathroom in his office, but yes, I still promise."

"You're still going to be a freak and stalk him today, aren't you?"

Damn. She really did know me too well. "Most of my stalking of Thorn will occur at our early dinner meeting with clients."

"You're impossible. Just don't act weird."

"Easier said than done," I muttered as I reluctantly started back toward the building.

After the "cock seen round the world" episode, I threw myself into my job. My new work ethic was also inspired by a closed-door meeting with Murray about what had gone wrong, in which I didn't act like a pussy and place the blame elsewhere. It was my fault for not checking the files like I should have even in the short amount of time I had. While Murray was grateful I'd managed to somehow save the day, he'd cited many issues he saw with my performance. Since I hated being reprimanded, I vowed to not let it happen again.

That was why I knew how important the Halliwell meeting was. It was my chance to right some of the wrongs, to show everyone I really did belong in my position—that I deserved to be vice president even if I didn't necessarily want or like the job. I needed to wow the hell out of them to make it happen.

The one area where I wasn't making any headway was my attraction to Isabel. You would think making a woman absolutely despise you would somehow turn you off—oh no. It just stoked the fire burning within me. Every snarl of her lip, every roll of her eyes, every frustrated huff made me even hornier, if that was even possible.

I wanted to bite that snarling lip. I wanted her eyes to roll back in her head because of the pleasure I was giving her. I wanted her to huff in frustration as I held her back from coming.

Yes, I was in deep shit with no end in sight.

When Isabel sashayed into my office after lunch, I groaned inwardly. Okay, so maybe I was exaggerating a little on the alleged sway of her hips. Maybe it's just how I wanted to imagine it in my mind. Most likely, she was more stalking into my office than seductively swaying.

"I wanted to check in to see how things were going on your end."

"They're fine."

"Would you like to run through the presentation?"

I nodded. "That would be great."

After we went through everything I planned to discuss with Halliwell, it was time to recheck the figures. As Isabel hovered over me to eye the screen, the curve of her breast rubbed against my shoulder. At the same time, the floral scent of her perfume filled my nostrils.

Jesus, she was way too close. With just a flick of my wrist, I could have fingered the hem of her skirt and trailed it up her thigh. I could have then slid my hand between her legs to touch the one physical part of her that was still a mystery to me.

When my cock began to tent my pants, I shifted in my chair to shield it from Isabel's eyes. *Fuck.* This was so very, very bad. Since out of sight and out of mind was best, I had to get her out of my office— the farther away from me the better.

When an idea popped into my mind, I immediately acted on it. "If I'm going to get through the rest of this, I'm going to need some strong coffee."

When I stared up at Isabel pointedly, fury momentarily burned in her eyes before she plastered on a smile. "I believe I showed you where the break room is last week, but if you've forgotten, it's down the hall and then take two lefts."

Yeah, that would make perfect sense if I weren't sporting wood at the moment. I needed her gone to have a moment for both my dick and myself to cool off. "I want an espresso from Starbucks."

She crossed her arms over her fantastic tits, causing me to inwardly groan again. "Then you're going to need to take the elevator and go down the block."

Okay, the current course wasn't working. It was time to crank up the assholery. "How much plainer do I need to make this, Ms. Flannery? I want a Venti espresso from Starbucks, and you're going to get it for me."

"Well, Mr. Callahan, there are a lot of things I want that I don't get. That's just life. Furthermore, I know you're still new to the workforce, but being a coffee runner is not part of my job description. You have an assistant, AKA a secretary for that, not to mention a Secret Service agent who is outside thumbing through *Cosmo*."

Jesus, Ty must be out of his mind with boredom if he's reading Cosmo. I pushed that thought out of my mind to focus on Isabel. "I never said it was part of your job. However, I do believe it is part of your job description not to be insubordinate to your superior."

Yep, I actually said that. When Isabel's face turned almost purple with rage, I was pleased to see my words were having the desired effect. After she jabbed her finger into my chest, it took everything within me not to drag her onto my lap.

"Look, soldier boy, I know you're used to barking orders and having your men and women scramble to obey them, but we're not in Afghanistan anymore, Toto. Now I'm going to walk out of here and tell your secretary you're about to piss yourself for an espresso."

God, that mouth...that luscious fucking mouth I wanted wrapped around my throbbing cock—*focus, Thorn.* I forced a smirk onto my face at her mention of Alice getting my espresso. "Alice isn't here."

"Excuse me?"

"She took a half day to go to the dentist." And thank God she did because I desperately needed Isabel to get the hell away from me.

Isabel's fists clenched at her sides as war raged within her mind. Although she clearly wanted to both choke me and tell me to go fuck myself, she valued her job too much to do so. A shudder went through her body before she hissed, "Fine. I will go get your precious espresso, but don't doubt for one minute that I'll be filing a grievance via the proper channels."

God, I loved her fire. She was the type of woman who made life interesting both in and out of the bedroom. "You make sure you do that."

When she whirled around and started stomping out of my office, I called, "Oh, Ms. Flannery?"

Slowly she pivoted around, her body shaking with silent rage. "Yes, Mr. Callahan?" she questioned in a strangled voice.

Now it was time to go for the jugular with my assholery. "I would offer you some cash, but I'm sure you'll want a receipt to corroborate your story."

She nodded her head at me before sprinting from the room. As soon as I felt enough time had passed for her to get on the elevator, I bolted from my chair and into the bathroom. Since my pants were still partially tented, my cock wasn't going down without a fight...or at least a release.

After locking the door, I unzipped my pants and dipped my hand inside. One thing I hadn't abandoned from my time in the desert was going commando. As I fisted my hand around my cock, Isabel's image automatically formed in my mind. Gritting my teeth, I willed it away, but it was no use. Somehow she had burrowed deep beneath my skin, and I couldn't seem to get her out.

Since the Starbucks was just down the block, I knew I didn't have a lot of time. I had to go for the down-and-dirty fantasy. As I closed my eyes, the images played step by tantalizing step in my mind.

After shoving Isabel's skirt over her hips, I bend her over my desk. Tearing away her lacy thong, I smack both of her ass cheeks—hard. She cries out with pleasure rather than pain, because she wants it as rough as I do.

Nudging her thighs apart with my knee, I slam into her slick walls. She's already dripping from need and from me going down on her. Of course I've tasted her—made her come twice. God, the cries of ecstasy...she's so wet...so hot.

I press my fingers deep into the flesh of her ass and pound in and out of her. I'm relentless as she demands I take her harder and faster, and we come together with my name echoing on her lips.

In a frenzy, my hand worked over my cock as I came with a shout. As I rode the spasms of my orgasm, I fought to catch my breath. When I finally finished shuddering, a wave of guilt washed over me. What kind of creepy pervert was I to jerk off in the middle of the day while fantasizing about my coworker?

With a grunt of disgust, I went about cleaning myself up. After washing my hands, I tucked my slackened dick back in my pants and zipped up. After unlocking the door, I peeked my head out to make sure Isabel hadn't returned. With the coast clear, I walked back over to my desk and plopped down in my chair.

Just as I started to get back to work, Ty popped his head in the door. "Are you all right?"

"Peachy. Why do you ask?"

"I thought I heard you shout as if you were in pain."

Fucking hell. Talk about not having a moment of privacy. "It wasn't me."

Ty peered curiously at me. "Okay. I just wanted to check."

"I'm fine. You can go back to reading *Cosmo*."

"Excuse me?"

Glancing back down at my files, I said, "Isabel told me you were reading *Cosmo*. Get any good sex tips?"

"Actually, I read an interesting article on how masturbating at the office can relieve stress and tension."

I snapped my head up to meet his amused gaze. "Wait, what?"

Ty waggled his brows. "I think I figured out the source of that shout."

"I don't know what you're talking about."

"Come on, Thorn. Considering how guilty you looked when I came in here, coupled with the fact that you're all flushed, it isn't hard to figure out." He shrugged. "It's not like I'm going to judge you."

"You don't find it rather creepy to be jerking off at work?"

"No. You took care of business discreetly. Creepy would be jerking off at your desk in the hopes someone would walk in and see you."

With a grimace, I muttered, "That is creepy as hell."

"Were you trying out Barrett's gift?"

I rolled my eyes. "Jesus, you two are like a couple of gossiping old women." When he cocked his brows at me, I replied, "Not that it's any of your business, but no, I was not."

"Pity. I wanted to get your thoughts on it. I was debating getting one for myself."

Motioning to my desk drawer, I said, "You're welcome to this one."

"Oh no, I wouldn't dream of depriving you."

"Aren't you kind," I said dryly.

"I try."

As Ty hung around my desk, he stroked his chin thoughtfully. His mannerisms told me there was something he wanted to say but he was debating whether or not it was worth it. "All right, spit it out."

"I couldn't help wondering if your previous meeting with Isabel had anything to do with you needing to rub one out."

Narrowing my eyes at him, I countered, "You know my stance on that."

"While that might be true for your brain, it doesn't necessarily mean your dick is on the same page."

"Unlike some men I know, my dick doesn't do my decision-making."

"That's a fucking farce of a statement considering you were just jerking off."

"If you don't have anything else to discuss with me besides my dick, I really need to get back to work."

"You sure are testy for someone who just got off."

"Goodbye, Ty," I muttered.

He flashed me a final grin before heading out the door. After starting out, he stopped and glanced back at me. "Heads up—she's baaaack," he said.

Maybe it was time to request a change in my security detail. Isabel appeared just seconds later, looking exceptionally beautiful with a flush in her cheeks from running around.

Right. Time to curb that bullshit. With a roll of my eyes, I asked, "Jesus, did you go to the Starbucks ten blocks from here?"

"No, I went to the one just down the street," she replied as she handed me the espresso. When our hands met, I couldn't help noticing the softness of her skin. *Jesus, I need help.*

"Well, it took you fucking forever. I might as well have ordered an iced coffee." As I took a swig, I noticed Isabel leaning forward. I supposed she was worried I was going to find fault with it. To let her off the hook, I pronounced, "It's good."

Relief flooded her face. "I'm glad to hear that."

Her reaction only fueled the gnawing guilt I felt about being such a bastard toward her. Inwardly, I battled with myself about coming clean with Isabel, admitting that me being an epic asshole was just a ruse and I was really sorry for being such a jerk.

In the end, I knew nothing good would come from being honest. Instead, I flipped the asshole switch again. "I suppose you're waiting on a thank you?"

Isabel smirked. "I wouldn't dare expect you to be grateful for someone going above and beyond to do you a favor."

I couldn't help smiling at her reaction. Since it wasn't within me not to express my gratitude, I said, "Thank you, Ms. Flannery."

"You're welcome," she said, her tone one of surprise.

Since it felt like we were about to have a moment, I quickly motioned to the paperwork before us. "Would you like to get back to work so we can be prepared to leave for dinner on time?"

Just like that, the moment was broken with the reappearance of my assholery. She narrowed her eyes. "There's nothing I would love to do more."

Once she exited my office, I sighed. If only there was a way I didn't have to see Isabel. Since I refused to admit defeat, I wouldn't dare ask to be moved to another department. For the time being, it appeared I was stuck between a rock and a hard place, or in my specific case, a rock-hard dick.

The shrill sound of my alarm alerted me it was time to get ready to leave for the dinner meeting with Halliwell. Normally, I was used to seven or eight o'clock dinners, but Halliwell had requested six o'clock, which made it feel like we were dining with the senior citizen crowd.

When I rose out of my chair, a stabbing pain crisscrossed its way across my abdomen. As I pressed my hand against my stomach, it slowly subsided. Considering I hadn't eaten anything but a few fiber-infused protein bars, I couldn't imagine why my stomach would be hurting.

After brushing my teeth and changing my tie in the bathroom, I headed back into my office. Isabel poked her head in the door—of course she would be punctual. "Would you like me to call for a cab?"

"That won't be necessary. We can take my car," I replied.

"Figures," she muttered under her breath.

As I grabbed my bag, I used my other hand to text my driver. Then I joined Isabel in the doorway.

"Do you have everything?" she asked.

"Yes, Mom, I do," I teasingly replied.

With a roll of her eyes, she turned and started walking to the elevators. I fell in step behind her with Ty at my side, and we made the trek downstairs and to the car in silence.

After Ty took a seat in the front, Isabel reluctantly slid into the back with me. As the car eased into traffic, I was assaulted by another stomach cramp. At what must've been my grimace, Isabel asked, "Are you all right?"

"I'm fine." When I glanced at her, she actually appeared concerned. Well, it was a mixture of concern and a bit of horror. "Don't worry, I'm not going to fuck this up."

She shifted in the seat. "I didn't say you were."

"You didn't have to—it was written all over your face."

Ducking her head, she smoothed her skirt. "I'm sorry. I'm sure you're going to do just fine."

Sure you are. We didn't say anything else to each other on the way to the restaurant. After the driver let us out, I followed Isabel into the lobby, where Halliwell's silver head stood out among the other patrons. "Robert, it's great to see you," I said as I thrust out my hand.

"It's wonderful seeing you, too. How's the civilian world treating you?"

"Pretty well. It's definitely been an adjustment."

"I can only imagine." He motioned to the two other men with him. "These are two of my associates at Halliwell Enterprises, Peter Nations and Gerald Hughes." After I shook their hands, Halliwell's gaze bounced from mine over to Isabel. "And you must be Ms. Flannery."

A warm smile lit up Isabel's face. "Yes, sir. It's a pleasure meeting you."

As he shook her hand, Robert said, "I've heard great things about you from Murray."

An appreciative flush filled her cheeks. "Thank you. I'm truly honored to hear my reputation precedes me."

"It does. I know you're quite an asset at Callahan." Robert smiled at me. "How fortunate for you to get to work closely with Ms. Flannery."

Since throttling a client would be frowned upon, I merely forced a smile onto my face. "Yes, it is."

When I dared to look over at Isabel, I could tell her smile was just as forced as mine. Halliwell seemed oblivious to any tension between us. "I'm so thrilled to hear what you have in store for me tonight."

"We're pretty excited ourselves."

"Mr. Callahan, your table is now ready," the hostess said.

The moment I stepped out to start walking to the table, I was seized by another stomach cramp, and this time, it didn't let up. Instead, it remained after we sat down. As I picked up the drink menu, I desperately tried focusing on something besides the pain.

When it got to the point where I could barely focus on the conversations around me, I put my menu down.

"Gentlemen and Ms. Flannery, I'm terribly sorry, but could you please excuse me for a moment?"

Halliwell nodded. "Of course."

"Go ahead and order me a sparkling water," I instructed as I rose out of my chair. When I threw a hurried glance at Isabel, I noticed she'd paled slightly while chewing on her bottom lip. I guess she was afraid my escape-artist stunt was derailing the presentation before it even got started.

As I started toward the bathroom, sweat broke out along my forehead while goose bumps simultaneously pricked their way along my arms. I'd experienced this feeling one other time. There's not really an equivalent of the FDA in Afghanistan to regulate all the side-of-the-road food stands. During my first tour, I decided to sample some of the local cuisine, and it was one of the worst mistakes of my life. We're talking a stomach calamity so severe I ended up getting an IV from the medic.

I'll spare you the gory details of what transpired over the next hour after I locked myself in a stall. Yes, that would be sixty minutes of agonizing stomach cramps with evacuation at both ends. Okay, that last bit was probably too much information.

Let me backtrack a little. I'd probably been gone about ten minutes when Ty appeared in front of my stall. "Are you all right?"

"That would be a negative."

"Do you need anything?"

"Got any Zofran in your pocket?"

"Sadly, no, but I could probably get some ASAP."

"That's okay. I'll make it."

"Are you sure?"

As another wave of nausea overtook me, I shook my head. "Not really."

"Hang in there. I'll call in the cavalry."

I didn't know how he did it, but it wasn't too long before Ty reappeared with some Zofran.

"You got a dealer on the side?" I teased as I reached under the stall for the bottle.

"I'm a man of many talents."

"How long have I been gone?"

"Half an hour."

"Fuck. I gotta get out there," I groaned.

"Thorn, you're puking and shitting your guts out. You're sure as hell in no shape to run a business meeting," Ty argued.

I shook my head. "But I've got to. We need this deal." *I desperately need this deal.*

"For what it's worth, it looked like Isabel started the presentation without you."

Although I should have been grateful for Isabel trying to salvage the meeting, I was utterly pissed it wasn't me. With a frustrated grunt, I uncapped the Zofran and popped a pill under my tongue. Pinching my eyes shut, I willed my gastrointestinal system to get a hold of itself so I could get the hell out of there and advance my career.

In the end, the meds didn't help much. Finally, at the sixty-minute mark, I raised a symbolic white flag by staggering out of the stall. "Okay, let's get out of here," I muttered.

Ty nodded before slipping an arm around my waist. After we exited the bathroom, I started back toward the table. "Whoa, where do you think you're going?"

"To apologize to Halliwell about having to leave."

Shaking his head, Ty replied, "That's not happening."

"I can make it," I growled.

"I don't doubt that. I'm referring more to the fact that you smell like a sewer, and you're covered in puke stains."

I scowled down at my shirt before muttering, "Fuck."

"Yeah, you're completely knackered."

With a defeated sigh, I let Ty pull me to the exit at the back door. Oh how the mighty had fallen. Once I got inside the car, I texted Isabel to let her know I was heading home.

She immediately called me. From the clanging sounds around her, I imagined she was standing outside the kitchen. "Thorn, I don't want you to worry one bit about the meeting. Halliwell appears ninety percent on board, so everything is fine."

"That's just peachy," I sourly replied.

"Listen, I know you hate not being here, but remember it's your work he's embracing."

Huh, that was unexpected. Over the last few weeks, any form of a compliment from Isabel to me was non-existent. I knew from the tone of her voice she was truly sincere and not just feeding me a line of bullshit to make me feel better. "Thanks. That means a lot."

"Just take care of yourself okay?" I couldn't help being surprised by the almost pleading tone in her voice. It was hard to imagine she remotely cared about my well-being.

"I'll try."

"You sound a little weak. I'm sure you're dehydrated. Maybe you should go by an urgent care and get some fluids."

That concerned comment completely floored me. Of course, my sex-starved mind immediately went to a fantasy of her wearing a skimpy nurse's uniform while she attended to my needs. I shook my head to rid myself of the vision.

I am seriously delusional. I smell like a rat's ass, yet I am thinking pervy thoughts about Isabel. But therein lay the problem—nothing seemed to divert my attention from wanting her, not even vomit and diarrhea. *Moron.* "Yeah, I'll have the doctor come by later if I'm not better."

"I'll text you when I leave to let you know how it goes."

"Thanks. I appreciate that."

"Take care, Thorn."

"Okay. Bye, Isabel."

"Bye."

In a state of shock at Isabel's compassion, I kept the phone cradled against my ear. While I'd initially been attracted to her beauty, I couldn't discount how attractive her sympathetic side was. She was the ultimate package of brains, beauty, and a beautiful heart and soul.

With a groan, I lamented the tragedy of her not being a total bitch who was devoid of all feeling and empathy. I'd known so many women who were ice queens wrapped up in a pretty package. If only that were the case with Isabel.

CHAPTER TWELVE

Thorn

The day after my gastrointestinal melee at Delmonico's, I found myself at the conference table with Isabel where we were finalizing the documents for the Halliwell project. After passing out that night at nine, I'd woken up the next morning to a victory text from her saying we'd won him over. Yes, she was kind enough to say "we" when the truth was she had done it. From what I was told through the grapevine, she completely charmed the pants off Halliwell and his investors.

Whenever it looked like things might be going south, her tenacity persevered to save the deal from crashing and burning, not to mention she had gone above and beyond to assure Halliwell of how sick I was and how committed to this account I was. In the end, she'd saved my ass twice, which was saying a hell of a lot considering how I'd treated her over the last few months. She could have hung my ass out to dry while winning Halliwell for herself, but for some reason, she hadn't.

In the end, it didn't surprise me one bit that she'd managed to save the day. Isabel was more than qualified to wine and dine clients. Hell, she was infinitely more qualified than I was. Her Southern charm coupled with a natural head for business made her a superstar. I had no doubt she was going to rise to the highest ranks at the Callahan Corporation.

After her initial concern, I'd fully expected her to gloat about sealing the deal, but she remained uncharacteristically humble about the whole matter. Who knows what she said about it behind my back, but to my face, she appeared almost sympathetic about what had happened.

Her concern for my welfare continued the next day when she brought both hot tea and ginger ale. She even went to get me chicken noodle soup for lunch. It was quite shocking considering how it normally infuriated her to have to bring me anything. Who would have thought a stomach ailment would reveal Isabel's softer side?

As I gazed across the table at her, I couldn't help wondering what other secrets she possessed. Even though we'd been working together in rather close quarters the last few weeks, I still knew so little about her—well, except for what I'd Googled one night on a whim. All of her professional accolades were there, from where she'd attended college to her impressive resume. From the company directory, I knew she owned an apartment not far from the office, which, based on the location, I imagined had set her back a pretty penny.

I was more interested in the personal side, though. Like me, she didn't have a Facebook or Instagram I could snoop on, but I did find a few pictures on her friend's Instagram. Apparently, Isabel caught a Broadway show from time to time, but considering this was New York, that didn't automatically flag her as a theater geek. Since she appeared to live at the office, I couldn't imagine she had a very active social life. That wasn't saying anything negative on her part. From what I'd heard, sacrificing your friends and family seemed to be the curse of the first ten years in investment banking for those who wanted to get ahead in the business.

While her accent was a dead giveaway that she wasn't an East Coast native, I knew little more than she'd grown up in a small town north of Atlanta, and I'd only unearthed that detail based on her resume in the company profile. It came as no surprise to me that she'd been valedictorian and racked up countless scholarships. I had been slightly shocked to find she was a former beauty pageant queen, though. Nothing about Isabel screamed big hair, fake tans, and poofy dresses, yet there it was in photographs from the local newspaper. She'd been just as beautiful back then, although there was an innocence about her she no longer possessed, and I don't mean a sexual one. It was more like the world hadn't had a chance to chew her up and spit her out yet.

When she glanced up and saw me staring at her, her brows furrowed questioningly. "What?"

"Nothing. I was just wondering if you were almost finished."

"No. It's going to be a long night."

I twisted my wrist around to glance at my watch. "Shit, I've got to be at the helipad in thirty minutes to catch a flight to D.C."

Isabel's brows furrowed. "Are you bringing Halliwell to the office to pick up the files?"

"No, I have a previous engagement this evening."

Her blue eyes narrowed into steely slits. "And you're just going to leave me to finish everything while you flit off?"

"For the record, I'm not *flitting* anywhere. As far as leaving you to finish everything, I will be taking my share with me to work on during the flight."

Unable to hide her curiosity, she asked, "You're going out of town?"

"Yes. I'm going to D.C. then catching a helicopter ride over to Camp David."

Isabel's eyes bulged. "You're going to *the* Camp David tonight?"

I chuckled. "I wasn't aware there was another one."

She shook her head. "There isn't. I was just...surprised." Impressed was what she wanted to say, but she wouldn't allow herself to utter those words in regard to me.

When her expression revealed she was hungry for more information, I said, "Dad asked Barrett and me to come to dinner. He's entertaining—"

"The Canadian prime minister and the president of Mexico."

"Yes, that's right." Tilting my head, I added, "I didn't know you were such a fan of my father's."

"I watch the news and read the paper."

"So you're not a fan?"

"As a matter of fact, I am. I even voted for him."

"That's good to know. I know he appreciates your support."

"Will you be helping to broker new deals between the North American superpowers?"

With a laugh, I replied, "No, I won't have that privilege. It's just an informal dinner. They'll save the important talks for tomorrow, which I won't be privy to." I shrugged. "I guess the whole point is for me to get paraded around as a war hero."

Isabel's expression saddened at my words, and it took a moment to register in my mind that I'd actually said them. I shook my head. I didn't actually believe that…did I? I certainly didn't think it about Dad, but was it something I thought his aides might've thought up? Both Dad's and my service was something his campaign had constantly capitalized on during the election.

Since I didn't appreciate the look of pity Isabel was giving me, I rose out of my chair and then began shuffling my files together. "Anyway, I need to get going. I'll bring these back by the office tomorrow on my way home."

"That's fine, but don't expect me to be here waiting on them."

"Really? I thought you lived here."

She rolled her eyes. "Contrary to popular belief, I actually do have a life outside the office. While I might not to be flying off to Camp David for an important diplomatic dinner, I still know how to cut loose."

I fought the urge to question her about exactly how she cut loose, desperately interested in finding out more about what made her tick. It was almost as hard imagining her in a club as it was to imagine myself there. At the thought of her bumping and grinding on the dance floor, my thoughts immediately went south. I imagined her *cutting loose* with me on my desk, on the couch, against the door, and upon every other surface possible. It was getting a bit ridiculous. *Why the fuck can't I get her out of my head?*

Instead of pressing her for more information, I slid my mask back on. "Thank you for that information, Ms. Flannery. I will definitely sleep better tonight knowing that."

Isabel's expression darkened at my smartass remark. "Good night, Mr. Callahan," she muttered before burying her head back in her laptop.

"Good night to you too, Ms. Flannery," I replied before heading out the door.

After making the trip down to D.C., Ty and I met up with Barrett and Addison on the White House lawn. We then boarded Marine Two to make the trek to the northern woods of Maryland where Camp David was located. A self-proclaimed history nerd, Addison practically bounced in the seat in front of me with excitement. While I did a little work on the Halliwell files, she rattled on about the historical significance of Camp David. "Did you know that the Hickory Lodge has a bowling alley, movie theater, and restaurant?"

"No, I didn't, babe," Barrett replied.

"Maybe we can catch a late movie after dinner?" she suggested.

Wagging his brows, Barrett replied, "I was thinking more of some midnight skinny dipping."

Addison rolled her eyes. "Seriously, Barrett, it's March."

"The pool is heated," he countered.

"Yeah, I still think I'll pass."

"But it's one more public place to cross off our list."

With a groan, I covered my eyes. "There's not enough bleach in the world to get that mental image out of my mind." While Barrett chuckled, Addison shrieked in horror. Leaning forward in my seat, I said, "In your defense, that comment was directed at thinking of Barrett naked."

She grinned at me over her shoulder. "I can see why."

"You just wish you looked as fantastic naked as I do," Barrett joked good-naturedly.

"I'm pretty sure I do."

"Keep dreaming, bro."

With a chuckle, I turned my attention back to the files and spent the rest of the journey working. When we landed, I shuffled my paperwork back into my briefcase. As I climbed down out of the helicopter, I saluted the Marine at the bottom of the stairs.

Compared to the elaborate trappings of the White House, Camp David had a much more rustic feel. It consisted of three main buildings. The Aspen Lodge was the fancy name for the president's cabin, and it was where Barrett, Addison, and I would be staying for the evening. The prime minister of Canada and the president of Mexico would be staying in their own cabins on the expansive two hundred acres.

Once we got inside, Mom's social secretary (not the one Ty had banged) showed us to our rooms. Then it was time to get changed for dinner. Just as I was finishing up, a knock came at my door. "Yes?"

Ty poked his head in. "Your father would like to see you before dinner."

Inwardly, I groaned. I might've been thirty-one, but any time I heard the words *Your father would like to see you*, I instantly felt like a teenager who was about to get his balls handed to him. After I checked my appearance in the mirror one last time, I headed out of the bedroom and down the hall.

Once I knocked on the door, Dad called out for me to come in. When I entered, he stood in the center of the bedroom with his valet sliding on the jacket of his tux. At the sight of me, he gave me his usual beaming smile. "Hello, Thorn."

Returning his smile, I replied, "Hello, yourself." I motioned to the man checking over Dad's tux. "This is new. I feel like I've stumbled into an episode of *Downton Abbey*."

Dad laughed. "This is Dwight. He's been around since the inauguration."

Now that I thought about it, I remembered the guy's face from the White House. Presidential valets were more personal assistants these days rather than just the guys who straightened ties. "Nice to meet you," I said as I extended my hand.

With a smile, Dwight shook it. "101st Airborne, right?"

"Yeah, that's right."

"I was a Ranger."

I returned his smile. "Then it's really nice to meet you."

"Likewise." Dwight then nodded at my dad. "Looks like you're all set. I'll go check on how dinner is progressing."

"Thank you."

Once Dwight left, I threw an anxious gaze at my father. "I understand you wanted to see me."

Dad motioned to the two high-backed chairs in the corner of the bedroom. "Let's have a seat."

I made a tsking noise as I sat down. "This can't be good."

"When is it not good for me to talk with my firstborn?"

"Come on, Dad. We're in formal wear at Camp David—I think we're past the point of pretending this is just an everyday chat."

"Fine then, I won't beat around the bush any longer. I understand you've been having some difficulties in your new position."

I sighed. "Seriously? What asshole thought it was necessary to burden you about my work performance? Last time I checked, you had a lot on your plate being the leader of the free world."

"It wasn't burdening me, son. I was the instigator. They were merely answering my request for information."

My breath hitched. "So you were checking up on me?"

"Of course I was. I wanted to know how you were settling in."

"Then why didn't you ask me directly?" As hard as I tried, I couldn't avoid my accusatory tone. It was one thing to be a grown man and have your father checking up on you; it was another thing completely to be a man who had led a unit into combat and now was having his abilities questioned.

Dad sighed. "I wanted to get an unbiased response."

Throwing up my hands, I swept out of my seat. "You couldn't do that by picking up the phone and talking to me?"

"I didn't think you would set out to lie to me, Thorn."

"It sure as hell sounds like it."

"I know what a perfectionist you are. If things weren't going smoothly, you would feel you were letting me down by telling me the truth."

Of course, he had a point there. I jerked a hand through my hair. "Let me guess—you've heard about my lackluster performance."

"Lackluster seems to give the impression that you haven't been trying." When I cocked my head at Dad, he replied, "I've heard you have struggled in your new role."

I winced hearing the words from his lips. After swallowing hard, I croaked, "Yes, I have faced difficulties getting acclimated to my new position."

Dad rose out of his chair to stand in front of me. "Thorn, it doesn't matter to me how well you're doing because I know you're trying your best. You have always given one hundred and ten percent of yourself. When you and Barrett were younger, I never had to worry about you fulfilling your potential like I did him. I know you will rise to the challenges."

I couldn't help being touched by Dad's words. He always knew just what to say to pull you out of the abyss. I supposed it was one reason he'd been elected president—people saw his empathy and compassion were truly genuine. At the same time, guilt flooded me with the realization that I hadn't been trying my best. I'd been giving my half-assed best.

After stuffing my hands in the pockets of my pants, I sighed. "While I appreciate your unwavering belief in me, I'm not entirely deserving of it."

"What do you mean?"

"Some of the issues I've experienced have been a direct result of my apathy toward the job." After sucking in a harsh breath, I told Dad about what had happened with Gregson and the infamous cocks.

"Hearing you admit to that makes me even more concerned for your emotional well-being than I previously was."

There it was, the statement coupled with the fear in his eyes—he was worried about the PTSD I might be experiencing. When I'd first landed stateside, he'd wanted me to see a therapist, which I refused even though it was a recommendation I gave to my men and women upon returning home. "Is this a plug for me to see a shrink again?"

"I'm also concerned for you physically as well. I understand you became ill during a client meeting."

Rolling my eyes, I said, "It was just some stomach bug, one of those twenty-four hour things."

"You had to excuse yourself from the meeting, and you were so sick that Ty had to help you to the car," Dad countered.

"I also shit my pants—did he leave out that little tidbit?"

The corners of Dad's lips quirked as he fought to not smile. "As a matter of fact, he did."

Great. I had just unnecessarily divulged something mortifying. "I'm not proud to admit it, but yes, I did shit my pants."

Dad chuckled. "That must've been a hell of a stomach bug."

With the atmosphere lightening between us, I couldn't help laughing as well. "It was. I haven't been that sick since I ate what turned out to be a rancid kebab on my first tour of Iraq."

"I've been there before myself. It's one reason I'm so careful about what I eat at state and informal dinners. The last thing I need is to pull a George Bush Sr. and puke all over everyone."

"No, that would not be good," I said as I laughed.

As our amusement faded, Dad gave me a pointed look. "I'm always here for you, son. Even though you're a grown man and a decorated officer, I'm still here for you."

I smiled. "I know, and I appreciate it—even if I don't act like I do."

"The Callahan Corporation is filled with capable, giving people. Don't be afraid to reach out to them for help."

"Is this about Isabel?"

Dad's brows furrowed. "Who is Isabel?"

"Isabel Flannery. Murray was grooming her to take the vice president position I was given. She's supposed to be helping me transition."

"I can assume by your use of 'supposed to' that you aren't allowing her to do her job?"

With a shrug, I replied, "Maybe."

"Why on earth wouldn't you take advantage of an available resource?"

Well, Dad, here's the thing: she's a drop-dead gorgeous woman who makes my cock want to stand at attention whenever I'm in her presence. Besides that horny detail, she's the first woman I've actually noticed since returning home, and I haven't noticed her just because of her beauty—I find her brain pretty damn attractive as well.

I cleared my throat. "She just rubs me the wrong way." *Oh Jesus, did I actually just say that?* There could be no wrong way for Isabel to rub me.

"Can't you at least try to make it work?"

If only it were that simple. After the asshole tirade I'd been on the last few months, I didn't think it was humanly possible to wave a white flag of defeat and make everything right with her, but I couldn't tell Dad that. Instead, I merely nodded my head. "Yes, I promise I will try."

"I'm not completely sure I believe you."

I laughed. "You know me far too well."

A knock came at the door before Dwight popped his head in. "It's time, sir."

Dad nodded. "We're coming." He then smiled at me. "Thanks for hearing me out tonight."

"Any time."

Dad patted my back. "Although you haven't been completely forthright with me this evening, I still feel it's in your best interest to warn you that your mother has plans to fix you up tonight."

"Just when I thought the evening couldn't get worse," I mused.

"While I don't agree with your mother's ambush tactics, she is a lovely young woman."

"Hmm, a lovely young woman of a certain pedigree who would make a suitable bride?" I shook my head. "Talk about feeling like I'm in *Downton Abbey* again. Does she come with a dowry?"

Dad chuckled. "Don't scoff. Your mother was a lovely young woman of a certain pedigree." Pure happiness radiated in his face. "And she's been wonderful for me."

I couldn't help feeling slightly envious at both his expression and his sentiment. More than anything in the world, I wanted what he and Mom had, but for some reason, it still remained elusive. "Okay. I'll try to keep an open mind."

"I'm glad to hear you say that." Smiling, Dad motioned for me to open the door. "Who knows? Maybe something good for you can come out of me being president. You could meet your future wife at Camp David."

I laughed. "Yeah, I'm not going to hold my breath on that one."

My mother pounced on me the moment Dad and I entered the living room. After throwing her arms around me, she enthusiastically cried, "Thorn, I'm so glad you could join us this evening. I made sure the cook prepared your favorite dessert."

Dipping my head, I whispered into her ear. "Save it, Mom—I know you're trying to fix me up."

After she tensed in my arms, she pulled back to pout at me. "Even though your father ruined it, I'm still planning on fixing you up, and I'm still happy to see you."

I laughed. While my mom had come from a pedigreed background, she wasn't one of those cold, unfeeling types who shuffle their kids off to boarding school. Even though we had a nanny and a cook growing up, Mom still packed our lunches most mornings, drove us to school, and came to every practice and game we were involved in. Dad wasn't exaggerating when he talked about how lucky he was to have her.

"I suppose I have no choice but to concede to your matchmaking unless I plan on running out of here, right?"

Mom nodded. "But I really do think you're going to like her."

Scratching my chin thoughtfully, I replied, "Now where have I heard that before?"

After she waved a dismissive hand at me, Mom said, "Come on, at least let me introduce you to her before you completely write her off."

"Fine."

Dinner was being served in the Laurel Lodge, which was half a mile down the path from the Aspen Lodge. My family, along with the Secret Service contingency, began making their way down the path in the legendary Camp David golf carts. It was a beautiful late March evening with unseasonably warm temperatures for Maryland.

Once we got inside, we were arranged to do a receiving line of our guests. Of course, Mom stuck me beside her so she could oversee my fix-up. After shaking hands with the prime minister and his wife, I glanced over to see the side profile of a gorgeous redhead.

I did a quick double take because I thought it was Isabel, but when the woman turned her face toward me, I saw that it wasn't. While she was extremely beautiful, not to mention stacked, I couldn't help comparing her to the other redhead in my life. Nothing good ever came from comparisons—something or someone always came up short.

Before I could reach out to shake her hand, Mom turned to me. "Thorn, this is Pippa, the prime minister's niece."

"It's nice to meet you," I replied with a warm smile.

Pippa returned my smile. "It's nice to meet you as well."

My mother glanced between us before continuing. "Pippa was an art history major at Cambridge. She works at the Smithsonian."

And there it was: exhibit A of how my mother had no idea how to properly execute a setup when it came to me. I could go ahead and wager that the lovely Pippa and I had absolutely nothing in common. While I had an appreciation for literature and the theater, I had absolutely no enjoyment of art. "How interesting," I said with more enthusiasm than I felt.

Thankfully, we had to keep the receiving line moving, so Pippa went on to meet Barrett and Addison. It was no surprise to me that she turned out to be seated to my right at dinner. "Are you happy being home from the Navy?" she asked.

"Actually, I was in the Army, and no, I really miss it."

Her brows furrowed. "You miss being away from home with only the basic necessities?"

Okay, apparently Pippa was never going to be one I could take on a hike or camping. She was far too posh for that.

"Yeah, I miss roughing it. I miss the camaraderie of my men, the ability to help those in need."

"That's nice," Pippa mused.

That was the extent of the depth of our conversation. While she had Isabel's same auburn hair, she didn't have the same fire within her. We continued making the usual polite conversation you engage in at a dinner party, but there was no romantic spark. Just as I had anticipated, there was absolutely no chemistry. Mom had struck out yet again.

Before the main course was served, I glanced up to see Barrett staring at me. When he popped his brows, I shook my head. He appeared slightly let down that there wasn't anything happening with Pippa. I was sure it would be disappointing to my mother, and I knew a relationship between the president's son and the prime minister's niece would have made a great diplomatic love story on Page Six, but unfortunately, it just wasn't going to happen. In a way, I wished there were fireworks with Pippa as it would have gotten my mind off of Isabel.

As I ate the Yorkshire pudding prepared in honor of the prime minister, I couldn't help imagining what it would be like to have her by my side. As intelligent as she was, I knew she could hold her own when it came to making conservation. She would have both my parents enthralled by how well she could work a room.

I especially liked imagining what she would look like in a tight-fitting cocktail dress, one that showed off the chest I was so well versed with. Jesus, I had to stop thinking about Isabel in that way. I would wager good money she wasn't spending her Friday evening fantasizing about me. If she was, it was likely more about inflicting bodily harm, and not of the sexual variety.

No, when it came to Isabel, I was thoroughly and completely screwed, and not in the good way.

After the dinner meeting with Halliwell, I vowed to never, ever sabotage Thorn again. There was something about seeing his face turn the color of the white linen tablecloth that made me see the error of my ways. There was no way I could have foreseen him having had that kind of reaction. I learned later he had been scarfing protein bars chock full of fiber that day, which ended up making for a lethal combination.

While I truly felt horrible about what happened to Thorn, I couldn't deny how good it had felt to win over Halliwell and salvage the evening. Hearing Murray praise my valiant efforts was music to my ears, and even Thorn had been complimentary about how I'd managed to rise to the occasion.

Of course, all the uplifting words rang a bit hollow. It was like cheating to win a race—there was no true honor in the victory. I'd taken out my competition with dog laxatives. Whatever morals and ethics I'd thought I possessed had completely flown out the window. Even Mila didn't question my anti-sabotage stance after she heard about Thorn's extreme reaction. Since she had initially egged me on, I think in a small way she felt like an accomplice.

In the end, I'd felt so bad about the laxative debacle that I skipped out on working Sunday morning to attend church. I was pretty sure I was going to need to attend services for a long, long time to atone for what I'd done. When I saw the sign for volunteer opportunities, I gladly offered my services.

Now a week had passed and things were somewhat back to normal. In other words, Thorn was being his usual asshole self, and I was grudgingly putting up with it. Even though I was utterly repentant about my actions with the laxatives, it didn't completely stop me from giving him attitude. In my mind, I argued that no one could get violently ill from sarcasm.

I'd been working steadily all day when I realized I desperately needed some documents from Thorn to finish off the project, so I made my way down to his office. "Alice, I need the Pedansky files from Mr. Callahan."

"I'm afraid he hasn't completed them."

Inwardly, I growled in frustration. "Is he inside?"

Alice shook her head. "No. He's out cold in the sleeping room." She glanced down at her hands. "I was afraid to wake him."

Yeah, I was sure she was. Thorn had been a douchebag to me, but Alice had also incurred his wrath from time to time. While I had told him numerous times to get bent, Alice was much too sweet to tell him off.

A low growl came from within my throat. "Don't worry. I'll wake him." After taking the folder from her, I stomped down the hallway to the office that was designated as the official sleeping room. When I'd first interned there, I had been shocked to find the secretive room away from prying eyes. Officially, it was where analysts took private calls. Unofficially, it had a nice, comfy couch along with mats under some of the desks. I'd come to understand that when you're working thirteen- and fourteen-hour days, you sometimes choose to eat at your desk and take a power nap during your lunch hour.

After I threw open the door, I scanned the room for Thorn. When I didn't see him on the couch, I started peeking under the desks, and I finally found him at the back of the room. Lying on his side, his back was to me. "Mr. Callahan, I need your signature on this file." Thorn's response came in the form of a loud snore. With a roll of my eyes, I tapped his leg with my foot. "Mr. Callahan?"

Okay, so Alice hadn't been kidding when she'd said he was out cold. I eased down on my knees beside him. After placing my hand on his shoulder, I shook him. The next thing I knew he'd shot straight up, his chest rising and falling in harsh pants like he'd been running. Before I could move away from him, he leapt at me, knocking me onto my back. As he pinned me with his body, his hands grabbed my arms and shoved them above my head. The wild look in his eyes caused me to shudder in fear. "Thorn, stop!" I cried.

At the sound of my voice, he blinked several times, and then the tension visibly melted from his body. Too afraid to move, I remained deathly still. The only sound in the room was that of Thorn's and my heavy breathing.

An eternity seemed to pass before he forlornly shook his head. "Jesus, Isabel, I'm so sorry."

I widened my eyes at him addressing me as Isabel and not Ms. Flannery. "Uh, it's okay," I croaked.

"Are you okay?" His voice vibrated with a concern I'd never heard before.

"I'm fine." I wasn't sure how long he planned to remain on top of me. Although I was still shaken up, there was a part of me that enjoyed the feel of him. He was all muscle and power and strength, and I didn't like just how much I was enjoying it. "Do you think you could get off me now?"

"Oh God, I'm so sorry." After scrambling to his feet, Thorn extended a hand to me. Normally, I would have smacked it away and told him to shove it, but my emotions were too jumbled for a smartass comeback. Instead, I slipped my hand into his and let him help me up off the floor.

I also wasn't just thinking about me. The look in Thorn's eyes would haunt me for years to come. He had to have experienced some epic shit to express that level of horror. I wondered how many service men and women came home so internally scarred. I'd never witnessed firsthand the struggles of my grandfather who had served in Vietnam. Had he had moments like that when he'd first come back? Moments where he would fight off a touch simply because human contact had previously meant danger?

"I think you could use a drink," I suggested.

He scowled. "I'm fine."

"Okay, well, *I* need a drink because I'm sure as hell not fine after what just happened." I jerked my chin at him. "Why don't you let me buy a drink for a distinguished serviceman such as yourself?"

Eyeing me suspiciously, Thorn crossed his arms over his chest. "Are you suggesting we skip out on work to drink?"

"Consider it a working dinner." I waved the manila folder at him. "We can go over the Pedansky file."

"Okay. I really could use a bite to eat."

"Great. I'm just going to get my purse. Meet you downstairs in five?"

"Yeah. See you then."

Exactly five minutes later, I walked up to Thorn in the lobby. Hanging a discreet distance behind him was Ty. "You're late," Thorn stated without a hello.

"I am not. Your watch must be fast." When I started walking to the door, Thorn fell in step beside me.

"Where are we going?"

"Rafferty's."

"That pub down the street?" he questioned almost disdainfully.

"Yeah, that one."

"It looks like a dive."

"That's because it is, but the food is good, and the drinks are stiff but cheap." I grinned at him. "Besides, as a Flannery, I have a soft spot for all things Irish."

He snorted. "I call bullshit on that one."

"Why is that?"

He smiled. "Because I'm Irish, and I'm pretty sure you hate my guts."

Shit. I wasn't expecting that one. Sure, it was a well-known fact in my mind and in my circle of friends that I hated him, but I certainly did not want him being so aware of it. "Hate is a pretty strong word."

Thorn opened the door of Rafferty's for me. "It's a strong emotion, and I'm pretty sure you feel that way about me."

"If I hated you, would I have offered to buy you a drink?"

"You're buying me a drink out of pity for what happened back in the sleeping room," Thorn stated matter-of-factly.

Before I could argue with him, the hostess stepped forward. "Hi there. How many?"

"Just two," Thorn replied. Then he jerked a thumb behind us at Ty. "He'll take a booth close by."

After giving us a strange look, the hostess then led us over to one of the booths. After handing us a menu, she walked down the row to seat Ty.

"For the record, I'm not buying you a drink entirely out of pity."

"Then you admit this is a pity party?"

I sighed. "I like to think it's more empathy than pity."

A waiter interrupted us. "What can I get you?"

"I'll have a vodka orange and an order of cheese fries."

Amusement flickered in Thorn's eyes. "You're having cheese fries for dinner?"

"I plan on adding a Caesar salad later," I replied.

He smiled at me before looking at the waiter. "I need a moment to look at the menu, but in the meantime, I'll take a shot of Jack."

With a nod, the waiter replied, "I'll be right back with your drinks."

Once he left, it finally hit me that I was alone with Thorn. Sure, I'd been out of the office with him before, but only in an official work capacity. There was very little official about being at Rafferty's having drinks, and it was in moments like these when he wasn't wearing his asshole mask that I could see how good-looking he was, how very sexy and desirable.

Damn, I hated myself for thinking those thoughts.

After clearing his throat, Thorn asked, "What's good here?"

"Obviously, I'm a fan of the cheese fries, and you can't go wrong with the chicken wings or any of the salads."

"I'll keep that in mind."

Propping my menu up on the table, I said, "Although you really don't impress me as the chicken wing type."

"And why is that?"

"I don't know, maybe because you're a little white bread."

Thorn chuckled. "Whatever alleged white bread I had in me disappeared when I entered the Army. You don't get four-course meals from the mess, not to mention how unappealing MREs really are."

"I stand corrected."

After tossing his menu back on the table, Thorn said, "I think I'll take your suggestion of the chicken wings."

"If you're a fan of spicy, go for the habanero sauce."

"Is that the hottest one?"

"No. That would be the nuclear. I'm pretty sure you'll lose feeling in your lips."

"It's not a true spicy sauce if you don't start to tingle," Thorn countered with an uncharacteristically crooked grin. It was the kind of smile that got me tingling below the waist. I wasn't sure what it said about me that I was getting hot over hot sauces.

After Thorn's unprecedented innuendo, an uncomfortable silence permeated the air. "So," I began.

"So," Thorn echoed.

"Should we address the elephant in the room?"

A panicked look flashed in Thorn's eyes. "Is it about what I just said?"

"No. I'm talking about what happened earlier in the sleeping room."

Relief momentarily flickered in his expression, but then his jaw tightened. "I would prefer to get at least one shot of Jack down," he replied with a tight smile.

"Okay, that's reasonable."

He cocked his brows at me. "You're not going to press me to do it now?"

"No. I'm sure you'll talk about it when you're ready, and if you don't, you don't. That's your business."

"Interesting perspective."

"I guess I can assume it's not one you hear often."

He gave an angry shake of his head. "Everyone keeps pressing me to talk about what I went through, as if running my mouth will make things any easier."

"My grandfather was in Vietnam, and he never liked to talk about it to anyone but my grandmother. I think she was the only one he really trusted except for his war buddies."

"That's understandable. There's an inexplicable bond between the men you serve with." He shifted in the booth. "I do want to say how sorry I am for what happened. I know I scared you."

"I won't lie and say you didn't shake me up pretty bad."

Anguish burned in his eyes. "And I'm so very sorry for that." He sucked in a ragged breath. "I never imagined I would react that way to someone waking me up. I haven't exactly woken up with anyone lately to test the waters."

Even though it shouldn't have, my mind immediately homed in on the fact that he wasn't waking up with anyone. Did that mean he wasn't *sleeping* with anyone? I couldn't imagine an impossibly good-looking guy like Thorn would go without sex for any period of time. The truth was he probably was a banger and booker, i.e. he got off and got out. I'd seen it numerous times, and I'd experienced it once or twice myself. It would make sense since his younger brother was a notorious womanizer—at least he had been until his recent engagement.

"Well, in some small way, I'm glad it happened with me. Now you can inform the next woman what might possibly transpire."

At my reference to sex, Thorn's lips quirked. "Now that's a hell of a turnoff. I'm sure after sharing that little tidbit, she'll be lulled into a peaceful sleep."

"Maybe the wrong woman would be turned off, but I'm sure anyone who had a heart and cared about you wouldn't."

"What about you?"

"Excuse me?"

"If a guy you were dating told you he might happen to attack you if you startled him awake, would you want to stick around?"

"I'd have to be a pretty cold-hearted bitch to leave. I mean, no one is exempt from bringing baggage into a relationship. Some people just have bigger or less attractive baggage."

Thorn stared intently at me for a moment. "I guess you're right."

Right then, the waiter returned with our drinks and the cheese fries. After we gave him our food orders, Thorn picked up the Jack and downed a long gulp. Following his lead, I took a pretty big sip of my vodka orange, which caused me to shudder.

"Is it not good?" he questioned.

I grinned. "It's too good. I think it's predominately vodka."

Thorn smiled. "Might as well go big or go home, right?"

"I'll drink to that."

I never intended to get drunk with Thorn. Let me rephrase that: I never intended to get drunk with my boss, but it happened. Somehow between me not eating lunch, the cheese fries, and two and a half vodka oranges, I got a little tipsy, and tipsy Isabel tends to run her mouth, which is exactly what happened.

CHAPTER FOURTEEN
Thora

It was pretty fucking surreal to be sitting across the booth from Isabel. As fucked up as our relationship had been so far, it seemed like we were experiencing the impossible: two relaxed people enjoying each other's company. Of course, it was a hard-earned relaxation after what had transpired in the sleeping room.

I couldn't help basking a little in Isabel's concern for me. Considering how she usually looked at me—namely, with loathing and disgust —it was a welcome change. Of course, I had brought all of that on myself. In the spirit of the true transparency of our current conversation, I knew it was time to be honest with her.

After we toasted each other with our drinks, I smiled at Isabel. "I really appreciate you offering to buy me a drink. It was very kind of you considering everything that has transpired between us."

Isabel swallowed the cheese fry she'd been munching on. "There's no need to thank me. Being there for people is just part of who I am."

"In the last few months, I guess we haven't really gotten to know each other, have we?" I asked.

Isabel's lips quirked. "I'd have to say I've become well versed with your asshole side."

"Touché." I took another swig of Jack. Half the fun I'd had was because of how she reacted to my assholery, her fire and fury, but I thought it would be better not to share that. Still, right then, right there, I wanted her to know that wasn't really me—not completely. "Would it surprise you to know I'm not normally an asshole?"

"No. It wouldn't."

I widened my eyes in surprise. "Seriously? And why is that?"

"I Googled you." *She Googled me?*

"And Google told you I wasn't an asshole? That must've been a hell of a powerful search."

Isabel laughed. "While it didn't come right out and say it, I found evidence that didn't support your complete and total assholery."

"Since I've never Googled myself, I can't imagine what you unearthed to disprove your theory."

"You've spent the bulk of your adult life giving back to your country. During the times when you weren't deployed, you worked with charities that served veterans' causes, and while you were away, you still managed to raise money." She cocked her head at me. "Considering your military background, that didn't surprise me too much. I have to say I was very impressed to see the work you did with the at-risk children of deployed servicemen."

"But those could have just been a ruse to paint me in a better light. The privileged always have to have good works to make themselves look better," I argued.

"Normally, I would agree with you. However, in your case, it wasn't for show. You gave your time to charities where you literally got your hands dirty, like building houses for homeless vets and their families." She paused to down a pretty hefty gulp of her vodka orange. "In spite of all your jerky ways, you really do have a good heart."

Fuck me. It was amazing hearing the adoration for me resonate in Isabel's voice. It was certainly a change of pace from the usual disgust and annoyance. "So I have a good heart except when it comes to you?"

Isabel shook her head. "I wouldn't say just to me. Most of your team members at Callahan have felt the sting of your assholery from time to time, although it does seem you've graced me with the brunt of it."

"That's because I've been a dick who took out his frustrations on everyone else."

"After I Googled you, that's the conclusion I came to."

I chuckled. "Ah, so you've got me figured out, huh?"

"It took some time, but I think so. If you had taken any other job but mine, I would've had overwhelming empathy for you."

"Really?"

She nodded. "Well, if you hadn't continued being a giant asshole to me."

"I would say that's a fair summation. "

"You really have been through a lot, Thorn. I mean, you had to leave the only professional world you've ever known not of your own volition, not to mention being injured recently." She exhaled a ragged breath. "I can't imagine how agonizing that must've been."

Wow. Isabel really got me. It spoke to the content of her character that she could somewhat overlook the way I'd treated her to still feel empathy for me. In that moment, I knew more than ever that I had to come clean with her.

"While I've been taking out my frustrations on others, the truth is I've been going out of my way to be even more of a bastard toward you."

Her brows popped in surprise. "You have?"

"Yes, I have."

"But why would you do that?"

There it was, the moment of truth. Was I really going to come clean? What would happen once I let down my carefully constructed façade? "That first day after our somewhat unorthodox meeting, I found myself..." I swallowed hard. "Attracted to you."

"You're joking."

With a nervous chuckle, I replied, "No, I'm not." I stared intently at her. "In fact, I thought you were the most beautiful woman I'd seen in a long, long time."

Isabel blinked at me. "Oh wow."

Trying to lighten the mood, I teased, "Yeah, that's pretty much what I thought when I saw you."

"I...I don't know what to say."

"You don't have to say anything. I just wanted to explain things to you."

"You needed to explain that I was beautiful?" she questioned almost shyly.

"No, but that fact set a course for everything else that's happened."

Her brows knitted in confusion. "I don't think I follow."

"Considering the current climate in the workplace being what it is, I feared that somehow my attraction to you might be perceived as unwelcome, or might even be considered harassment. I decided the best way to cover my tracks was to treat you like crap. I figured if you hated me, you wouldn't possibly think I was interested in you."

Isabel's mouth formed a perfect O of surprise. "I can't believe it," she finally murmured after an uncomfortable silence hung around us.

The awkward moment was broken by the waiter appearing with our food. After we both ordered another ill-advised drink, we were once again left alone.

"Look, Isabel, I'm sorry if I've shocked you. I just felt I should clear the air after what happened earlier." When she didn't respond, I shook my head. "I'm sorry. I shouldn't have said anything." I reached for my glass, downed the rest of it, and hoped like hell the waiter would return soon with my drink.

Isabel leaned on the table with her elbows. "I want to make sure I have this correct: for the last two months, you've been an unimaginable bastard to me because you liked me?"

"Well, it wasn't so much that I *liked* you. It was more that I didn't want you to realize I was *attracted* to you."

"This isn't elementary school, Thorn—you didn't have to be a dick to show you liked me."

I held up my hand. "Okay, once again, I feel I need to clarify: attraction is different than liking someone. Yeah, it's usually a necessary first step on the path to liking someone, but in this case, we're just talking about attraction."

"Wait, does that mean you don't like me?" she asked teasingly.

Jesus, this woman was frustrating. "From what I see of you as a person and fellow employee, yes, I do like you. When we met that first day...well, you're gorgeous." When Isabel appeared once again taken aback by my compliment, I jabbed my knife and fork into my steak. "Come on, you have to be aware of how the male population views you."

"Yes and no, but from you, of all people..." *Me? Of all people?*

"Let's be honest here—your actions didn't make me believe you were interested in me at all."

"Which was just an act."

"Well you're a damn good actor." *So it appears.*

"Surely this isn't the first time you've ever dealt with a man not falling all over himself when you're around."

She sighed. "Hardly. Considering my past with men, I disagree."

After chewing on my bite of steak, I shook my head. I didn't want to think about her *past* with other men, but what the fuck was wrong with them if they didn't treat her like a queen? "Apparently, you've been interacting with boys and not men."

A shy smile curved on her lips. "Maybe, though at the end of the day, I'm not totally blameless. I've been impossibly driven from the time I entered middle school. I knew I wasn't going to make it out of my hometown if I got distracted by guys."

"I don't think I've ever heard you speak about your home."

"It's thirty minutes north of Atlanta in Dawsonville."

While I already knew where she was from, I wanted to know more about it. "Small town?"

"Pretty much. Lots of rural parts, which is where I grew up." She pushed her salad around with her fork. "My dad dropped out of high school at sixteen, and my mom got pregnant with me right out of high school. We lived in this dinky metal trailer until I was in middle school when we traded up for a double-wide. I didn't shop at the mall like other kids—we bought at GoodWill or Wal-Mart, not to mention we were on free lunches all through elementary school."

"I know a lot of men and women who came from towns and situations like yours." I gave her a pointed look. "They were just as good, if not better than the others when it came to doing their jobs. Money and prestige doesn't make someone a better person. In fact, many times it ruins them."

"I guess you're right. In my case, it just gave me a drive to overcome so I'd never have to worry about how I was going to pay the bills or feed my family."

"It certainly is an interesting path to investment banking."

She laughed. "Maybe it's some deep-seated desire from growing up poor to control money, to be able to dole it out or withhold it."

"Is that what it is?"

With a shake of her head, she replied, "Because I was good in math, I knew I wanted to do something in finance. It was more like the pieces started falling into place once I was in undergrad." She jerked her chin at me. "What about you? Did you always want to be a soldier?"

"Yes. From the time I was a kid, I wanted to be just like my dad. I used to parade around in his old dress greens."

"Did you follow in his footsteps with the family business?"

"Yes, in a way. He never pressured me to do something in finance. It was just something I'd grown up with, so it made sense, but in the back of my mind, I always knew it was just the fallback career. To be an officer, I needed a degree, so I chose finance."

"It doesn't sound like it's something that makes you happy."

I sighed. "It really isn't. I mean, there have been times I've been happy to be in the office, but overall, it's not something I really see myself staying in."

"Why should you stay in a career you don't like? There's got to be something within your father's administration that you could do— something that would feed your soul."

"You aren't trying to get rid of me, are you Flannery?"

A flush entered her cheeks. "At one time, I would have said yes." She reached across the table to lay her hand on my forearm. For a moment, she seemed almost shy, timid. "But after experiencing what I did with you tonight, it's not about me. It's about you finding your place in the world."

Fuck. We're sitting on opposite sides of this booth, yet just a touch on my arm has me turned on. It wasn't just her touch, though; it was her empathy. She got me. My place in the world had been snatched away from me. Sitting in an office making banal decisions about big corporations' finances wasn't me.

Fuck me. How was it possible I hadn't even contemplated anything outside of the Callahan Corporation? It was like I'd had blinders on thinking it was the only thing available for me. I hadn't even thought of pursing a job within Dad's administration. There had to be a place for me somewhere within veterans affairs. Sure, I'd be taking advantage of nepotism once again, but I was a hell of a lot more qualified to be involved with the military than investment banking, not to mention my heart would truly be in it.

"You know what? I think you're really onto something." I shook my head. "I can't believe I didn't think of it myself."

"As my dad would say, sometimes we can't see the shit until we step in it."

I barked out a laugh at her unexpected comment. "That's very deep. Your dad sounds like a very wise man."

She grinned. "I like to think so."

"Over the years, I've stepped in a lot of shit—both literally and figuratively."

The amused look in her eyes faded. "Is that sort of what happened with the roadside bomb?"

"Ah, I see you came across that when you Googled me."

When she nodded, I shifted in my seat. It wasn't any easier to hear it from her lips rather than speaking it myself. In an instant, my mind slammed me back in time to the Humvee on the highway outside Kabul, to that moment when everything changed in an instant, when seconds meant the difference between life and death.

The sound of the explosion rang in my ears, the agonized screams and panicked shouts of those around me, the searing pain of the shrapnel as it tore into my skin. "I lost two of my men," I croaked absently.

"Yes," she murmured softly.

"I'm sure you only read their names and ages. Maybe their hometowns were listed." I winced as I ran my hand over my face. "The media singled me out because at the time, I was the son of a senator who was running for president. Yeah, I was an officer, but what the hell did that really matter? It's not like a bomb has any respect for rank. They were great guys. Carlos had a voice that could've won *American Idol*, which was good since he was always singing. Perry was just two months shy of going home. He was planning on proposing to his girlfriend."

When I looked back at Isabel, there were tears in her eyes. "I'm so sorry."

"Thanks."

After she swiped her cheeks, she asked, "While I think I know how you're doing emotionally, how are you doing physically after your injury?"

I tapped my shrapnel-scarred leg. "It still gives me some trouble from time to time, especially when I push myself too hard during a run or a workout. It also hurts a bit when I'm sitting at my desk for too long."

"I'm sorry." Isabel immediately winced. "I'm sure that sounds completely lame. I don't even know the right thing to say in a situation like this."

Most people don't. "It's okay. I appreciate the sentiment."

"What was it like?"

"Getting bombed?" When she nodded, I sucked in a harsh breath. No one had ever asked me that—no one wanted to know. After a few moments searching for the right words, I replied, "Intense."

She shook her head. "I can't even imagine."

"It's strange because it seemed to occur both fast and slow, like time slowed down for a minute and then sped up. One minute we were just rolling along on this desert road, and the next minute this sound was busting my eardrums. Even though I'd been through training on how to handle myself and my unit, nothing can ever fully prepare you for the rush of that moment."

"Not to mention you sustained injuries as well."

"It must've been the adrenaline because after the initial pain, I don't remember hurting any more. I just remember jumping into action to make sure everyone was okay and we weren't about to come under any enemy fire. The only reason I stopped was because my leg finally gave out, and I literally collapsed."

"Were you scared?" she questioned softly.

I stared intently at her. Because of the relationship we had, I felt I owed it to Isabel not to bullshit her, and for the first time, I felt I could talk about my experiences, even though I wasn't sure why. "Hell yeah I was scared. In the moment, I think I was more scared for my men than I was for myself, but when the medivac arrived to fly me out, I started to worry I might not make it. I started thinking of all the things I hadn't achieved yet, how hard it would be on my parents and siblings if I died." I glanced out the window. "I guess it was all the typical things that rush through your mind when you're staring death in the eyes."

At the sound of a sniffle, I jerked my gaze back to Isabel. *Oh hell.* She was crying—like, her chest heaved as mascara-blackened tears streaked down her cheeks. I threw a panicked glance around to make sure no one was staring at us—or more importantly, to see if they were staring accusingly at me like I was a villain who'd made her cry. Thankfully, no one was even looking our way.

Warily, I focused my attention back on Isabel. I could lead a company of men through a warzone, but I was fucking clueless when it came to female emotions. I reached up to loosen my tie, which seemed excessively tight at the moment. "Isabel, are you okay?"

Shaking her head, she dabbed her eyes with her napkin. "No, I'm not."

"Was it something I said?" That simple question revved up the waterworks. Jesus, I was worse at this comforting thing than I thought. Shifting in my seat, I cleared my throat. "Look, I know we haven't had the easiest relationship so far, but I'm genuinely concerned about you at the moment."

"You won't be once I tell you what's wrong."

"I doubt that."

"Trust me on this one."

As her chest heaved several more times, I reached out to take her hand. "Will you please just tell me what it is?"

She stared from my hand back up to me. "You're going to hate me," she whispered.

"I highly doubt that." I squeezed her fingers. "Come on, don't leave me in suspense any longer."

"I've been sabotaging you at work."

I blinked at her. "Excuse me?"

"Surely you of all people know what the word sabotage means."

"Of course I know what it means—I just don't know what the hell it has to do with the two of us and work."

"Fine, let me spell it out for you: I've been trying to make you fail at your job so the powers that be would move you to another department and I could have the job as vice president."

After everything I'd been through in life, it took a lot to shock me, but there in the booth at Rafferty's, you could consider me absolutely fucking gobsmacked. "You've been sabotaging me," I repeated.

"Yes."

"But how?"

"Remember that day you lost all your work in Excel?"

"Yeah…"

She pinched her eyes shut as if she were in tremendous pain. "I deleted your work and then resaved it."

I sucked in a breath. "You didn't."

"Yes, I'm afraid I did." Her eyes opened, and she stared sadly at me. "But that's not the worst thing."

"There's more?"

"Oh yes…much more." She swallowed hard. "That porn website during the presentation? I knew that was going to happen."

My mouth fell open in shock. "You did?"

She nodded. "When you decided not to check the analysts' work, I went through everything to make sure it was okay. I saw that the site pulled up *cocks* instead of *coccyx*, but I decided to leave it in there to punish you for not taking things as seriously as you should have."

Never in a million years would I ever have pegged Isabel for being so underhanded. Of course, at the same time, I couldn't blame her for doing what she'd done. It was pure and simple sloppiness in my work ethic that I hadn't checked the files. She had every reason to let me burn in front of the investor.

In my silence, Isabel added, "I know it's terrible. I should've taken it out the moment I saw it. I'm so very, very sorry."

"While it was epically shitty of you to delete my work, I can see your point in leaving the error in the file. A good vice president ensures that the best possible product is put forth before investors."

Isabel blinked at me in surprise. "Really?"

"Yes, really."

She shook her head. "While that might be true, you won't be so understanding when I tell you what else I did."

"There's more?"

"Yes, something horrible."

Although she was a spitfire, I couldn't imagine her doing anything truly terrible. "Okay, tell me."

An agonized expression flashed across her face before she frantically shook her head back and forth. "No...I can't."

"Come on, Isabel. Since when are you afraid of anything?" I countered.

"Fine," she huffed before drawing her shoulders back. "Last week when you got sick and had to miss the dinner meeting?"

"Uh huh," I replied.

"That was me."

"How could that possibly have been you?"

"When you were such a dick about me getting you coffee, I wanted to punish you. After I realized I had some dog laxatives with me, I dropped two in your coffee."

"Holy shit." Okay, I take back what I previously said: apparently Isabel could be *epically* vindictive when it came down to it. I couldn't fathom that she would ever do something vile. It seemed to go against every facet of her character. "I can't believe it."

In an anguished whisper, she replied, "I can't believe I did it either."

As I sat there staring in disbelief, a battle raged within me. On one hand, I was ready to storm out of Rafferty's and immediately go to human resources to report her. Attacking me professionally was one thing, but Jesus, she'd attacked me personally when she'd put dog laxatives in my drink. She deserved to face the music for what she had done.

But then I started thinking about all the horrible things *I* had said and done to her since coming to work at the Callahan Corporation. I had never spoken to or treated another female so deplorably. It wasn't how I'd been raised, it wasn't how I served in the military, and it wasn't acceptable, not to mention the fact that I'd taken the position she'd spent years working her ass off for. My perfect plan of being an asshole to turn her off had instead backfired against me. I'd forced her hand, causing her to retaliate. I'd seen it all before in the military.

Fresh tears glistened in Isabel's eyes. "You served our country honorably, Thorn. You had to leave the job you loved. You saw friends die and were injured. And me? I'm *pissy* that I didn't get the job I wanted. I'm a horrible person. I just want you to know, you don't have to turn me in to HR—I'll resign myself."

When she started bawling again, a laugh bellowed out of my chest, one that surprised the hell out of both Isabel and myself. I mean, it was one thing to see Isabel as a crying drunk, but when you added in all the petty shit she'd been doing, I suddenly found it fucking hilarious.

"You think this is funny?" she hiccupped.

"Yeah, I do."

"You have a weird sense of a humor."

"Come on, Flannery—when you really stop to think about it, you sabotaging me is a freaking riot."

"You're not mad?"

"Of course I'm mad—I'm fucking livid, but at the same time, I guess I can understand why you did the things you did."

She shook her head. "Regardless of what you did to me, there is still no excuse for sabotaging you." With a sniffle, she added, "I'm morally and ethically bankrupt."

"No, you're not."

"Yes, I am. My whole life, I've never cheated to get ahead. I've always played by the rules. Now I've completely debased my character."

"You did a few dirty deeds to your bastard boss. It's not like you put out a hit on me." I cocked a brow. "Did you?"

Isabel stared at me in horror. "Of course not. I never wanted to hurt you physically—I just wanted to make you look bad at your job so they'd transfer you somewhere else."

"I'd say that statement isn't entirely true if you were willing to feed me dog laxatives."

She grimaced. "I really don't know what came over me. It's truly horrible, and I'm so very, very sorry."

"If there's anything I've learned from this, it's to not rely on anyone else to get me coffee or food."

"I don't blame you." After she swiped her nose with her napkin, she gave me a tentative look. "Do you think you can ever forgive me?"

"Do you truly want my forgiveness, or are you just afraid I'm going to report you?"

"I won't lie and say I don't fear the repercussions of HR, but I hope you believe me when I say I want your forgiveness from the bottom of my heart."

After gazing at her for a moment, I realized she was sincere. I also knew her well enough to know she spoke the truth. She had merely been retaliating against my shitty behavior.

"I propose this: let's put the past behind us. I'll no longer be Thorn, the epic asshole, and you'll no longer be Isabel, the epic saboteur."

The corners of her lips quirked up. "Really?"

"Yes, really."

"I concur, and for the record, I'd like to note that I stopped doing any underhand deeds after what happened to you with the dog laxatives."

I laughed. "I'm glad to hear I don't have to check for any booby traps or other forms of ill will when I get back to the office."

"Nope. Everything is cool."

"And us? Can we be cool?"

"I'd like that a lot," Isabel replied.

"Normally I would suggest we drink to commemorate our new peace treaty, but I think it's safe to say you've had enough."

Isabel giggled. "What gave me away? The hysterical crying or confessing all my sins?"

"It was a little of both."

"For future reference, don't ever let me have more than one vodka orange, even if I've had a big meal."

"I'll try to remember that."

Tilting her head at me, Isabel said, "Instead of a toast, we could always shake hands."

"That sounds like a good idea." I extended mine across the table. "Here's to working together for the greater good of both our careers as well as the good of the Callahan Corporation."

Isabel slid her palm against mine. "I wholeheartedly agree." As we shook hands, she gave me a sly look. "Since we're noting things for the record, I'd like to add one more thing."

"And what's that?"

"I was also attracted to you."

Holy. Fucking. Shit. Isabel was attracted to me. Wait, was that just the past tense, or did she still feel that way?

Just as I started to ask for clarification, she jerked her hand from mine as her eyes widened in horror. "Oh God, I think I'm going to be sick."

With that statement, she bolted from the table. I hoped it was the excessive alcohol mixed with the cheese fries and not her declaration about my attractiveness that had made her nauseous. Pulling my wallet out of my jacket pocket, I tossed a hundred on the table. As I rose out of my chair, Ty appeared at my side.

"Everything okay?"

"Well, we reached a truce in our relationship with each other."

"That's good."

"And then she told me she was attracted to me."

Ty's face lit up. "No shit."

"Don't get too excited—she just ran off to puke."

"You really know how to sweet-talk them, don't you?" Ty joked.

"Oh yeah, I'm a total ladies' man."

Since Isabel and I never made it back to work after our cathartic evening at Rafferty's, I ended up heading to the office at seven the next morning. After grabbing some breakfast from one of the food trucks, I buried my head in my computer and didn't look up for the next couple of hours. I was just making headway when my phone buzzed.

"Mr. Callahan, Ms. Flannery is here to see you."

I glanced up from the computer to stare at the phone in surprise. *Damn.* Had I forgotten we were supposed to meet this morning? So much for having my shit together. "Does she have an appointment with me?" I asked tentatively.

"No, sir. She just said there's something she'd like to speak to you about."

Exhaling a relieved breath, I replied, "Send her in."

After saving my work, I rose out of my desk chair and started across the office. The door opened to a reveal a much fresher and more put-together-looking Isabel than I'd last seen. From her determined gait, I couldn't help but be intrigued.

When she smiled at me, warmth radiated in my chest, which immediately made me feel like a giant dope. There I was, a thirty-one-year-old man getting all giddy like a teenage boy just because my crush smiled at me. I was seriously hopeless.

"I hope I'm not interrupting anything, Mr. Callahan."

"*Mr. Callahan?*" I cocked my head at her. "It was my understanding that after I held your hair back for you to throw up, we had moved past unnecessary formalities."

A flush entered her cheeks, and I was sure she was remembering what had happened the night before. Just before we got in the car to go home, Isabel had gotten sick again. With only a trashcan in sight, I'd been a knight in shining armor by holding her hair back. "We did. It's just…I wasn't sure if the informalities of an informal dinner correlated to the workplace."

"Considering how you also saw me yesterday evening, I think we're good to go."

"For the record, I'd once again like to apologize for throwing up." She shuddered. "I'm pretty sure I haven't thrown up in a trashcan on the street since I was in college."

I laughed. "I'm pretty sure we all have an incident with a trashcan on the street from our younger days."

"True, but I would have much preferred to leave those memories in the past. It certainly was an epically mortifying moment to end an embarrassing evening."

"It's okay." Sensing we needed a subject change, I asked, "Now what is it you wanted to see me about?"

"Yes, about that." After licking her lips nervously, Isabel began pacing around in front of me. I hadn't ever seen her so unhinged. "In spite of the alcohol I consumed, I didn't get a lot of sleep last night."

"Please don't tell me you were afraid I was going to report you to HR."

A nervous laugh bubbled from her lips. "No, that's not what kept me up."

"Then what was it?"

"I was thinking about ways I could atone for some of the underhanded things I did to you."

At the idea of atonement, my mind did a nosedive straight into the gutter. I immediately imagined that Isabel had come to offer herself as a token of repentance. Even though I shouldn't have imagined it, I was more than happy for her to work a little sexual healing on me.

I cleared my throat, which had run dry. "You want to atone for your sins?"

"Very much so."

"Last time I checked, I wasn't a priest, so I'm not sure how you can atone outside of confession."

She laughed. "Considering I'm Baptist, confession isn't really in my wheelhouse."

"I see. What did you have in mind?"

"If you'll come to my office, I have a present for you."

I was hoping to get down and dirty in my office, but what the hell. A change of scenery wasn't too bad. Of course, I would have preferred taking her back to my apartment or to a hotel to ensure we had enough privacy.

"Fine. Lead the way."

Isabel appeared both energized and nervous at my declaration. As I followed her down the hall, my mind was assaulted with so many different fantasies. When we reached her door, I licked my lips in anticipation. The moment I stepped inside, I did a double take. Sitting in her desk chair like he owned the world was a dog.

"What in the hell is that?"

"That's a dog."

I rolled my eyes. "Yes, I'm aware of that."

"He's a Belgian Malinois," she pronounced.

"While that wasn't my next question, it's good to know."

"Ah, I get it—you're wondering what he's doing here, or more precisely, you're wondering what the hell he has to do with my atone-ment," Isabel said.

"Ding ding ding."

"He's here because I thought he would be good for you."

"Does he have special skills in shaking clients down? No wait, let me guess—he's an attack dog who's been trained to take a literal bite out of our competition?"

"Har, har. That's not it at all."

I crossed my arms over my chest. "Then please enlighten me."

"Conan has been trained as an emotional support dog—"

With another roll of my eyes, I countered, "That's just a bullshit term people use to get special perks for their pooch, like getting them on an airplane."

Isabel shook her head. "While some people abuse the label, Conan is not like that. He's been specifically trained to aid combat veterans."

Panic pricked its way up my spine. I now knew where the conversation was going, and I didn't like it one fucking bit. Weak men needed emotional support dogs, and there was no way in hell I was weak. My fists clenched at my sides. "For your information, I'm not a basket case who needs a dog to keep him from spazzing out. Yeah, I saw some tough shit, and as such, I was experiencing some PTSD. It happens to every soldier who has been through combat," I spat.

"No—that's not it at all."

Her expression softened, which only pissed me off more. "Look, I'm sorry I overreacted last night when you woke me up, but it doesn't mean I'm some broken guy who needs a dog to put him back together. I just need a little more time to get acclimated to being back home."

"You and I both know it's more than that," Isabel said in an uncharacteristically soft voice.

Fuck me. I shuddered at the intensity of emotion in her blue eyes. How was it possible for someone who was basically a stranger to see straight through to my soul? I thought I'd been doing a stand-up job faking it. After all, everyone else seemed convinced—but not Isabel. She knew the truth. How was that even possible?

"Let's say just for a moment I entertain this insanity and get the dog—how do I know this isn't part of an elaborate plan to get me labeled as unstable for the workplace?" In that moment, asshole Thorn appeared without me even having to try.

Sweeping her hands to her hips, Isabel countered, "If this was all just a ruse to get you kicked out of your job, wouldn't I have done it before I told you I'd been sabotaging you?"

She had a point there. "Maybe."

"Come on, Thorn. I need you to believe I'm doing this out of the goodness of my heart, because that's the truth. It's for you and for him."

"Him?"

"Conan's a former shelter dog. This is a chance at a new life for him."

Shifting my gaze, I eyed Conan. "What was a beautiful dog like him doing in a shelter?"

"His owner died, and when none of his relatives would take him, he was sent to the shelter."

"That's a fucking shame. He's gotta be a purebred."

"Yes, he is, but I've seen it so many times over the years at the rescue."

"Rescue?"

She nodded. "I used to volunteer with Ruff Redemption. Obviously, I don't have as much time to contribute nowadays, but I try to help out with their big fundraisers. They're who I turned to last night when it dawned me on how I could try to redeem myself."

Isabel the dog whisperer—this was an interesting development. I'm not really sure why it surprised me. She obviously had a huge heart, so I shouldn't have been surprised to learn she did volunteer work; I just didn't imagine her working with needy creatures with four legs rather than two.

"I never pegged you for a dog person."

"Come on, I'm a country girl, remember? You don't grow up on ten acres without at least three or four dogs running around, not to mention the chickens, goats, and the occasional piggy that went to market for our bacon, sausage, and pork chops."

I laughed. "I would give money to see you back home and running around with chickens."

"I would make sure you had a good pair of boots first—I'd hate for you to get chicken shit all over your nice shoes."

"That's kind of you."

A heavy silence permeated the air around us. After a few painful moments, Isabel questioned,

"Why won't you at least give him a chance?"

It was such a simple request, and I didn't know why it seemed to be so difficult. After everything I'd been through, what could possibly be so hard about a dog? In reality, though, it went so much deeper than just welcoming a four-legged creature into my life.

I clenched my jaw as I worked to replace the wall of defense around me. "You just don't get it. I've led men and women into battle. I've always been in charge and in complete control. To take him on would mean I'm no longer in control." I gave an angry shake of my head. "It means I'm weak."

"It doesn't have to mean that at all."

"That's easy for you to say."

Isabel crossed her arms over her chest. "Have you ever stopped to think that this is bigger than just you?"

"What are you talking about?"

"As the president's son, you're in a unique position to be able to bring attention to a worthy cause. Think about all the service men and women who are suffering at the moment. Maybe they're looking for someone to be a role model for them. If you can come home from combat and master the corporate world, maybe they can find the strength they need as well."

"I can do all that without looking weak with the dog," I countered.

"But maybe they're wanting a dog or they already have one. You could show them that it isn't a sign of weakness—that it's a sign of *healing*." She gave me a tentative smile. "You could still be a leader, just a different type."

Fuck me. As much as I hated to admit it, Isabel was right on so many levels. I desperately needed something to pull me out of the darkness I'd felt since leaving the military. I also needed to deal with what I had experienced in combat. Maybe I could invest in a four-legged therapist, and in turn, I could get my head on straight while helping others at the same time.

Time ticked slowly by as Isabel and I stood in a sort of standoff. Finally, I exhaled a ragged breath. "You make a valid point to which I concede any further arguments," I finally admitted.

"Does that mean you want to meet him?" Isabel asked, a hopeful gleam burning in her blue eyes.

With slight hesitation, I replied, "Sure."

A beaming smile broke out on her face. *That* smile I'd never seen before, and I wanted to know how to put it on her face regularly. *Gorgeous.* Turning from me, she said, "Come, Conan."

At her command, Conan hopped down from her office chair and came hustling around the side of the desk. When Isabel instructed him to sit, he sat directly at my feet. Turning his head, he stared up at me expectantly. "Shake hands," Isabel said.

When Conan held out his paw to me, a tiny sliver of the ice built up around my heart melted a little. Just like Isabel, I'd always been a dog person. When I was growing up, there was never a time when we didn't have a dog in the house, and Satchel and Babe, my parents' black labs, were already making a name for themselves at the White House. Mom was determined to follow in the late Barbara Bush's footsteps by writing a book narrated by them.

I reached out my hand and took Conan's paw in mine. "Hey, boy," I murmured.

His eyes seemed especially kind as they sized me up. I wondered what he was thinking. Could he automatically tell some of the shit I'd been through? Did he have some doggy sixth sense about people who were broken in some way?

"What do you think?"

"As a dog lover, I wanted to give you an enthusiastic yes, but I'm torn."

Isabel put on what I could only describe as her businesswoman face. "What are your reservations?" she questioned diplomatically.

"I've never had a dog of my own. When I was growing up, my parents took care of our dogs. All I had to do was love on them or throw tennis balls for them. I have no fucking idea what they eat or what kind of care I'm supposed to give them."

"Is that all? I can help you with that, not to mention Google will answer any dog-related questions you might have."

Well, damn. Talk about feeling like an idiot. "Okay, that's all well and good, but don't you think I'm taking on a little too much? I mean, here I am just trying to get myself acclimated back to civilian life. What do I have to give him?"

Isabel smiled. "Even though you don't see it, you have more to give him than you can possibly imagine."

While I especially liked having her vote of confidence, I still wasn't completely sold. At the moment, my life didn't lend itself to taking care of anyone else. Let's face it: I barely had my shit together as far as adjusting to my new circumstances, so how could I possibly be emotionally and physically present for another living creature? "Okay, but what do I do with him while I'm here at work? It's not much of a life for him to stay in a kennel all day."

"Duh, he'll come to work with you."

"And do what? Answer phone calls and make copies?"

"He'll do the job he's been trained to do: he'll support you."

"I already have Ty to do that," I argued.

"Not in the same capacity." She gave me a wry smile. "I highly doubt Ty would lie at your feet or lick your face after a hard day."

"You never know. He just might if the money was right." Although, if there was any licking involved, I'm fairly sure I wouldn't want it to be Ty or Conan...

"While Ty is phenomenal in his ability to protect you from danger, Conan comes with a completely different skill set. He is able to detect when you're about to have a panic attack or episode, thus lending emotional support."

As I felt the walls of Isabel's office closing in on me, I stared into Conan's eyes. Like Isabel had stated, he appeared to already be in tune with my emotions. His head cocked to the side as he whimpered slightly and everything within him seemed to strain to come to my side, but since he hadn't been commanded, he remained still.

"Where did he get his name?"

Isabel grinned. "I thought you might like the fact that he has an Irish name. It was actually the name his former owner gave him."

"So, I'm correct in assuming it wasn't a coincidence?"

"Let's just say it was a happy coincidence that Conan was just graduating from the training program and also had an Irish name."

"Conan Callahan has a nice ring to it."

"Yes, it does."

I drew in a deep breath before exhaling it slowly. "Okay, I guess I could take him for a trial run, see how things go."

"That sounds reasonable. He's pretty much set up for the rest of the day, but we could always make a quick run to the pet store during our lunch."

"You want to have lunch with me?"

It shocked the hell out of me when pink tinged Isabel's cheeks. After she'd admitted she'd found me attractive, I couldn't help wondering if the embarrassment came from the fact that she had said too much. Was it possible she felt more for me than just friendship? I sure as hell hoped so.

After tucking a strand of hair behind her ear, she replied, "Well, you know, a working lunch—for Conan."

Ah, there it was—the letdown. I didn't usually lose out to the furry guy, but this was apparently my lucky day. "Okay, a working lunch it is."

After buying Conan a shitload of toys as well as food and a new bed, Isabel and I headed back to the office. The moment of truth came when we got off the elevator onto our floor. That was when the prying eyes apprised Conan at my side. Even if they didn't know me or know about my service record, it took them only a moment to realize just exactly what the dog was. His vest that proclaimed "Service Animal: Do not pet" told them everything they needed to know.

I won't lie, that first walk down the hallway was fucking tortuous. Several faces immediately lit up at the sight of a dog on the floor, and I could feel the conflict within them about wanting to pet and love on Conan, but it was the other looks that got to me. My skin burned underneath my suit with their curious stares. I knew it would be a long time before I got accustomed to the looks, and an even longer time before I got comfortable with them.

When I finally stumbled into my office, I exhaled the agonized breath I'd been holding from what seemed like the moment I stepped out of the elevator. As Isabel chewed on her bottom lip, I could tell she was debating telling me she was proud of me or praising me for making my first public appearance with Conan.

It was Ty who spoke up instead of Isabel. He smacked his hand on my back before squeezing my shoulder. "Way to go, brother."

I cocked a brow at him. "You approve?"

"That surprises you?"

"A little. I mean, you were in the Army and never needed a dog to help you cope."

"Trust me, I needed help coping—I just didn't go about it in a healthy way like you are." He shook his head. "I also wasn't an officer, nor did I have my life dictated for me. I left the Army of my own volition. You didn't get that chance."

Ty's comment rendered me momentarily speechless. It wasn't that I had expected him to give me some bullshit answer to stroke my ego, but I hadn't expected such raw honesty. "Thank you," I murmured.

"You're welcome." With a grin, Ty jerked his chin at Isabel. "Of course, I think all the thanks goes to her. She's the one who came up with all of this."

With a smirk, I replied, "Oh, I'm not sure how much thanks I actually owe her. This is all part of her redemption."

Isabel's eyes bulged as she began sputtering. "I-I d-don't think it's n-necessary to go into all that now, d-do you?"

I laughed at her coming so unhinged at just the suggestion of me revealing her dirty deeds. "No, I don't think it is."

The tension in Isabel's body gradually receded. "Good. Well, if you don't need me anymore, I'll head back to my office to get some work done."

"We're good."

After Isabel patted Conan's head, she started out of my office.

"Isabel?"

"Yes?" she asked as she turned around.

There was so much I wanted to say in that moment, so much that *needed* to be said, but in the end, I just went with, "Thanks."

She stared at me intently before replying, "You're very welcome."

Once Isabel left, Ty followed shortly after. Then it was just Conan and me. After I sat down in my desk chair, he eased down beside me. When I glanced down at him, I could've sworn he was smiling. I reached over and patted his head. "Good boy," I murmured.

CHAPTER SIXTEEN

Thora

As Conan and I fell into a steady routine together, it was hard to imagine a time when he wasn't part of my life. Whatever worries I'd had about me acclimating to his presence or him acclimating to my life quickly dissipated. He meshed easily within my schedule, and I had to admit he was a pretty laidback dude who constantly went with the flow.

While he followed all of his commands to the letter, he wasn't so fond of his kennel. On his second night with me, he burrowed into the covers of my bed and gave me the saddest dog face known to man. I immediately relented and let him sleep with me. Truth be told, I enjoyed having him beside me. Immediately, I noticed I had fewer nightmares, and my sleep was much more restful.

My morning run became our morning run, and on the days the weather didn't cooperate, he would almost wistfully watch me on the treadmill. When I was at the office, he would lie by my desk or on the couch across from me. I started eating lunch at my desk so I could use the time to take breaks throughout the day to throw a ball around for Conan or take him for a short walk.

It didn't take long for the media to get wind of my ownership of a support dog, and I'd been snapped by the paparazzi almost immediately. After our first night together, I'd called Dad to let him know I was getting an emotional support dog. He didn't press me to do any PSAs or anything that might reflect well on his administration. Instead, he told me he was proud of my decision and said he looked forward to meeting Conan.

In the end, I took the initiative and phoned the head of the Department of Veterans' Affairs. What happened next was somewhat of a media blitz with both print and television interviews, and Conan turned out to be quite a ham for the cameras. Just like Isabel had predicted, the campaign did a hell of a lot of good for veterans suffering from PTSD, and I was immensely proud of the fact that I'd decided to step out of my comfort zone for the good of others.

One thing I hadn't expected from getting Conan was how he would bring Isabel and me closer. Although he was neutered, Conan took to Isabel's dog, Daenerys, like she was his long-lost soul mate. Suddenly, since our dogs were BFFs and hanging out together, so were we. I'd never realized all the dog-friendly places around the city until Isabel pointed them out to me.

With my eyes blurring and my stomach growling, I glanced down at Conan. "I think it's time we break for some grub. What do you think?"

I laughed when he licked his chops in reply.

"I think I'll go see if Isabel wants to grab something." At the mention of Isabel, Conan's ears picked up. "Sorry, bud, but Dani isn't with her. She's at doggy daycare, remember?" As I rose out of my chair, he gave me his depressed face. "How about I make it up to you with some table food?"

He wagged his tail as he hopped to his feet then we made our way out of my office and over to Isabel's.

Cheryl looked up at me. "I'm sorry, Mr. Callahan, but she isn't inside."

"Do you know where I can find her?"

"Last I heard she was headed to the conference room."

"Thanks, Cheryl." I then changed direction to find Isabel. I couldn't imagine what she was up to in the conference room.

When I opened the door, I froze midway into the room. Isabel was leaning over the conference table, which meant her delectable ass was on display through her tight skirt, but even better was the teasing glimpse of her black thigh-high stockings.

To me, there was nothing sexier than a pair of stockings, and I was especially partial to lacy thigh-highs. Maybe it was because they ended just before a pussy. While I enjoyed sinking my teeth into the band before dragging them down a woman's legs, I also loved the feel of the friction on my own thighs as I pounded into her.

In that moment, I imagined my tongue licking along the lacy band as I plunged two fingers deep inside her. Just before my dick started to tent my pants, Conan had to ruin my perfect fantasy by charging ahead to goose Isabel in the ass. With a shriek, she jumped out of her skin, sending plastic eggs flying into the air before raining down around her. Whirling around, she wagged a finger at Conan. "Bad, bad boy!"

"Conan, come," I instructed.

As he trotted back over, the dog had the nerve to smirk at me, like somehow he knew, even being neutered, he had more balls than me because he'd dared to go where I only wished to go. *The bastard.*

With an apologetic look, I said, "Sorry. I swear I've been working with him on that."

Isabel nodded. "It's okay."

After I instructed Conan to stay, I walked over to the table. "What's all this?"

Isabel held up a hand. "Before you give me shit about using work time for an outside project, I'm only working on this during my lunch hour."

I frowned at her. "I wasn't planning on giving you a hard time. I was simply curious why the conference room was filled with plastic eggs and candy."

"It's for my sister's Easter egg hunt next weekend."

"I didn't know your sister had children."

A pained expression came over Isabel's face. "She doesn't. That's the reason behind the egg hunt."

"I'm not sure I follow you."

"After trying for many years, my sister, Christina, and her husband found out they can't have children—some unspecified fertility issue."

"Man, that sucks. I'm so sorry."

"Thank you, and yes, it does. Private adoption costs a ridiculous amount of money—the kind Christina's teaching salary and Brent's policeman salary just don't cover. A year ago, they started an adoption fund on GoFundUs. They did little things like yard sales and car washes, and even though I made a donation, I promised them the minute I got my promotion, I'd give them whatever they needed to reach their goal." Isabel's eyes widened as her hand flew over her mouth and she shook her head. "I'm sorry, I shouldn't have mentioned that."

Talk about feeling like a giant tool. My getting Isabel's promotion had even more repercussions than I'd first imagined. I wasn't just the dasher of her dreams; I'd also managed to screw things up for her sister and brother-in-law. "No, it's okay. I'm the one who's sorry."

"Really, it's not your fault. It wasn't like you went out of your way to take the job."

While I still felt pretty shitty about everything, I decided it was better to move on. I motioned to the table. "So the eggs are part of the adoption fundraiser?"

Isabel nodded. "They're supposed to egg a hundred yards this weekend. Since I couldn't get home in time to help Friday night, I'm stuffing these and FedExing them to Christina. Then I'll head home next Saturday to help hide the eggs."

"What kind of profit are they looking at from this?"

"Well, the eggs and candy have all been donated, so it should be a couple thousand."

"That's amazing. Will that get them close?"

"No. They're still about ten thousand off, but I know they'll make it eventually, even if I have to donate more money anonymously since they refuse to take any more of mine."

"That's one way to do it."

Isabel stuffed a pack of M&Ms into one of the eggs. "What about you? Do you have big Easter plans?"

"As a matter of fact, I do. I'm flying to D.C. on Friday night to partake in some egg hunting myself. Actually, it's going to be rolling eggs instead of hunting them."

"The White House Easter Egg Roll?"

"The very one."

She smiled. "That's so cool."

"I didn't know you were a fan of the Roll."

With a laugh, Isabel replied, "I'm not necessarily. I just remember it from back in the day in an episode of *Murphy Brown*."

"The one where she accidentally catnaps Socks the cat?"

Isabel's eyes widened. "You watched *Murphy Brown*?"

I laughed. "My mom was a fan. As far as me watching it, I could ask you the same question."

"It shouldn't be too shocking that I was in love with a show that featured a strong career woman with an attitude."

"You're right. I can totally see why you would have watched it."

"Now you've got me wanting to watch some reruns," she mused.

"Me too. Maybe we can catch an episode or two the next time we get Dani and Conan together."

She smiled. "Sounds good to me." With an amused twinkle in her eyes, she said, "Why am I having a hard time imagining you interacting with the kids at the Roll?"

"Maybe that's because you're imagining asshole Thorn around them, but he doesn't actually exist, remember?"

"That's true."

I picked up one of the eggs and tossed it in my hand. "For the record, I do like kids."

"Now that I really think about it, I can totally see that about you."

"You can?"

"A lot of your charity work involves children, and you have a very giving heart."

"Thank you." I motioned to the table. "Speaking of my giving heart, I could help you if you'd like."

Her brows shot into her hairline. "You want to help me stuff eggs?"

"Sure. I mean, I'm going to want to order in because I'm starving, but I can totally help."

"I'm kinda hungry myself. The only lunch I've had is a few packs of M&Ms I've stolen."

"Then I think we should totally order in some good Thai and stuff the hell out of these eggs."

Her eyes lit up. "The spicier the better?"

I laughed. "You read my mind."

"I'll go get the menu."

"Okay, sounds good."

As soon as Isabel left the conference room, I pulled my phone out of my suit pocket. It was time to try to right a wrong.

Ty answered on the second ring. "Yes?"

"I need you to do some legwork for me."

"Sure. What is it?"

"I need to procure some information on Isabel's sister."

"Seriously?"

"Yeah, why?"

"Oh, I don't know—maybe because it sounds a little stalky to me?"

I laughed. "I promise there's a noble, not-at-all-creepy reason why I need it."

"If you say so."

"Specifically, I'm going to need some information on a GoFundUs account."

"Got it."

As Isabel appeared back in the doorway, I said, "I gotta go." After plastering on a smile, I prepared to stuff the hell out of some eggs.

After a crazy week at work, I was more than ready to escape the city for a little family time. I would have considered it some R&R time as well, but I knew my sister planned to use and abuse me. After catching a seven a.m. flight, I arrived in Atlanta at nine-thirty.

My younger sister by eighteen months, Christina, was waiting for me at the luggage carousels. Although we were close in age, we were nothing alike when it came to appearances. While I had my mother's fiery auburn locks, Christina had inherited my dad's coal-colored hair. She'd also inherited his dark eyes. In spite of our physical differences, we'd grown up the best of friends. We'd always had each other's back and supported each other one hundred percent in all our endeavors.

"Izzy, you're the only person in the world I'd get up this early on a Saturday morning for," Christina teased as we hugged. It felt odd hearing my old nickname. No one outside of Georgia ever referred to me as Izzy.

With a laugh, I replied, "Consider it good practice for when the baby arrives. I'm pretty sure they don't sleep in."

She grinned. "I have a feeling that'll happen a lot sooner now because of you."

I furrowed my brows. "What do you mean?"

"Your donation."

"The eggs?"

Christina rolled her eyes. "Fine, play it cagey if you want to."

I didn't have a chance to question her any more because my bag came sliding down the ramp of the luggage carousel. After hauling it down, I trailed behind Christina as she filled me in on all the details for the night's egging.

When we arrived at our parents' house, Mom had a Southern breakfast of champions waiting on me, including homemade biscuits with sausage gravy and bacon from one of the neighbor's hogs. I stuffed myself to the gills before collapsing on the couch for a nap.

The TV blaring woke me up. Popping open one eye, I saw my dad lounging in his favorite La-Z-Boy recliner, his tobacco spit cup in one hand and the remote control in the other.

"Hey, Daddy," I murmured drowsily.

"Hay's for horses," he teasingly replied.

My dad might've dropped out of high school at sixteen, but grammar had always been important to him. "Hello, Daddy," I corrected.

"Hello, Belle. Did you have a good flight?"

Nodding, I pulled myself up into a sitting position on the couch. "Yes, I did."

After glancing at the clock over the mantle, I realized it was almost three o'clock. "I can't believe I slept so long."

Daddy smiled at me. "You needed it. I'm sure you're still burning the candle at both ends."

"As a matter of fact, I am."

"I sure am proud of you, Belle, but I wish you could slow down a little."

"I don't think it's in my DNA to slow down," I replied with a wink. All my life, I'd never known anyone to work as hard as my dad—except maybe my mom.

"While that might be true, I never thought you'd be keeping farmer's hours up there in New York."

"Regardless of the long hours, it's worth it."

"I'm glad to hear that. I know your mother and I are awfully proud of you, even if you do insist on doing too much for us."

"But I want to do those things. Goodness knows you guys sacrificed enough for me over the years."

"We did it out of love, Belle, not for any paybacks."

"I know. I'm just grateful I'm in a place where I can help out."

"As long as it's not taking away anything from you."

I laughed. "It's not, I promise."

We were interrupted by Christina and Mom blowing through the door with their arms laden down with groceries. "You have a nice nap, Sleeping Beauty?" Christina asked.

Stretching my arms over my head, I replied, "It felt more like a coma."

"From your snoring, it sounded more like hibernation," Daddy teased.

I tossed one of the throw pillows at him. After quickly deflecting it, he rose out of his chair. "I guess I better get back to work. Those veggies aren't going to plant themselves." He handed me the remote control on his way out. "You rest up. Your sister has a big evening planned for you."

"Thanks, Daddy. I will."

While Mom and Christina put away the groceries, I started flipping through the channels. For years, my parents had considered cable a luxury, and my first gift to them after paying off my student loans was pre-paying for five years of cable. Even though they said it wasn't necessary, I knew they secretly enjoyed the hell out of it.

When I got to C-SPAN, it showed children scattered across the White House lawn. "Thank you for joining us for today's coverage of the White House Easter Egg Roll," a news announcer declared. I whirled around to see the smiling faces of President and Mrs. Callahan. "While the Easter Egg Roll is usually held on Easter Monday, President Callahan is breaking with years of tradition to have it this Saturday. His motives are genuine since he plans to spend Easter and the following days visiting deployed troops. Not only is Mrs. Callahan in attendance, all three of the Callahan children are as well."

My breath hitched at the sight of Thorn. Even though I'd known he was going to be at the Roll, there was something to be said for seeing him on television. I didn't know how it was possible, but he seriously looked even sexier on the screen, which was saying a lot considering how panty-melting he was in person. Of course, it didn't hurt that when the camera panned onto him, he was crouched down comforting a little girl who had fallen. My dormant ovaries definitely stood up and took notice.

I jumped when Christina squealed beside me and jabbed her finger at the screen. "Is *that* your boss?"

"Yes, that's Thorn—uh, I mean, Mr. Callahan."

"Holy shit," she murmured.

"Yeah, he's cute."

Christina swiveled her head before pinning me with a *you're full of shit* look. "*Cute*? Seriously, Isabel, I would think an educated woman like you could come up with a better adjective."

"Handsome?"

Her eyes rolled back in exasperation. "He far exceeds handsome. I can't imagine what he looks like in person." When she dragged her bottom lip between her teeth, I didn't *even* want to know what she was picturing in her mind. "I'm a happily married woman, but if Brent gave me a pass, I'd be climbing that piece of perfection like a spider monkey."

"Ew!"

With a wag of her brows, Christina said, "Seriously, Belle? Haven't you ever had a naughty thought or two about him bending you over your desk and pounding you until you scream?"

Duh, of course I have. Not only that, I'd imagined banging him on and off of every piece of furniture in my office, not to mention using one of his expensive ties to bind him to his desk chair and then having my way with him.

"Um, no, I haven't," I lied.

"Bullshit."

"Excuse me?"

"I know we don't get to see each other a lot, but I still know all your tricks. I'm your sister, remember?"

"What's your point?"

"Whenever you're lying, you do that shifty thing with your eyes."

"I do not."

"Oh yes you do."

I exhaled a defeated sigh. There was no reason to keep arguing with Christina considering she had the goods on me. Sometimes I felt like she and Mila should've have been sisters considering how alike they were. "Fine, I might've had an impure thought or two about him, but only lately—not when he was being such a jackass when he first came to work."

Christina shook her head. "Considering what he did for the adoption fund, it's hard to believe some of the stories you've told me about him being such a jerk."

I blinked at her. "What are you talking about? Me flying down here to help with the egg hunt has nothing to do with Thorn's kindness and everything to do with my frequent flyer miles."

"I'm talking about the ten thousand dollars he donated to our GoFundUs."

Holy. Fucking. Shit. There had been few times in life when I'd found myself truly speechless, but now was one of them. "Did you just tell me Thorn sent you ten thousand dollars?"

She nodded. "When I realized you weren't just being cagey by denying the donation, I did a little research. The anonymous donation had an IP address from New York, and after some digging, I found the initials TC. I knew it had to be someone from your work, so with some further snooping of your office directory, I realized the only TC remotely connected with you in any way was Thorn Callahan." While I continued staring at her wide-eyed and open-mouthed, Christina added, "I'm planning on sending a thank you card for him with you. I'd also like to call him as well."

"Thorn gave you ten thousand dollars," I said lamely.

"Yes! Like I seriously pissed myself when I got the email about a new donation. Here I was thinking it might be a few hundred dollars, but oh no—it was *ten thousand.*"

"That's unbelievable."

"I know. The amount was why I first thought it was you, like maybe you'd gotten the promotion after all."

"I wish."

Christina shook her head. "You've done plenty for me over the years."

"But I can always do more."

"And I know you will when the baby gets here."

I smiled. "Yes, Auntie Isabel will spoil it rotten."

"I know you will." Christina then shook her finger at me. "Back to the donation—thanks for calling and giving me some warning. I could have had a heart attack from the surprise."

"I couldn't have called you because I didn't know."

She gasped. "He didn't tell you?"

Slowly, I shook my head. "No. He didn't say a word to me."

"That's weird."

"Yeah, it is." I stared at the television. "Especially now that we've gotten to be friends."

"Oh, you have?"

Without looking at her, I countered, "Not friends with benefits. Just friends."

"If you say so." When I finally met her intense gaze, she cocked her brow. "I don't know many people who would give their *friend's* sister ten thousand dollars."

"That's just who Thorn is. He has a really big wallet to go along with his big heart."

Tapping her chin, Christina said, "I wonder what else is big on him."

I laughed. "Would you get a grip?"

"I would love for you to get a grip of his impossibly big manhood."

Groaning, I pulled myself off the couch. "I swear, if you didn't teach computer programming, I would be convinced you and Mila were the same person. You're both far too concerned with me getting busy with Thorn."

"Maybe it's not so much that we're perverts, but that we just want to see you happy."

"And happy equates with screwing my boss?"

"It does when your boss looks like he does."

I threw up my hands. "Once again, you're impossible."

"Fine, you can run now, but I plan on continuing the discussion about Thorn's manhood after you get ready."

"Lucky me," I grumbled before I strode toward my childhood bedroom to escape any more teasing about my boss's dick.

CHAPTER EIGHTEEN

Thorn

My mom hadn't so much requested my presence at the White House Egg Roll as she had informed me when to be there. The truth was I wouldn't have said no—well, unless I'd previously caught wind of her plan to try to force another setup on me. Thankfully, though, she was far too busy executing the plans for her first Egg Roll as First Lady so my love life wasn't on her radar at the moment. Thank God.

Of course, I'd expected to just work the crowd and smile for the cameras while parading Conan around. The First Family's dogs were always a part of the Roll, and Satchel and Babe would be entertaining the kids along with Conan. What I hadn't expected was for my mother to volunteer me to serve as the Easter Bunny during the 12:15 to 2:15 group. I'm not sure what she was thinking. There was no part of me that screamed *enjoys being in a furry costume while interacting with kids*. I would have thought it was some sort of punishment for my Pippa fix-up crashing and burning if it weren't for the fact that Barrett was slated to take over after me.

The moment I slid the rabbit head over my own, Conan's eyes widened as his ears perked up. "It's just me inside here, buddy. I'm fine." Since the dog didn't appear too convinced, I reached out a furry hand to pet him, but he quickly dodged out of the way. "I guess your love only covers me when I'm not in a giant bunny costume, huh?"

At the feel of someone poking my ass, I whirled around to see Barrett grinning at me. "Look at you hopping down the bunny trail."

"Har fucking har," I replied through the head.

"Hey, watch your language—there are kids around," he chastised.

"If there weren't kids around right now, I'd haul off and knock the hell out of you."

Leaning in closer, Barrett said, "From your attitude, I can surmise you haven't been using my gift."

"I'm not using a pocket pussy to get off."

"Does that mean you're using your hand?"

"Fuck off, Barrett," I muttered before walking away.

The truth was I had been using my hand more than I wanted to admit, but the more I jerked off, the more sexually frustrated I became. In the field, a good rub out would relieve tension and keep me satisfied for a day or two, but not anymore. These days, the moment I came, I only wanted more.

I think the problem had to do with the image I was getting off to. Although I hated myself for it, Isabel seemed to star in my fantasies more than I liked. Okay, fine, she was the only one I fantasized about. While I knew exactly what her breasts felt and looked like, I had to use my imagination for the rest of her. In my mind, we'd banged in my office, her office, my apartment, and the back seat of the car.

What the hell is wrong with you? How much more perverted can you be having an illicit fantasy about your coworker while on the White House lawn? There are kids around, you creep.

I pushed all thoughts of Isabel out of my mind and poured my energy into being the best damn Easter Bunny possible. At the end of the two hours, I was completely and totally spent. It took everything I had to give the energy necessary to the kids who were thrilled to see me, not to mention that extra bit to the kids who were scared shitless of me. When Conan went straight into the lay-down position, I knew he was exhausted as well. He'd had a lot of tiny hands on his body in the last two hours.

When Ty came to escort me back inside, I fought the urge to start singing the "Hallelujah" chorus in my head. Once we got inside to the bathroom, I made quick work of getting freshened up before I headed back outside to see the next group of rollers.

While Barrett and I had been called on to do bunny duty, Addison and my sister, Caroline, were recruited for story time. After giving a wave, I stopped in front of Caroline, who was getting ready to read *Where the Wild Things Are*. When several of the little boys clambered to sit closer to her, I couldn't help snickering. Anyone with eyes could see how beautiful my baby sister was. She and I both had the same sandy blond hair and blue eyes that came from our mother, as well as similarly reserved personalities. At twenty-three, she was about to head to Oxford to do an internship.

Caroline waved before glancing past me to where Ty was standing. I frowned when pink tinged her cheeks, and she appeared slightly flustered. Peering over my shoulder, I noted his reaction, exhaling a relieved breath when I saw he wasn't even looking at her. Instead, he was in Agent Ty mode, keeping his eyes on anything that might be a potential threat to me. If he had been looking at Caroline with anything other than concern in his eyes, *I* would have been a threat to *him*.

After I moved on from story time, I went over to where the Egg Roll had just ended and knelt down in front of a dark-haired little boy. "Did your egg make it?"

The boy jerked his head up to give me a grin that was rather gummy since his top front teeth were missing. "Yep, it did," he replied before thrusting out the egg for me to see. Of course, Conan lunged to snatch it away, and I had to jerk him back.

"Sorry about that. He's an egg thief."

The boy laughed. "I like his bunny ears."

"I'm glad you do. I don't think he's a fan."

As I stared into his dark gaze, another face appeared before my eyes—one that appeared to be the same age and size, but the little boy in my mind wasn't smiling. Blood ran from his nose and mouth while his dark eyes held a glassy stare. I hadn't felt for a pulse. I knew he was gone, *another* countless, innocent life taken in battle.

The world started to close in around me. Fighting to breathe, I clawed at my tie, trying desperately to loosen it. Conan whined and nudged my knee with his muzzle. When I scrambled to my feet, I accidentally dropped his lead. As I started power walking through the crowd, Conan kept right by my side, occasionally knocking my hand with his head.

The voices around me became muted like I was under the surface of water. At each laughing child, I saw the mangled body of an Afghan child. With every smiling mother, I saw the lifeless eyes of mothers taken from their children. Although sweat poured down my face and back, an icy chill radiated over my body. With the side door in sight, I silenced all the commotion around me. Just a few more steps and I could escape.

"Where you going?" Ty asked beside me.

"Just need to get out of the sun," I choked out.

As the door came within reach, Ty stepped in front of me. Clenching my jaw, I was just about to tell him to get the fuck out of my way when he brought his hands to my shoulders before staring me straight in the eyes, surprising me.

"Take a deep breath. You're not over there anymore. This is now."

I can hear the screams. I can smell the dirt and blood and gunfire smoke. I need to escape.

"Take another deep breath. You're not there, Thorn. You're here with your family and those who love you."

Why do they have to fucking kill the children? It's beyond cruel. I can't breathe. The air—

"Thorn, deep breath. Breathe with me, now, Thorn. In and out. In and out."

Lifeless eyes...the softness of a dog's head beneath my fingers...

"We're here with you, Thorn. Deep breath in and out. Breathe with me, buddy. You got this."

Ty. Conan. Sunshine. Clean air. Laughter. Happy voices. Two things I can see, two things I can sense, two things I can hear.

"Thorn—"

"Yeah, Ty. I'm here. I'm okay." I looked down at Conan leaning against my leg, looking straight up at me with what I swore was compassion in his eyes. *How does he know?*

I glanced at Ty's stern yet insightful expression. It wasn't sympathy I saw, and his reaction was the exact reason why I'd wanted him as my Secret Service agent. He got the soldier life, and he got me. I bobbed my head in acknowledgement. "Thanks."

Ty patted my arm before pulling back a few feet to give me some air. I picked up Conan's lead before rubbing his ears. "Thanks for having my back, boy." His scratch fest was interrupted when my phone buzzed in my suit pocket. Reaching into my jacket, I took it out. When I glanced at the messages, my breath hitched for the second time in a few minutes. Isabel had called. After tapping the voicemail icon, I brought the phone to my ear.

"Um, hey, it's me. I know you're busy right now at the Egg Roll, so I didn't expect you to answer this, and don't feel like you have to call me back or anything. It's just...I was talking to Christina, and she told me about an anonymous donation made to her GoFundUs. I don't think I ever told you what a major snoop she is." After a nervous giggle, she continued on. "Seriously, Christina might just be a high school technology teacher, but she could probably get a side job with the FBI or CIA. Anyway, she tracked down the IP address to New York and then started stalking our company directory. She is so grateful. Like a true Southerner, she has a handwritten thank you note for me to bring you on Monday."

I chuckled as Isabel drew in a breath.

"Besides relaying the message from Christina, I also wanted to tell you how grateful I am for you helping them out. You totally went above and beyond. It really means a lot to me." There was a pause. "Anyway, I just wanted to call and tell you that. I hope you're having a good time at the Roll. See you Monday."

Somehow, hearing her voice right at that moment was also just what I needed. *She is light.* I wanted to hear the sound of her voice again, so I called her back right then. It rang several times before she finally answered.

"Hello?"

"Hey, it's Thorn."

"Oh, hi," she replied over the wail of a guitar.

"What is that noise?"

"It's called classic country music—none of that new auto-tune bullshit," she replied.

I snorted. "Where are you?"

"At my Uncle Bud's pool hall."

"I thought you were going home to egg yards tonight."

"We are. My brother-in-law had the bright idea that we should do it slightly inebriated."

Before I could say anything, a male voice drawled in my ear. "Why you always gotta be usin' those highfalutin' words?"

A vision came charging through my mind of some backwoods stud putting his paws on Isabel. "Who the hell is that?"

"The aforementioned brother-in-law."

I exhaled a relieved breath as the male voice said, "There you go again."

"Oh shut up, Barry. Break out the dictionary from time to time instead of *Field and Stream*."

I chuckled at her sassy reply.

"Anyway, I'm glad you called me back because I really wanted to tell you again just how grateful I am for what you did for my sister."

"It's the least I could do."

"The least? No, it goes above and beyond," Isabel protested.

"Well, considering you were going to use your raise to give them money, I felt it was the right thing to do for both your sister and you, like a peace offering."

"Regardless of what you might think, it's a hell of a gesture, Thorn."

"What's a little money between acquaintances? I mean, you got me a dog, and I gave your sister some money. We're all good now."

She laughed. "I guess so. Speaking of dogs, how's Conan liking the Roll?"

"Besides the fact that he's tried to eat a few eggs, he's been a real trooper. My mother put bunny ears on him for Christ's sake."

"She did? Oh you have to send me a picture."

"Okay, I will."

"Is that him?" a strange voice demanded.

"Yes," Isabel hissed.

"Let me speak to him."

"I don't think that's—"

I jerked the phone back as a loud scratching noise invaded my ear. "Mr. Callahan?" the unfamiliar female voice questioned.

"Yes."

"This is Christina Pike. I'm sending you a proper thank you note with Isabel, but I just wanted to tell you how grateful my husband and I are for your generosity."

"You're more than welcome. I hope it helps."

"Oh it will. We have enough money now to move forward and get matched with a birth mother."

"That's great."

"I would say if it's a boy, we'll name it after you, but my husband is dead set on naming him after his daddy."

"Barry Jr.?" I asked.

She laughed. "No. We're not having any BJs, AKA Barry Juniors, around here. It would actually be Henry, after my late father-in-law."

"Ah, I see. Henry is a fine, distinguished name."

"Thank you. Of course, if it's a girl, we're going to name her Isabel Faith and call her Faith."

"That's very kind of you to name her after Isabel."

"She deserves it. She's done so much for Barry and me."

"Yes, she has a very giving heart."

"She's gorgeous, too."

"Christina!" Isabel cried.

I chuckled at her indignation. "Yes, she is very beautiful."

"Oh, have you noticed?"

"It would be hard not to, wouldn't it?"

"I would think so. I don't know how she stays single, do you?"

The scuffling sound started up again, and then Isabel came back on the line. "It's been good talking to you, Thorn, but we really have to get going. We have a lot of yards to egg tonight."

"Now that's not a statement you hear every day."

She laughed. "You and Conan have a nice Easter tomorrow, okay?"

"Thanks. Same to you."

"Goodbye, Thorn."

"Bye, Isabel."

After talking to Isabel, I headed back out to the Roll feeling ten feet tall and bulletproof. Who would have thought a petite redhead with a fiery personality would become part of my armor?

CHAPTER
NINETEEN

Thora

The next six weeks flew by in a flurry of work. While it had taken some time, I was finally starting to come into my own in my position. Of course, I couldn't have done it without Isabel. The truce we'd enacted ensured that we had each other's backs at the office, and I didn't think I would have come as far as I had without it.

Our friendship continued to grow and extend beyond the office, and we were always grabbing lunch or dinner together. Sometimes we dined with some of the others from the floor. I started getting to know a lot of the analysts and associates, which helped me in the long run when it came to projects.

We also made sure to get Conan and Dani together as much as possible. They were becoming inseparable. Since I felt stronger than ever, I'd even gone so far as letting Conan go to doggy daycare a few days a week. While he was in heaven, the others around the office missed his presence.

When it came to Isabel and me, I'd never really had a friend who was a woman. I supposed that was partly a hazard of being in the military, where I was predominantly surrounded by men. Over time, there wasn't anything I felt I couldn't say to Isabel. She never forced me to talk, but whenever I did open up, she was always there to listen.

Of course, in the back of my mind, my attraction to her still burned bright. I always noticed the curves of her hips in the straight skirts she wore, the way her breasts strained against some of the silk blouses she wore. I felt like a fucking creep every time her image came to my mind when I was jerking off. I'd started trying to watch porn while I took care of business, but somehow I ended up gravitating to the subgenre of redheads.

Did I want more than just to fuck her? Hell yes I wanted more—I just didn't know how to approach it. In the end, I was too afraid of the collateral damage that might occur if I crossed the line.

The night found us once again working late at the conference room table. We were both buried in our laptops when I heard a growl from below the table. After throwing a quick glance at Conan, I turned to Isabel. "Was that your stomach?"

An endearing flush colored her cheeks. "Yes, it was. I didn't really have lunch today, unless you consider a bag of Doritos out of the vending machine a meal."

"Okay, we need to get you fed."

She huffed out a breath that fanned some of the loose tendrils of her hair out of her face. "I'm not Conan—you don't have to ensure I get fed and watered."

"I'd wager you're probably dehydrated as well by your lack of bathroom breaks this afternoon."

Isabel widened her eyes. "Excuse me?"

Now it was my turn to be embarrassed. "Sorry, it's a throwback to the military. You don't..." I was going to say pee, but I realized that might be a little crass. "You don't excrete waste when you're dehydrated."

After staring at me for a moment, Isabel barked out a laugh. "Did you just say 'excrete waste'?"

"And what if I did?"

An impish look burned in her blue eyes. "Thorn, I think you can say pee in front of me. I mean, you've seen my boobs."

Fuck. She would have to bring that up, immediately bringing a delicious flashback of said boobs to my mind. "Fine. You've haven't pissed enough this afternoon. Better?"

She grinned. "I can totally hear you saying that to your men."

"I said it to my women as well. I didn't sugarcoat anything overseas."

"I can't imagine you did. It's not like you sugarcoated much when you started here."

"Touché." I jerked my thumb at the door. "Come on. I'm hungry, and you're starving."

Her brows furrowed. "Don't you think we should order in to conserve time?"

I shook my head. "I think some fresh air would do us some good."

Conflict flickered over her face, which I imagined stemmed from two things. First, she was such a professional that she hated to cut loose when there was so much work to be done, and secondly, she was wondering about the parameters of us having dinner, i.e. did it look like a date? Since she had her work clothes on, it seemed her brain could only see me as vice president. Our boundaries were clear—colleagues only—yet when we were hanging out outside of work, we were friends who relaxed together quite easily.

I felt as though I needed to ensure that I understood the boundaries, so I cleared my throat. "It won't just be us—Ty will be there too." After glancing down at my feet, I added, "And Conan."

Isabel laughed. "Okay."

"What sounds good?"

"Even though it will run the risk of putting me to sleep, I'd love anything loaded with carbs."

"Pasta?"

Her eyes lit up. "Mm, yes."

"I know just the place."

"Il Felice or Brigante?"

"No. I'm talking a true authentic Italian restaurant on Mulberry Street owned by a guy whose parents came through Ellis Island."

"You want to go to dinner in Little Italy?" Isabel asked almost incredulously.

"From your tone, you would think I'd suggested chartering the company jet and flying to Rome for dinner. Last time I checked, it was a twenty-minute drive over to Little Italy, give or take a bit with traffic."

"I just assumed you meant we were going to grab something close." Eyeing me curiously, she replied, "You could really charter the jet on a whim?"

"Sure I can."

She shook her head. "That's crazy."

"If you want to go to Rome, just say the word."

"I'd love to go to Rome, but not tonight."

"Have you ever been?"

"Not yet. I've done most of the UK, but I haven't made it to Italy yet. It's one of those bucket list things." With a determined look, she added, "I hope to make it soon."

I nodded. "My mom loves traveling internationally. I think I was barely a year old when I got my first passport."

"Wow. I didn't get one until I was twenty-five." She smiled. "I gave myself a trip to London for getting my MBA."

"Well that's a good thing because you're old enough to remember the trips. The pictures of me in diapers at the Vatican are the only way I even know I went to Rome—well, at least until we went back when I was a teenager."

"It's hard to imagine you as a sweet little toddler in diapers."

"Who said I was sweet?" I jokingly asked.

"Were you a terror?"

"Actually, I was a pretty laidback kid, which turned out to be a good thing for my parents because Barrett sure as hell wasn't." I reached into my suit pocket for my phone. "Here, let me call for my car."

"Your car? Fancy."

"I'm fine with taking the subway, but it gives Ty hives with the potential security issues."

Isabel's expression grew serious. "Does he really think someone would hurt you?"

"Not really. There's always a slight risk being a sitting president's child, but I don't think there's ever actually been an attack."

"Just on Princess Anne," Ty piped up from the doorway.

"Excuse me?" I asked.

He grinned. "Sorry, that's my British side speaking there. While there haven't been any attempts on the lives of a president's child,

Princess Anne was almost kidnapped back in 1974, but she used her balls of steel to fight off the guy trying to get into her car."

I gave him a pointed look. "See? None here in the States."

"That doesn't mean I'm going to let up in my duties. It's a crazy world we're living in now," Ty countered.

"I'm surprised you don't get more women throwing themselves at you," Isabel said with a smile.

"Who says that hasn't happened?" I replied teasingly.

If there were stereotypical Italian restaurants in Little Italy, Mauricio's was one of them. It had the Italian flag prominently displayed along with black and white pictures of long-dead Italians, and a violinist played *O Sole a Mio* in the candlelight.

The moment we swept through the door, the owner, Mauricio himself, clapped his pudgy hands and came over to us. "Mr. Callahan, how lovely to see you."

"Thanks, Mauricio. There isn't an issue with my companion joining us, is there?"

Instead of looking at Conan, Mauricio threw a playful glance at Isabel. "Is she housetrained?"

"Barely," Isabel retorted with a smile.

"Ah, a lovely redhead with a personality to match her hair." Mauricio reached over and grabbed Isabel into his arms. She stiffened slightly as he planted kisses on both her cheeks.

"Can we get two tables please?"

"Of course. Give me one moment."

Over the last few weeks, Isabel had gotten used to the arrangement when we went out to dinner with Ty. At first, she couldn't believe Ty wouldn't be sitting with us, but now she was used to him taking a table close to the door so he could survey the scene.

After we sat down and gave our wine order, my phone buzzed in my pocket. I glanced at the text and fought the urge to roll my eyes before shoving it back in my suit.

"Hot date?" Isabel asked.

I snorted. "Not quite. It was my mother."

"I see."

"You would think it was her getting married this weekend instead of Addison and Barrett."

"Oh, that's right. With the media coverage, it feels a little like our own royal wedding."

"I'm pretty sure this one will have a lot less pomp and circumstance."

Isabel smiled. "Don't tell me you got up early to watch Harry and Meghan's wedding."

"I did get up early, but that was to attend the wedding."

Her eyes widened. "You *know* Prince Harry?" she demanded in a strangled voice.

"He and Barrett were thick as thieves back in the day. We got to know each other when I attended the Invictus Games with Barrett."

"I...well, wow." She slowly shook her head. "Sometimes when I'm with you, I forget who you are."

"And who is that?"

"Someone famous."

"Hardly," I scoffed before taking a sip of wine.

"Come on—your father is the president of the United States, and you hang out with princes."

"For the record, I've only met Prince Harry. I'm pretty sure none of the others have any clue who I am," I argued.

"It still makes you pretty extraordinary when you think about it."

I shook my head. "Leading an extraordinary life isn't about those things. Sure, it's pretty amazing that my dad is one of the most powerful men in the world, but the person he is inside is far more noteworthy. Regardless of how high he climbed in the political world, he always managed to keep his integrity. At the same time, he managed to be a hell of a good father." Jerking my chin at Mauricio, I said, "His father was extraordinary too. He came to America with only the clothes on his back, and through the sheer will of his character, he built this restaurant. He didn't die a very rich man, but he left a legacy for his children and his community with the content of his character."

Isabel swept her hand to her chest. "I don't think I can possibly verbalize what I'm feeling at the moment."

"You're speechless? I think we should check to see if hell has frozen over."

"I'm serious."

With a shrug, I replied, "It's just how I feel."

"If someone told me two months ago that you would ever say something so deeply beautiful, I would have laughed in their face."

"That's because I was executing Operation Asshole, remember?" I tapped my chest. "I'm the same person I've always been."

She smiled. "I'm thankful you decided to wave a white flag of surrender on that one."

"What about you? Who do you know who is extraordinary?"

"By your definition, I would have to say my parents."

"You really haven't told me much about your family."

"They're just good, simple people."

I couldn't help being curious about why Isabel seemed hesitant to give me any details about her family. "It's okay. We can leave it at that," I said diplomatically.

After nibbling on her lip, she replied, "I might as well tell you the truth. I mean, I don't know how cagey you can be when you're sitting across from a guy whose dad has access to the FBI and CIA."

I laughed. "For the record, I would never have my father dig up dirt on you."

"And I appreciate that." She took a sip of wine. "My dad is a farmer who makes his living for the year off a roadside vegetable and fruit stand. In the winter, he does odd jobs around town, like handyman stuff. My mom drives a school bus so she can help him during the summer, and they still live in the same double-wide trailer they bought when I was in middle school."

"Your dad works with his hands, and your mom cares for kids." When she gave a quick jerk of her head, I replied, "That sounds like honorable work to me."

Tears momentarily shimmered in her eyes. "Thank you. They've worked hard all their lives, but most of all, they've been really good parents. They always sacrificed to make sure Christina and I had what we needed."

I tilted my head in thought. "And now you do all you can for them."

"Yes, I do."

"I'm sure they're immensely proud of all you've accomplished."

Isabel's face lit up with my compliment. "Yes, and they are very vocal about their pride. I often hear it two or three times a week when we talk."

"It's wonderful you can maintain a close relationship even though you're so far away."

"It is, but you're no stranger to long distances with your family, either."

"Very true. I've seen them more in person the last few months than in the past several years, but we managed through Skype chats and phone calls. I can't imagine what it must've been like for soldiers in the pre-technology days."

"It had to be brutal for them and for their families."

As I thought about technology, my mind focused on the contents of my mom's text. I hadn't told Isabel about Mom informing me she was going to set me up if I wasn't bringing anyone to the wedding. The last thing in the world I wanted was another one of Mom's setups. Being single at a wedding is uncomfortable enough, especially when you throw in trying to get to know someone.

Then an idea popped into my head. What better person to attend the wedding with than Isabel? She could rub elbows with the best of them, and I knew the minute my family met her, they'd like her as much as I did.

"So, I was just thinking…"

"About what?" Isabel asked as she swiped her mouth with her napkin.

"I still think you owe me for all the sabotage."

Isabel's eyes widened. "I got you Conan—isn't that enough?"

At the mention of his name, Conan raised his head. "Yes, he is the gift that keeps on giving. At the same time, I'm wondering if, considering the severity of your actions, I shouldn't ask more of you."

"I'm not sure I like the turn this conversation has taken," she huffed as she tossed her napkin on the table.

I furrowed my brows at her. "That I expect more of you?"

"That you expect...*that* from me."

I held up my hands. "Whoa, wait a minute—*that* is not what I was insinuating at all."

Isabel's forehead wrinkled in surprise. "It's not?"

"Uh, no. It's not."

"Oh, God, I'm so sorry," she muttered as her face turned the color of an overripe tomato.

I gave her a teasing grin. "I'm not sure you should be apologizing to the man upstairs when it's me you just insinuated wanted sexual favors from you."

"Mentioning God was about the mortification I felt because I assumed that."

"And why exactly did you make that assumption?"

She shrugged. "I don't know. There was something about the tone of your voice...asking me to do more for you..." She gave me a pointed look. "You are a man, after all."

"Thank you for noticing that." I cocked my head at her. "And men are natural sex fiends?"

"That has been my experience."

I laughed. "Well, that's not me." *Great, Thorn, way to sound like a complete eunuch in front of Isabel.* Rushing on, I added, "I mean, don't get me wrong—I like and appreciate sex, but I don't let it rule my life."

The corners of her lips quirked at my last comment. "Now that we've cleared that up, what is it you would like me to do that is *not* sexual in nature?"

"I want you to come to Barrett and Addison's wedding with me."

Isabel's jaw practically dropped onto the table. "What?"

"I'm pretty sure you heard me."

"Sure, I did, but forgive me for still being slightly shell-shocked after the previous course of our conversation, not to mention that an invitation to the White House bears repeating."

"Oh come on, it's not that big of a deal."

"I think we've already covered what a big deal it actually is."

I shrugged. "To me, it's just my little brother getting married, not some huge society event."

Isabel eyed me curiously. "You really don't have a date?"

If she hadn't said it almost incredulously, my manhood would have been insulted. "As a matter of fact, I don't."

"I see."

"Does that surprise you?"

She nodded. "I would assume you had a whole harem of women at your beck and call."

With a laugh, I replied, "No, I don't."

"And how is that possible for a rich and handsome man like you?"

I shrugged. "I don't know. It's just one of the great mysteries of life."

"I'm serious."

After taking another sip of wine, I looked at Isabel. "You think I'm handsome?"

Isabel rolled her eyes. "Stop deflecting."

"Fine. I really don't know why I don't have a date for the wedding or a harem of women at my beck and call. I guess it boils down to the fact that that's just not who I am. I'm not a hookup guy. I only like to be with real women who aren't looking to be with me because of my money or looks. I want to be with someone who sees past all that to the person I am within."

"I can imagine that's pretty hard to come by with all the phony women around Manhattan."

If only she knew the truth of that, knew the number of times I'd been stopped when out running or even just walking with Conan. Women had actually come straight over and propositioned me. Before I left the States for my first tour, women weren't that brazen. At first, I'd thought it was funny, if not odd, but with each folded cell number or up-close-and-personal hug while getting a selfie with me, I became angry. It was as if I'd lost my identity on two levels: as a major in the Army, and as Thorn Callahan the man. Phony women were pissing me off.

Then there was the beautiful one in front of me.

"Yes, it is. With Dad's presidency, it's gotten even worse. Women want to be photographed with me for the instant fame, or they want to date me for my money—to see what expensive gifts and lavish vacations I might bestow on them."

With a sympathetic look, Isabel said, "I can't imagine how hard that must be. Women should be able to see what I see."

Unable to help myself, I fished for a compliment. "And what is that?"

"A man of worthy character and a kind, giving soul."

Speechless, I could merely stare at Isabel. Statements like that made me question just how much I liked her—they made me love her…and as more than just a friend. "Thank you."

"You're very welcome. I truly mean that—I wasn't just saying it to stroke your ego."

"Yes, I knew you were sincere."

"Good."

Since we desperately needed a change in the conversation, I asked, "Why aren't you dating anyone?"

"Oh no, don't change the subject. This conversation isn't about me."

"Guess what—it is now."

She huffed out a frustrated breath. "You can be so infuriating."

"It's part of my charm," I mused.

With a shrug, she replied, "I could say I don't know why I'm not dating anyone, that it just boils down to one of the great mysteries in life, but that would be a lie. Like the vapid bimbos who search you out, I seem to find the men they should be dating. Men always end up being threatened by my career. They're turned off by a strong woman who is self-reliant. They want so much to be needed, and they want to control. They can't imagine how I could possibly compliment their lives."

"Fuck me. That's a dismal summation," I replied.

Isabel gave me a rueful smile. "Just callin' it as I see it. But, like I've said before, my career doesn't leave a lot of time for dating. Of course, when it's someone really worthwhile, you make time."

"Yes, you do." I shook my head. "And I stand by my previous statement about how you've only dated boys and not men. There's a man out there who will appreciate your strength and drive as much as they do your beauty." With a wink, I added, "You're a hell of a package, Flannery."

"Wow, you sure know how to stun a girl," Isabel murmured.

"I like to consider it one of my talents. "

"Thank you. That's one of the most beautiful things a man has ever said to me."

"While I'm grateful to oblige, you should have heard it a lot more by now."

She took a long gulp of her wine. "You really want me to go to Barrett's wedding with you?"

"Yes. Not only would I enjoy hanging out with you, it would save me from my mother trying to fix me up."

Tilting her head, Isabel said, "But what if she introduces you to the one?"

She had no idea—no fucking idea how incredible she was. She had no idea how completely captivated I was by her, that every intelligent and insightful word she said left me in awe, that I watched her body every moment I could wishing I could touch, kiss, and worship her. She had no idea that even if my mother tried to introduce me to someone, my eyes wouldn't stray from the beauty I saw during the day at work and at night in my dreams, no idea I was pretty sure I was sitting across from *the one* but didn't have the balls to tell her.

I shook my head. "My mother is a lot of wonderful things, but she is not a good matchmaker."

Isabel smiled. "If you're sure I'm not depriving you of the future Mrs. Thorn Callahan, then I would love to go to the wedding with you."

"You would?"

"Hell yes." A wicked gleam flashed in her eyes. "Can you imagine the bragging rights I'm going to have back home after this? Most of the people in my town have never been to D.C., least of all to a wedding at the White House."

"Forget just a wedding—you'll be staying at the White House."

Isabel appeared momentarily stunned. "Shut up. Are you serious?"

I laughed. "Where did you think I'd put you? In a hotel down the street?"

"I hadn't had time to really think about it, but yeah, I assumed all the family and dignitaries would be at the White House."

"They'll be across the street at Blair House. I'm pretty sure we can find you a room in the residence."

"Holy shit—the family residence? Like where the Lincoln Bedroom is?"

I couldn't help being amused by how excited she was. "Yes. I'm actually staying in the Lincoln Bedroom this time."

Covering her widened mouth, Isabel shook her head. "This is just too much."

"Do you think you'll be able to contain your emotions and make it through the weekend?" I asked teasingly.

"I don't know, but I'm going to try!"

After Thorn asked me to be his date to Barrett's wedding, there was no way I was going to get any more work done. Once I got back to the office, I made sure all my files were saved before I ducked out. I was too emotionally jangled to go home, so I headed the opposite way.

Since it was after nine, I knew Mila would still be at the theater. When we'd become roommates, she'd given me passes to come backstage. Plus, most of the crew knew me by now, so the pass wasn't even always necessary.

I waited around in the wings until intermission was over, when I knew Mila would be free. When I swept through the door of the makeup room, she glanced up at me in surprise. "Well, hello."

"Hey," I replied as I crossed the room over to her station.

"I didn't expect to see you tonight." Cocking her head, she added, "Did I forget we were supposed to meet for dinner?"

"No. You didn't forget anything," I replied.

"Then to what do I owe the pleasure of your visit?"

I plopped down in the makeup chair. "Thorn asked me to go with him to his brother's wedding this weekend."

Mila swept her hand to her chest. "You're shitting me."

"Yeah, that was the same reaction I had."

Placing her hands on the sides of the chair, she leaned in and grinned at me. "Holy shit, Bells. That's amazing! Okay, amazing doesn't quite capture how truly monumental this is."

"You're right. It's totally and completely amazing."

"Well, what did you tell him? I mean, you sure as hell better have said yes."

"I did."

As Mila did a happy dance around my chair, she exclaimed, "Yes, yes, yesssss. This is so freaking epic!"

"I'm glad you think so."

"You have to promise to take a million pictures and videos."

With a mirthless laugh, I replied, "I'll try."

After pausing her dance, Mila eyed me suspiciously. "Okay, so what gives?"

"I don't know what you mean."

"You're acting like Thorn asked you to attend a funeral rather than a wedding."

"It's not the wedding that's the issue."

"Then what is it?"

"It's the fact that we're going *together*."

"What's wrong with that? It's not like you two don't hang out all the time. I'm not going to lie, I've been totally jealous of Thorn for getting to spend so much time with you. It shouldn't make a difference just because you're crossing state lines."

"Don't you get it? This is different. This is a wedding where his family and friends will be attending. This is a..." I swallowed hard. "A date."

"Is that what he called it?"

"No."

"Then what's the problem?"

The truth was I really didn't know, or I couldn't accurately put it into words. I just knew my emotions were all jumbled up. "I guess it's because part of me wants it to really be a *date* date, and the other part of me is terrified that it is."

"You really like him, don't you?"

"Of course I do. We're good friends as well as coworkers."

Mila gave me a pointed look. "That's not what I meant. You yourself just said you wanted it to be a real date." She squatted down in front of me. "Admit it—you've fallen for him."

I shook my head. "No. It's not like that with us. I'm just being a girl and wanting it to be a date."

"Come on, Bells. This is me you're talking to. You can cut the bullshit façade about you two just being friends or just being coworkers. I've seen the way you light up when you talk about him." She nudged my knee with her hand. "And I can totally see why. He's a hell of a catch—good looks, money, and a really good heart."

Yes, he was all of those things. Over the last few weeks, I'd come to see that for myself. I didn't need Mila telling me. But, in the end, we were screwed by our connection to Callahan. "It's just too complicated."

"It doesn't have to be. You're a woman, he's a man—the parts all fit into place."

I laughed at her summation. "He's my boss."

Mila shrugged. "So? As long as you're consenting and it's not him trying to take advantage of you, what's the problem?"

"There's a no fraternization policy with executives."

"So be discreet."

I shook my head. "If I cross the line with Thorn, it could destroy everything I've worked so hard for. Any future promotions would be seen as nepotism. Not only would I be fucking the boss, I would be fucking the man whose family owns the corporation."

"No one who knows you could ever say that. Your work over the years speaks for itself. Who gives a shit if you happen to be *dating* the boss?"

When Mila said it that way, it really did seem easy, but I knew how fraught the situation actually was. It wasn't just about tuning out the negative voices around us at work. There was much more at stake. "What about if things didn't work out between us? How could I possibly stay at Callahan?" I shook my head. "I can't even imagine trying to find a job somewhere else. That place has been my life—the only thing I've ever known."

Mila rolled her eyes. "Why do you have to be such an uptight worrier? Why can't you just go with the flow and enjoy the moment?"

"Because that's not who I am, and may I remind you that over-thinking has served me well so far."

"Well, it's time to cut loose and just have some fun."

"Don't you know how much I wish I could do that?"

"You can, Bells." She tapped her temple. "You just have to turn off the voices in your head for a bit."

I sighed. "I wish it were that easy."

"For right now, the only thing you need to be worrying about is what you're going to wear."

Oh shit. In the midst of worrying about how to label Thorn and me, I had totally forgotten about the fact that I was in desperate need of a shopping excursion. Could I possibly be less of a woman for not thinking about a dress? "Oh God, you're right. What am I going to wear?"

"Something both classy and sexy."

"And just where exactly do I find that?"

"I might happen to have a few connections to designers."

Smacking her arm playfully, I said, "And you're just now telling me this?"

Mila grinned. "You've never asked." She pulled her phone out of her back pocket. "I'll message a few people. We should have you stylin' in no time."

"Thanks, Mi."

She winked. "You're welcome." Tilting her head, she said, "You'll need something for both the rehearsal dinner and ceremony, not to mention casual outfits to wear there and back."

"Why do I have the feeling my wallet is going to be weeping after you get through with me?"

"Oh, it'll be weeping tears of joy for how amazing you're going to look." A wicked gleam burned in her eyes. "Since I don't have a lingerie hookup, we're going to take a trip to Le Perla to make sure you have something smokin' hot underneath your dresses."

"I have underwear at home," I protested.

"You don't have Thorn-seducing underwear."

"For your information, I don't need any *Thorn-seducing* underwear."

"Hell yes you do, for your sake and his. You can consider me your fairy godmother for this coming weekend, and I'm going bibbidi-bobbidi-boo you some sex!

CHAPTER TWENTY-ONE
Thorn

The Wednesday before the wedding found me squeezing in my final tux fitting with Barrett during my lunch hour. Ty was along, not only in his usual capacity, but also because he was going to be a groomsman. Given his attention would be diverted for a lot of the wedding and we would have other agents surrounding us at every moment, he knew he'd be able to relax his guard somewhat on the day.

As I slid on the tailored jacket, I met Barrett's blue eyes in the mirror. "Remind me again why you needed a new tux?"

Barrett grimaced. "How could I possibly stand at the altar with my future wife in a tux I had potentially banged some other woman in?"

With a snort, I replied, "Only you would have the potential for *that* problem."

"So true," Ty murmured in agreement.

"Whatever. It's important to remember the past is the past. I've been reborn with Addison."

"Are you trying to say you were revirginized?" I asked.

Cocking his brows at me, Barrett said, "Do you know how long I went without sex while Addison and I were on the campaign trail?"

I tapped my chin thoughtfully with my index finger. "Oh, I don't know—maybe as long as I went without while I was deployed?"

Barrett weighed my words for a moment before nodding. "Fair enough." As the tailor appraised the fit of my jacket, Barrett asked, "As for the wedding, you're taking Friday off, right?"

I nodded. "Yep. The whole day is just for you, the groom-to-be."

Barrett chuckled. "I'm so touched. Does that mean we can get facials and mani-pedis?"

"Anything for you, little brother."

"Do you want to fly down with Addison and me on Thursday?"

There it was, the moment of truth. Considering how busy our lives were, I hadn't yet had a moment to tell Barrett I was bringing Isabel. He was still under the impression I was sticking to our previous plan of me going down to D.C. on Thursday so I could attend a pre-wedding party with him and Addison.

Instead of bachelor and bachelorette parties that might lead to embarrassing headlines for Dad, Barrett and Addison had decided to do a joint party with all the bridesmaids and groomsmen along with close friends, and they'd rented out the drag club Addison's brother owned. I still found it so ironic that Addison, the daughter of missionaries, had a drag queen as a brother. Thankfully, when the press caught wind of it, they had been as accepting as our family had.

"Yeah, I'm still on for flying down with you guys."

Ty cleared his throat. When I glanced over my shoulder at him, he gave me a pointed look like, *Would you get on with it and tell him about Isabel?!* Since we were practically attached at the hip, Ty was privy to the knowledge about me asking Isabel to the wedding.

"Here's the thing…it won't just be me on Thursday."

"What do you mean?" Barrett asked.

"I'm bringing someone with me to the wedding."

Barrett's brows shot up so far they disappeared into his hairline. "You are?"

"Is it seriously so shocking that I have a date?"

He rolled his eyes. "Of course not. We'll be happy to have her along too."

"Don't you want to know who it is?"

"It's Isabel, right?"

Now it was my turn for the high brows of shock. "How could you possibly know that?" I whirled around to stare at Ty. "Did you tell him?"

He held up his hands. "No, I didn't."

Turning back to Barrett, I said, "Did Mom tell you?"

"Nope."

"Then how in the hell did you know I was bringing Isabel?"

Barrett placed both his palms on my shoulders. "Because I knew from that day in your office how fucking over the moon you were for her."

"But that was months ago."

"Your feelings haven't changed, have they?"

"No, they haven't."

"And you haven't done jack shit to try to take things to the next level, have you?"

It was ridiculous just how well Barrett knew me. He rivaled Isabel in that respect. "You know why I haven't," I protested.

"Because you're a pussy?"

While Ty snickered, I growled at Barrett's remark. "If being conscious of both Isabel's and my career and friendship makes me a pussy, then yes, I'm a pussy."

"Come on, you're classier than that—you're Mr. Pussy if you're anything," Barrett teased.

Jesus, he could be such a dick. "Seriously? Are we back in high school?"

"By the way you're acting with Isabel, it would appear that way."

"How am I acting like I'm in high school with Isabel?"

"Because you're fucking scared of her."

I narrowed my eyes at Barrett. "I've never been scared of anything, least of all a woman."

"You are with this one, at least with your feelings." Barrett patted my back. "Trust me, brother, it takes one to know one. I was scared out of my fucking mind with Addison, but I took the plunge, and I've never been happier in my life."

"I wish it were that easy for me. You seem to be forgetting you didn't have any work-based complications from 'taking the plunge', as you call it, not to mention the fact that we've built a pretty strong friendship in the last few months."

Instead of being sympathetic to my plight, Barrett shook his head. "Stop being a pussy."

I threw up my hands in frustration. "I'm not. I'm being practical and responsible. I'm—"

"Being a pussy," Barrett and Ty said in unison.

Glaring at Ty, I said, "Et tu, Brute?"

Ty chuckled. "Sorry, Caesar. I'm siding with Barrett on this one."
Traitor.

As much as I railed against them, deep down I knew they were correct. I'd been practical and responsible all my life and it had been reinforced in the military, so it wasn't like a skin I could just shed upon entering civilian life.

"Just what exactly would you two have me do?"

"Look, I know you're not an overly verbose guy like me, but you need to tell her how you feel."

Ty stroked his chin. "You don't even have to tell her—you could show her."

"By showing up to her room with a boner?" I asked tersely.

With a roll of his eyes, Ty replied, "I was thinking something more along the lines of a kiss. I mean, the boner isn't a true representation of how you feel. You don't just want to fuck her—you want to date her."

He was right. With a groan, I swept my hands over my face. "How is it I'm thirty-one years old, have been in combat and seen the world, and one woman has the ability to completely emasculate me?"

Barrett grinned as he shook his head. "Man, you've got it bad, brother."

"Tell me about it."

Rubbing his hands together, Barrett said, "Okay, we need to come up with a plan."

"Excuse me?"

"You're a military guy, so let's strategize for how to tell Isabel how you feel."

"Oh hell no. This is way too much like high school."

"But don't you want to take things to the next level?"

"Yes, but I don't want to do so by slipping her a note that says, 'Check yes, no, or maybe,' which is what this plan sounds like."

Ty snickered. "I think in this day and age, the equivalent of that is a text."

"Better yet, a dick pic," Barrett chimed in. Jesus, my future sister-in-law was marrying a teenager.

I pinched the bridge of my nose. "I'm not sending Isabel a dick pic."

"You're right. That would come off a little strong," Barrett replied.

"And it would be physical evidence in a sexual harassment suit when it comes out that she doesn't feel the same way about me as I do about her," I countered.

"Well, that's not going to happen," Ty said.

"A sexual harassment suit?"

He gave me an exasperated look. "I mean, Isabel won't deny feeling something for you."

"Why?"

"With all the time I spend with you and therefore with her, I've seen the way she looks at you, the way she smiles and laughs. I might be single, but I know when a person likes someone." He patted my back. "She does, mate."

My ego did a fist pump at his declaration. "You really think I ought to pursue her?" I asked Ty.

He nodded. "It would be the best thing in the world for both of you."

As I turned back to look at my reflection in the mirror, I weighed his words. Maybe he was right—maybe they both were. I wanted her in my life, not just to fuck, and if I was truly honest, not just to date, either. I wanted the mornings and the nights. I wanted it all. It was time to stop being a pussy and pursue Isabel.

When Friday rolled around, I could barely control my emotions. I was experiencing a dizzying flurry of both excitement and nervousness about going to the wedding. Okay, so it wasn't just about going to the wedding. It was about going to a wedding at the White House. I mean, I was just Isabel Flannery from Podunk, Georgia, i.e. a nobody trying to appear to be somebody.

I don't know how I managed to get any work done. I was taking a half day off to fly to D.C., and although Thorn had invited me to accompany him for a party Thursday night, I had too much to take care of before blowing town for the weekend. I hated telling him no, especially when a defeated expression came over his face. I wasn't sure why it seemed to matter to him so much. It wasn't like I was bailing on going to the wedding with him.

Since he knew I was a bundle of nerves, he offered to fly up on the jet to pick me up, which was incredibly kind. Oh yeah, did I mention we were taking the corporate jet? I'd never jetted anywhere before. Talk about feeling like country come to town.

A hop, skip, and a jet ride from New York City later found me nursing a glass of wine in one of the guest bedrooms with Conan for companionship. After we'd flown in, Thorn had to go straight to the rehearsal while I had hung back in my room to get ready for the formal dinner that would follow the rehearsal.

After showering and doing my hair and makeup, I slipped into my dress and waited anxiously for Thorn to come get me. As I stared at my reflection in the antique mirror, I had to admit I looked pretty. I had chosen a navy-blue cocktail dress that fell just below my knees. Although the straps were wide, it did show a little more cleavage than I'd have preferred to display at the White House. I didn't want to offend anyone or come off looking slutty.

When a knock sounded on the door, I almost jumped out of my skin. "Wish me luck, Conan," I said. He gave a thump of his tail in approval.

I couldn't hide my surprise when Ty stood outside rather than Thorn. "Sorry to disappoint you, but Thorn's been held up with some last-minute best man details. He asked me to escort you to dinner."

I smiled. "That would be great. Thank you."

Like the true British gentleman he was, Ty offered me his arm. As we swept down the hallway of the Center Hall, I turned to Ty.

"Can I ask you something?"

"Of course."

"How did you manage the first time you came here?"

"Do you mean was I overwhelmed?"

"Yes."

Ty nodded. "Sure I was. How can you not be overwhelmed by the significance of being in the White House? Especially when you're someone like me—a poor kid from across the pond."

"That's exactly how I feel, except I'm a poor kid from the backwoods."

"In the end, it's important to remember that so many of the people who lived here or walked these hallways were immigrants, many of whom came from humble beginnings. The White House speaks to the American dream of carving out a better life."

"Such a beautiful sentiment. I had no idea you were so deep."

Ty grinned. "I have my moments."

"You know, it's easy to see why both Thorn and Barrett put so much faith in you."

His brows rose in surprise. "It is?"

"Yes. It isn't every day you find someone willing to take a bullet for you, least of all have that person be your friend."

"Thank you, Isabel."

"You're welcome."

He winked at me as we started down the stairs. "We're almost there, so don't be nervous."

"Does it show?"

"The fact that you're shaking is a pretty good giveaway."

I exhaled a frustrated breath. "I want to be cool, calm, and collected. I negotiate billion-dollar deals, for Christ's sake. I shouldn't be intimidated by dinner in the White House."

"You'll do just fine."

"I hope you're right."

"Just stick with Thorn. He can show you the ropes."

"Trust me, I want to stick to him like a sweaty shirt, but at the same time, I don't want to be in the way. After all, tonight is about him and his family, which makes me sort of an interloper."

"Stick to him like a sweaty shirt?" Ty questioned.

With a laugh, I replied, "Sorry, it's a Southern expression."

"Ah, I see." As we reached the bottom of the stairs, he paused. "If there's one thing I know about the Callahan family, it's that no one is an interloper. They go out of their way to make everyone feel welcome. I know they'll do the same for you."

"I hope so."

He grinned. "I have a feeling any attractive, single friend of Thorn's will be very, very welcome."

When I got his meaning, I almost stumbled in my fancy new heels. Did Thorn's family think we were more than just friends? Had he led them to believe that? "I can't imagine them not being nice to any of Thorn's friends."

At my emphasis of *friends*, Ty tilted his head at me, eyeing me curiously. I fully expected him to go off on me in true Mila fashion about my epic denial. Instead, he remained silent, which was almost worse than him laying his truth on me.

"There you are," Thorn said, his voice echoing through the hallway.

Ty led me to him. "Here she is."

Thorn grinned. "Thanks for delivering her to me."

Ty smiled in return. "Any time." He gave us one last knowing look before walking off toward the State Dining Room.

When I looked at Thorn, he was gazing intently at me. "You look absolutely gorgeous."

A rush of warmth cascaded over my body at both his compliment and the way he was looking at me. "Thank you. I do manage to clean up nicely from time to time."

"Yes, you do." He held his arm out to me just as Ty had. "Ready to eat?"

"I'm both starving and ready to puke," I mused.

"Don't be nervous," Thorn urged.

"Easier said than done."

"Everything is going to be just fine." He leaned in closer to me. "Take a deep breath."

"Are you serious?"

"Yes, I am."

"I didn't peg you as one for New-Agey stuff like breathing techniques and meditation."

"It's more like common sense than it is any *New-Agey stuff.*"

Since I knew Thorn wasn't going to let it go, I sucked in a deep breath and then exhaled it slowly.

"Again," he commanded. I followed his instructions three more times. When I finished, he cocked his brows at me. "Better?"

"Actually, yes."

"Just remember to keep breathing."

Following Thorn's instructions, I began to regulate my inhalations and exhalations as best I could. As we arrived at the doorway, I drew in one last breath and exhaled it super slowly.

"Ready?" Thorn asked.

"Yep. Let's get this show on the road," I replied, sounding a lot surer of myself than I felt.

Once we were inside and I found my seat, which was thankfully next to Thorn, I found my nerves slowly dissipating. By the time the second course was served, I was actually enjoying myself. Ty had been right about Thorn's family—they went out of their way to engage me in the conversation, and in turn, to make me feel welcome.

It was almost love at first sight with Barrett's fiancée, Addison, or at least love at first theater mention. Barrett and Thorn just rolled their eyes at the two of us, along with Addison's brother, Evan, as we went on and on about our love of Broadway.

As the third course plates were being cleared, Thorn leaned closer to me. As his breath warmed my cheek, he asked, "Wanna get out of here?"

A shiver of anticipation ran down my spine at his invitation. "But they haven't served dessert yet," I protested.

"You're choosing cake over busting out of this snoozefest?"

I laughed. "No, it's not that. I just thought it would be poor form if we left before dessert."

Thorn's brows shot up. "I never took you as an Emily Post devotee."

"I'm from the South—we live and die by manners."

"I see." Thorn glanced around. "Do you really think anyone will notice if we bail?"

"You are the best man and the president's son."

"It's just the rehearsal dinner. It's not like I'm advocating we bust out early from the ceremony."

I laughed. "Fine. I guess it wouldn't hurt."

Before I could rise out of my seat, Thorn pulled out my chair for me. "Such a gentleman," I mused.

"Part of one of the etiquette classes I took during school."

"You actually had a manners class?" I asked as I stood up.

Thorn nodded. "Yes. They taught us how to eat and drink correctly as well as how to waltz."

"Wow, you really are a triple threat when it comes to money, good looks, and dancing."

With a chuckle, Thorn replied, "You might reconsider that statement after you see me dance tomorrow."

"I can't imagine there's anything you don't excel at."

"Trust me, there are a lot of things, and dancing is one of them." As we exited the dining room, Thorn pointed to the hallway. "This floor is known as the State Floor because it's where all the formal shit takes place."

I laughed. "Somehow I can't see that line coming from a guidebook."

"Maybe an edition of *White House for Dummies.*"

"True." I glanced at the lofty ceilings. They had to be close to twenty feet high, and it was a bit overwhelming.

"This floor also connects the East and West Wings."

When we started down the corridor, I glanced back to see Ty wasn't behind us. "Ty won't be joining us?"

Thorn smiled. "No. He doesn't have to trail my ass as stringently while we're inside the White House." He nodded to one of the agents posted in the hallway. "These guys take care of that."

"Ah, I see."

Motioning to a staircase, Thorn asked, "How about we start at the bottom and make our way back up?"

"Sounds good to me." As we started down the marble stairs, I turned to smile at Thorn. "It's really nice of you to take me on a tour."

He flashed me a wicked grin. "It's not a completely unselfish act. I haven't had a chance to see everything yet myself."

"There's nothing wrong with killing two birds with one stone," I mused.

"While Addison is pretty much a walking guide book on this place, you're stuck with me—the guy who knows just enough to be dangerous."

"I'm sure you'll do just fine."

"Well, I might cheat by picking up a guidebook in the library."

"You had me at library," I swooned.

Thorn grinned. "I should've known you were one of those girls."

"Well, my nickname is Belle, and we all know how much she loved books and libraries."

With a frown, Thorn replied, "I can't say that I do."

"You don't know *Beauty and the Beast?*"

"No, I don't."

"Oh my God! We will have to remedy that ASAP when we get back home."

"I'm not watching cartoons with you."

"We can watch the live-action one."

"Whatever," he mumbled. He sounded like a petulant teenage boy. It was going to be fun showing him *Beauty and the Beast*. No doubt I'd come up with other movies to annoy him with.

We reached the landing of the stairs. "This is the ground floor." He pointed into the first room on the right. "The Vermeil Room houses a bunch of fancy silver as well as some official portraits of First Ladies."

I peeked inside the ornately decorated space. "Interesting."

Thorn continued on until he paused outside the second door on the left. "This would be the room with some china stuff."

I laughed as I caught up to him. "I think you mean the China Room where the patterns of the First Ladies are kept," I replied as we stepped inside.

"That sounds more official." He cocked a brow at me. "And just how did you know that? Were you holding out on me earlier with your White House knowledge?"

"Yes and no. My knowledge of this comes from the movie *The American President* with Michael Douglas and Annette Benning."

"I don't think I caught that one. Let me guess—it's a romance?"

"It is for the most part, but it also leans heavily on the political aspects of being the president."

"So do they get busy in the China Room?" Thorn teasingly asked.

With a laugh, I replied, "No, they only share a kiss before he has to go bomb Libya."

"Man, that's a bummer."

"They do 'get busy' later, but's it's one of those fade-to-black scenes, nothing too raunchy."

"Doesn't sound like my kind of movie then."

"Well, I can imagine your kind of movie doesn't have much of a plot except for a plumber with a bulge arriving at the house of a half-naked blonde."

Throwing his head back, Thorn laughed heartily. "Are you insinuating I only watch porn?"

"Maybe." Okay, maybe I liked to fantasize about him getting off while watching porn, like perhaps he had a thing for redhead porn. Yes, I realize I was completely pathetic.

"I'm a man of varied tastes, Ms. Flannery. I like war movies, Westerns, biographies, and comedies. I just don't dig cartoons or chick flicks like *Beauty and the Beast*."

I held up my hands. "I stand corrected."

"You know, we could catch a movie tonight if you'd like."

"Back in your room?"

Thorn's eyes flared at my somewhat suggestive comment. *Seriously, Isabel? What were you thinking suggesting going back to the man's bedroom?* I was pretty sure in a mansion like this they'd have a few TVs lying around in living rooms.

"I mean, in the family residence," I quickly corrected.

"Actually, we have our very own movie theater in the East Wing." Thorn jerked his thumb to the right.

"Oh, that's right."

"Would you like to see it?"

I smiled. "I'd love too." When Thorn started back to the door, I grabbed the sleeve of his suit. "But first I want to see the rest of the ground floor." I waggled my brows. "Most importantly, I want to see the library."

"It's your lucky day, because it's just across the hall."

With a squeal, I broke away from Thorn to run over. I burst through the door with the same level of excitement as a kid on Christmas morning, and when I got inside, I skidded to a reverent halt. Even though the room was tiny compared to the Beast's library, I had to appreciate the historical significance. Many presidents had given speeches in this room, and it was surreal to be in the presence of something so...time honored.

"Take one," Thorn urged.

I whirled around. "Excuse me?"

"Take a book," he repeated.

"That's what I thought you said." I shook my head wildly back and forth. "I can't take a book from the White House library."

"Why not? I don't think they'll miss it."

"Oh, I'm sure there's a meticulous record somewhere, not to mention some sensors and alarms would go off."

Thorn snorted. "I hardly think it's like the Declaration of Independence."

"You never know."

With a smirk, Thorn said, "You're such a rule-follower."

"Yes, and I'm not ashamed one bit," I replied as I perused some of the shelves. Although I could have spent hours in that room, I could tell Thorn was getting impatient. "Lead on, fearless guide."

After we got back out into the Center Hall, Thorn gestured down the hallway. "If I remember correctly, there's a kitchen down there, along with a map room, some sort of receiving room for dignitaries, the doctor's office, and Secret Service offices."

I wrinkled my nose. "Sounds kinda boring."

"Which is probably why I don't remember much of it," Thorn remarked.

Motioning to the staircase next to the library, I asked, "Where do those stairs go?"

"Down to the basement."

I peered into the darkness. "Anything cool down there, or is it creepy?"

"From what I remember, there's a flower shop and a carpenter's shop—oh, and the bowling alley."

Jerking my gaze to his, I declared, "Yeah, I gotta go down there."

"For what? The flower shop?"

"No, the bowling alley."

Thorn stared at me in surprise. "You can't be serious."

As I started down the stairs, I called over my shoulder, "Oh, I'm serious as a heart attack."

Thorn hustled to catch up with me. "I never thought I would see the day you would get all fired up about a bowling alley," he murmured.

Glancing around, I said, "Are we under some steps?"

"Yep, the ones of the North Portico."

"That's so cool."

In my mind, I imagined a bowling alley befitting the size of the White House, maybe with some cool strobe lights and a thumping stereo system. Instead, it was just a one-lane deal housed in a fairly small room.

Regardless of the size, I was still pretty thrilled to see it. "If I lived here, I'd totally hang out down here."

"You bowl?" Thorn asked incredulously.

"Heck yeah. Don't you?"

He chuckled. "No, I can't say I do, nor do I think I ever use the phrase 'heck yeah'."

Rolling my eyes, I replied, "It's a Southern thing, and I'm not too surprised to hear you didn't spend your summers in the Hamptons at the bowling alley."

"Har har."

"Growing up, the bowling alley and skating rink were *the* places to be." A smile curved on my lips as forgotten memories flooded my mind. "My parents kept this can on top of the fridge where they always put spare change. At the end of the month, they gave it to Christina and me to use for bowling and skating. Somehow a few ones and fives made it in there too."

"Once again, your parents sound pretty extraordinary."

I appreciated both the words and the reverent tone he used when he said them. "Thank you."

Sensing the need to lighten the mood, Thorn motioned to the bowling lane. "Want to bowl now?"

"Seriously?"

He shrugged. "Why not? Then you can be the only one back home who has bowled at the White House."

With a laugh, I said, "Ooh, bragging rights—I like it."

"Give me one second," Thorn said as he walked over to the control pad. After hitting a few buttons, the lights on the lane lit up, and the mechanized pins reset. Thorn flashed me a grin. "It's all yours."

With an excited squeal, I kicked off my heels and padded over to where the shiny black balls were lined up. After slipping my fingers into the holes, I thrust the ball upward with one hand and lifted my other hand to my chest. As my stocking feet slid on the slippery floor, I lamented not having an attractive pair of bowling shoes to wear. The last thing I needed to do was bust my ass in front of Thorn.

Pulling my arm back behind me, I focused on the pins. I slung my arm forward and released the ball, sending it spiraling down the lane. A loud crack echoed through the room as the ball smashed into the pins, knocking them all out in a perfect strike. I jumped into the air and let out a victory whoop.

The sound of applause caused me to whirl around. Thorn was grinning from ear to ear while clapping for me.

"Thank you," I said before curtsying. "Now it's your turn."

Shaking his head, Thorn held up his hands. "Oh, no. I think I'm good."

"Come on, just try it."

He gave a frustrated grunt at my insistence. "Fine," he muttered.

Thorn picked up one of the balls then went over to stand in front of the lane. After flinging his arm back, he brought it forward with equal momentum. Unfortunately, it slammed straight into the gutter. "Yep, I suck at bowling."

"No, you don't suck. It's not like you just start off being perfect.

You have to practice." I handed him another ball before pushing him back into position. "Now this time, you want to do it slow and easy."

Standing behind him, I eased his arm back. As I held his bicep, I couldn't help noticing how huge the muscle was beneath his shirt. I liked the feel of him under my skin, and I couldn't help imagining what it might feel like to cling to those bulging muscles as Thorn made love to me.

"Am I just supposed to stand like this forever?" Thorn questioned.

Shit. I'd totally zoned out for a moment while fantasizing about him and his muscles. "Uh, no. I just wanted you to take a moment or two to focus on the pins," I lied.

"Okay, I've focused on the pins. Now what?"

"You're going to bring your arm forward with strength, but I want you to go slower than the last time."

Once I let go of Thorn's bicep, I stepped to the side. He stepped forward and let the ball go. This time it careened down the lane to knock over five pins.

"See—you totally have this!"

He grinned. "I guess I just needed a good coach."

I laughed. "Considering I'm the least athletic person of anyone I know, I hardly think I'm coaching material."

"You were great." *Apart from when I imagined touching him naked.*

With a little curtsy, I replied, "Thank you."

"Do you want to torture me with more bowling, or would you like to see more?"

"I think I'm good to continue once we bust into the chocolate shop next door."

Thorn chuckled. "How did you notice that?"

Tapping my nose, I replied, "I sniffed it out."

"Come on, let's get you some chocolate." *Ah, music to my ears!*

When we made a pit stop at the chocolatier, we found we weren't alone. Members of the staff were working on souvenir chocolates for wedding guests to take home, and they kindly gave us a sample before we headed upstairs.

Instead of going up another flight of stairs to the residence, we headed to see what the East Wing had to offer. We made our way through what Thorn called the Visitors Foyer, where the non-VIPs entered the White House, to the long hallway called the East Colonnade.

"What's that?" I asked, pointing to what appeared to be a lighted garden.

"That's the Jacqueline Kennedy Garden."

"Oh," I murmured as I pressed my hands against the glass.

"You must be a Jackie Kennedy fan."

"Yes, I am. I loved her style."

Tilting his gaze to the ceiling, Thorn said, "Speaking of First Ladies, the second floor is pretty much just a bunch of offices, including my mom's."

"Sometimes it's hard to believe your mom is the First Lady."

"Why do you say that?"

"She's so down to earth."

"Even though she comes from a pedigreed family, she's always been that way. She's a true mom, and she took care of us instead of a nanny."

"I can totally see that about her. I have to say she did an amazing job. Look how the three of you turned out."

Thorn smiled. "I'll make sure to tell her that." He jerked a thumb at the door across from us. "And this is the theater."

I walked across the Colonnade to peek inside. "Okay, forget the bowling alley—if I lived here, I'd be hanging out in the movie theater all the time."

Thorn shot me a look. "Get serious, Flannery. You know you'd always have your head buried in work."

"I would make a point to carve out some 'me time', which would include movie time."

"Yeah, I'll believe it when I see it."

With a roll of my eyes, I replied. "Whatever."

"Shall we continue?"

"Yes, we shall."

"How about I show you the swimming pool?"

"Sounds good."

For some reason, I expected the pool to be indoors. Maybe it was because I was thinking of the old one Roosevelt used, but this one was tucked away from prying eyes and shielded by trees. "Have you been swimming here yet?"

"Not yet."

"Too bad we don't have our bathing suits," I mused.

Waggling his brows, Thorn replied, "We could always go in our undies."

"That would be a negative considering I'm not wearing a bra with this dress." *Shit.* From the look that flashed in Thorn's eyes, I knew I really shouldn't have shared that little tidbit.

A moment passed before he shook his head. "You wouldn't have done it anyway."

"Excuse me?"

"Even if you had a bra on, you wouldn't have gone in."

I swept my hands to my hips. "And just how do you know that?"

"Because you're too straight-laced. You're a rule-follower, not a rule-breaker."

"I seem to recall breaking quite a few rules when I sabotaged you at work," I protested.

Thorn grinned. "While that is true, my assholery influenced your decision. In this case, there's nothing to really influence you."

"Besides having bragging rights about jumping into the White House swimming pool with formal wear on?"

"I don't think it's in quite the same league." He reached over to tap my forehead. "Somewhere in that mind of yours is a raging battle about how impractical it would be to ruin your expensive dress, not to mention what everyone will think of you when they see you all wet and bedraggled."

I snorted. "Did you actually just use the word 'bedraggled'?"

"Hey, don't knock my extensive vocabulary."

"I'm not knocking it. I'm impressed."

"You're also deflecting."

"I am not."

After crossing his arms over his chest, Thorn cocked his head at me. "So, was I not completely correct about what's going through your mind?"

Of course he was. Although we'd only known each other four months, somehow he had the ability to see through to me as well as Mila or Christina did, but I didn't necessarily want him to know that—at least not yet.

"No. That's not what I was thinking at all," I argued.

With a smirk, he replied, "Yeah, right."

I glanced from him back to the water. I desperately wanted to not only prove him wrong, but to show myself that I could be spontaneous. Sure, the cost-conscious part of me was horrified that I might ruin a perfectly good formal dress with a dip in the pool, but there would be other dresses. There wouldn't be other chances to swim in the White House pool. At the end of the day, I could pull some strings and use the dress as a tax write-off.

And yes, I was worried about what people would think if they saw me looking bedraggled, as Thorn had pronounced, especially if they gave me a pretentious, snooty-type look like I was obviously trash since I didn't know how to act respectfully—but hey, I would most likely never see them again, so why did I give two shits about what they thought?

After kicking off my shoes, I gave Thorn one last fleeting look before breaking into a run. As my feet left the tile floor, I closed my eyes before letting out a victory squeal. The cool water hit my skin, sending slight shockwaves through me before the rest of my body was enveloped in the recesses of the deep end.

With a grin, I couldn't help thinking, *Carpe diem, motherfuckers!* Rules be damned. One day I could tell my grandchildren about how I'd thrown caution to the wind and swam in the pool at the White House.

Kicking my feet, I surged back toward the surface. When I emerged, I wiped the water from my eyes. Thank God I'd chosen waterproof mascara and eyeliner, or else I would've been looking like a raccoon.

"That was impressive," Thorn said behind me.

I whirled around to see him behind me in the water. "I'd say the same for you," I said with a grin.

Chuckling, Thorn said, "Since you already showed me up at bowling, I couldn't let you do it again."

"I see how it is." As I treaded water, I gazed up at the sky illuminated with stars. "What a gorgeous night."

"It is, isn't it?"

"You know, I don't ever seem to stop and look at the stars except when I'm away from home."

"Maybe it's because they're harder to see with all the skyscrapers in the city."

"Could be, or maybe it's because I just don't take enough time to actually look up at them. I need to be enjoying the little things in life," I remarked.

"Like swimming in formal wear in the White House pool?"

I laughed. "This isn't a little thing—it's a huge, colossal-type thing." I gazed back at the stars. "Just taking a few seconds to stop and look at the world around you...that's the little things."

When I looked at Thorn, who was quiet, he had a faraway look in his eyes. "I felt the same thing when I was deployed. Everything would be so wild and chaotic, and then it everything would seem to calm for a few moments. It was then I noticed the mosaic of colors when the sun stretched across the morning sky, or the different colors of sand." He nodded at me. "The little things really do matter."

As I stared into Thorn's eyes, I knew I was never, ever going to meet another man like him—one who could be as emotionally deep as the ocean while in the next breath be as irreverent as a comedian, not to mention the kindness and generosity he had shown Christina, and in turn, me. Forget the good looks or the money; I was so very attracted to the person he was within—the person he really was and not the asshole he had pretended to be.

While it was exhilarating to feel that way about another person, it was also equally frightening. I didn't know how to take the next step with him. Hell, I didn't even know if there should *be* another step for us considering everything that was at stake. I hated how convoluted everything felt.

As Thorn slowly swam closer to me, my heartbeat accelerated. That intensity of his was focused completely on me, as if he, too, couldn't wait another moment to get closer. The water was cold, and I wasn't wearing a bra, but I was on fire just from the look he was giving me. I felt desired. He looked at my lips and my breathing became choppy. I wanted my lips on his, on him. Damn it all to hell, I wanted him to kiss me—I *needed* him to kiss me.

As I willed it to happen, Thorn dipped his head. Just as his lips were about to meet mine, a voice boomed behind us. "Here you are." *Oh shit—Ty.*

Immediately, Thorn jerked away from me, and I whirled around to face Ty.

"Is there a problem?" Thorn asked.

While he appeared apologetic, Ty was also businesslike. "You went off the grid."

"Ty, I'm on safe grounds," Thorn replied tersely.

"While that's true, Barrett was looking for you."

Thorn groaned. "Are you serious?"

"Yes. Something about you needing to get the rings from the safe."

"Like I can't do that in the morning," Thorn grumbled.

"He also wants you to go with him and your dad to have a nightcap with the guests staying at Blair House."

While I'd always been a fan of Ty's, I seriously disliked him at the moment. After all the time it had taken to get Thorn and me to this moment, it had been ruined in just the blink of an eye. From the expression on Thorn's face, any *moment* we'd been having was gone. He'd been trained to look to responsibilities first. He was *that* man. Normally, I respected the hell out of it, but right then, I wished he wasn't.

He wouldn't be trying to kiss me again any time soon.

"I guess the tour is over," I said.

Thorn shook his head. "Barrett can wait."

"That might be true, but I don't think your guests can." I nudged his arm with my shoulder. "Go on and do your duty. I don't want your brother or your dad getting ticked that I took you away."

"At least let me get you a robe and then escort you back to your room."

"Escort me? There you go being proper again."

With a wink, Thorn replied, "I owe it all to prep school."

"Okay, Mr. Prep School, I'll let you do that as long as you promise to take me in a back way where no one can see me looking *bedraggled*."

Thorn chuckled at me referencing his word. "Yes, I can make that happen."

As I slipped on a fluffy, terrycloth robe from the pool house, I had the fleeting thought of wanting to stuff it in my suitcase. On the way back, the conversation between Thorn and me was lighthearted, but there was an undeniable tension in the air. From time to time, I would glance back to see Ty staring intently at us. I couldn't tell if it was just because he felt bad for interrupting or if it went deeper, like he really wanted to see the two of us together. *That makes two of us, buddy.*

Just as he'd promised, Thorn escorted me back to my room, and thankfully, he knew enough about the back stairwells to get us there without being seen by anyone—well, except for a few Secret Servicemen and some janitorial staff.

Ty gave us some space to say good night.

"I've got some best man stuff again in the morning, but I promise to come up and get you before the ceremony."

"Okay. I'll be ready at noon."

He nodded. "Good. I'll see you then."

Just as I was about to go into my room, Thorn stopped me, dipped his head, and planted a kiss on my cheek. The touch was tender and sweet, his lips warm and soft. It was both a poignant gesture and one that set me on fire.

"So? How did it go after you and Isabel cut out of the rehearsal dinner?"

For the second time in a week, I found myself enclosed in a small, mirrored room with bright lights and under Barrett's interrogation about my love life. It was T-minus two hours until the wedding, and we were putting the final touches on our appearances before taking pictures.

Thankfully, Barrett had the presence of mind to wait until it was just the three of us as his other groomsmen had already started out of the main house toward the Rose Garden.

At my brother's question, Ty groaned. "Go ahead and say it: I cockblocked you."

Barrett glanced between the two of us. "What's he talking about?"

I crossed my arms over my chest. "Everything was going pretty fucking perfect between Isabel and me. I was just about to finally kiss her—"

"You still haven't kissed her?" Barrett demanded.

With a roll of my eyes, I replied, "As a matter of fact, no, I haven't. Jesus, it's only been a couple of days since we talked about this. What did you expect me to do? Go storming back to the office and lay one on her?"

Flashing me a grin, Barrett replied, "I would have."

I snorted. "Yeah, well, I think we've established I'm not like you in the love department."

"So you were about to kiss her and Ty cockblocked you?" Barrett pressed.

Ty threw up his hands in exasperation. "For the record, I didn't knowingly cockblock him. My target went missing, and I went in search of him—it's that simple."

"Didn't you have the slightest idea that maybe Thorn and Isabel were getting busy since they ducked out of the rehearsal dinner early?"

"No."

Barrett shook his head at Ty before turning to me. "Then today is the day."

"Yes. It's your wedding day—that's the *only* day it is."

He jabbed a finger into my chest. "Correction: it's my wedding day *and* the day you seal your fate with Isabel. Don't let me down."

"Un-fucking-believable," I muttered.

Thankfully, the wedding planner appeared and saved me from any more of Barrett's berating. Sure, he was absolutely correct in demanding I quit dicking around when it came to Isabel, but it wasn't the day to have that as my focus. I needed to have my head on straight so I could flawlessly execute my duties as best man and get Barrett successfully married. Then...*I am coming to get you, Isabel.*

That was my new plan.

As I sat on a plush chair in the Rose Garden, I fought the urge to pinch myself for the millionth time for so many reasons. It wasn't just about the fact that I was in attendance at the wedding of the year, or that I was rubbing elbows with some of the highest-ranking political figures in the country, as well as some celebrities. It was more about how truly surreal it was. I was attending as the plus one of the president's eligible-bachelor son.

Speaking of Thorn, if I had thought he was delectable in a tailor-made suit, Thorn in a form-fitting black tux was positively combustible. After breakfast with his parents and sister, he'd spent most of the morning occupied with best man duties while I caught up on some work. When he came to escort me to the ceremony, I almost had a heart attack. At the sight of him, every illicit and impure thought I could conjure flickered through my mind. It took everything within me not to climb him like a tree right there in the family residence. Of course, if I'd tried that, I probably would have been tackled by a member of the Secret Service.

As a string quartet played Broadway show tunes—a subtle nod to the bride's former involvement in musical theater—Thorn led me to my seat. You can imagine my surprise when I found I was seated on the third row among his family—like the row behind aunts, uncles, and cousins. "Wait, I shouldn't be sitting here," I hissed in protest.

"Just shut up and sit down," he replied with a wink.

Normally, I would have told him to shove it, but the last thing I was going to do was make a scene in the Rose Garden. Instead, I eased into my seat without further argument. When I looked back at him, he gave me a panty-melting smile before he headed back down the aisle to continue escorting people to their seats. Of course, the skin on my back felt singed by the curious stares behind me. I knew they wondered who I was to have such a prestigious seat. More than that, they were wondering if I had ties to Thorn.

Time ticked closer to the start of the ceremony. When Thorn came walking out of the side door with Barrett, he sought my gaze in the crowd. The moment our eyes met, he smiled, and I instantly warmed not from the June heat, but from his gesture.

Even though I didn't know Barrett and Addison that well, I found myself tearing up from time to time during the ceremony. Call me a sentimental sap, but I was touched by the love they exhibited for each other. From Barrett shedding tears at the sight of Addison walking down the aisle on her father's arm to Addison's brother belting out a heartfelt rendition of *At Last*, it was an utterly gorgeous ceremony, the kind I dreamed to experience myself one day.

As the other guests filed into the East Room for the reception, Thorn instructed me to stay and hang out with him while the wedding party took pictures. I was glad he had suggested it since I didn't know a single soul inside. Once they had taken approximately one gajillion pictures, Thorn offered me his arm, and we started back inside the White House.

"What a beautiful wedding," I mused to make small talk.

"It really was." Thorn shook his head. "I still can't believe Barrett's married."

"He seems over the moon for Addison."

"Oh yeah, he is. It's just he used to be a notorious womanizer. He never cheated on women or anything like that, he just played the field." He winked at me. "A lot of fields."

I laughed. "I see."

Thorn's expression grew serious. "I guess it just goes to show the old adage is true about the love of a good woman changing you."

Under the intensity of his expression, I fought to breathe. Somehow it seemed he wasn't just talking about Barrett, like maybe he was referring to himself as well. It made my heartbeat accelerate.

"I suppose so," I murmured, my mouth suddenly dry. As a waiter passed by, I snagged a flute of champagne. I tried sipping it daintily though I wanted to throw the entire thing back in one gulp.

Thorn's hand came to the small of my back, and then he led us to our table. The next hour passed with a three-course meal followed by Barrett and Addison cutting the cake. I threw back more champagne while tearing up through Thorn's best man speech. The love that flowed between the two of them reminded me of Christina. There wasn't anything I wouldn't do for her, and the same could be said for Barrett and Thorn. Even though we'd lived far away from each other for many years, our bond was still just as strong. It seemed to be the same way with Barrett and Thorn.

After the cake was cut and distributed, Barrett and Addison shared their first dance. On the next song when other couples started to join them, Thorn turned to me. "Would you like to dance?"

I smiled. "I'd love to."

He took my hand and swept me from my chair. After we got onto the dance floor, my hand slid around Thorn's back as his came around my waist. My breath hitched being so close to him. My senses became overwhelmed with his nearness—the smell of his cologne in my nose, his callused fingers against mine. I wanted to be even closer to him, wanted to feel his skin against mine. Everything I felt for him seemed heightened, like the emotion surrounding the wedding was sending my feelings into overdrive.

Trying to get my mind on track, I focused on the band, which was playing a Big Band era song.

"I love this music," I said to break the silence between us.

"You do?"

I nodded. "Glen Miller, Cole Porter, Tommy Dorsey—all the big band leaders. Sometimes I think I was born in the wrong era. I've always hated clubs with all the sweaty bumping and grinding, but give me a dance with a jitterbug or slow dancing, and I'm there." Gazing up at him, I asked, "What about you? Do you ever feel you were born in the wrong time period?

Thorn tilted his head in thought. "I prefer modern conveniences, but the soldier in me would have loved to be around for WWII."

"Who wouldn't want to kick Nazi ass, right?"

He chuckled. "Exactly, and I would have loved to serve under some of the great generals, like MacArthur, Patton, and Bradley." He jerked his chin at me. "Speaking of WWII, I could totally imagine you as Rosie the Riveter."

I grinned. "While I love the music of the time period, I'm not sure I would have made it as a WWII-era woman. I would have been really pissed to stop riveting once the boys came home."

"I can totally see that about you. I can also see you being a strong, supportive woman by keeping the home fires burning."

"Of course I would've been. I would've made sure to tie a yellow ribbon around the old oak tree for my man." Tilting my head, I asked, "Did you have someone to tie a yellow ribbon?" I instantly regretted my question when a pained expression came over Thorn's face. "I'm sorry, I shouldn't have asked that."

"No, it's a perfectly okay question to ask. Considering how quickly my ex broke things off with me during my deployment, I doubt it. She wasn't really the yellow-ribbon type."

"It sounds like she wasn't *your* type. Any woman who was with you should have grasped the importance of your career."

"You're right. She never really appreciated that facet of my life."

Conversation seemed to fail us then. Maybe it was because of my awkward question, or maybe it was because we seemed to have moved from tiptoeing around the invisible line drawn in the sand between us to taking giant steps.

When the music stopped, I remained in Thorn's arms. To be honest, I could have stayed in his arms for the rest of the night. The screech of the bandleader's microphone tore my attention away from Thorn. "Ladies and gentlemen, please make your way to the exit to observe the fireworks as the bride and groom prepare to leave for their honeymoon."

"Fireworks? Now that's a sendoff," I mused.

"A little over the top for my taste, but they didn't ask me," Thorn replied as we started to the door.

"I think it's romantic."

Thorn cocked a brow. "A sonic boom filling the night sky is romantic?"

"The bright colors set against the starry sky are beautiful."

"If you say so."

"I do. Fireworks are part of celebrations, and what better thing to celebrate than a wedding?"

Thorn grinned. "Just when I think you aren't a girly girl, you go and say something like that."

I waved my hand at him. "I'm perfectly fine being a girly girl *and* a ball-buster."

"You've got the ball-busting down for sure."

Before I could argue with Thorn, a loud boom went off over our heads followed by streaks of blue and purple. At the top of the lawn, Barrett stood with his arm wrapped around Addison's waist, their faces tilted to the sky. I stood by my previous claim that it was really romantic.

When I glanced over at Thorn, he was no longer by my side. Instead, he had ducked under the tree behind us. I hurried over to him. Doubled over at the waist, he appeared to be trying to regulate his breathing. "Are you okay?" I shouted over the fireworks.

He didn't respond at first. Instead of pressing him with another question, I merely stood there and waited for him to speak to me. I didn't try touching him either. The seconds ticked agonizingly by. Finally, he raised his head. "Conan is probably freaking out in my room," he mused.

A relieved breath whooshed out of me. He was back with me, and his spirits seemed good since he was joking around, but I also knew something about self-deprecating humor. "Are you okay?" I repeated.

"I will be."

I reached up to cup his cheek. "I'm so sorry."

"It's okay. You have nothing to apologize for."

"It's just..." Words seemed inadequate at the moment. "I hate to see you in pain."

"And I'm grateful you care," he said softly.

"I do. I care a lot."

Thorn's eyes flared at my words. It was as if he'd been waiting for my consent, because he pounced on me, sending us crashing against the trunk of the tree. His hands came up to cup my cheeks. "I care a lot, too," he said.

The next thing I knew, his mouth was on mine, and even with my eyes closed, I was seeing fireworks. The kiss started soft with his warm lips pressed against mine, and then it deepened into something desperate, like he wanted to climb inside me, and God help me, I wanted him to. As his tongue swept past my lips and into my mouth, I moaned, and my hands came up to grip his corded shoulders.

When he finally broke the kiss, my chest heaved, and I trembled all over from need. *Oh God.* Thorn had kissed me, and it had been even better than I'd dreamed or fantasized about. I hadn't actually fantasized about kissing him under a tree on the White House lawn under a multi-colored display of fireworks; what I had imagined had been much more private, but it'd had the same level of intimacy.

At the same time, I hadn't imagined the kiss coming out of such emotional desperation on his part. One minute he was lost in a PTSD episode and the next he was kissing me. Did he really want to kiss me or was I just a distraction? My emotional grid went haywire with a mixture of confusion and hurt and fear.

Yes, I was a grown woman who felt fear about a kiss. In fact, I was scared out of my fucking mind. As much as I wanted the kiss and as much as I wanted him, there was also the fact that we had taken a quantum leap out of the friend zone. We would never be able to go back to the way things were. That fact truly horrified me, not to mention what would happen at work.

All of those out-of-control emotions were swarming in my mind when Thorn pulled away to stare into my eyes. Laden down with the baggage of the moment, I couldn't tell him how I felt about him. I couldn't tell him how much I'd wanted him to kiss me or about my growing feelings for him.

No, I promptly did the stupidest thing in the world, not counting the dog laxatives.

I ran.

Yes, ladies and gentlemen, I completely panicked, whirled away from Thorn, and then sprinted away as fast as my expensive heels could take me. Why, you ask? Oh please. It would take an hour-long session with my therapist to figure that one out.

I ran away from the best kiss of my life—the best *man* of my life—and I didn't stop running until I was locked in my room.

CHAPTER TWENTY-FIVE

Thorn

FUUUUCK reverberated in my mind as I watched Isabel's retreating form. How could I have possibly read the situation so wrong? No, everything had told me the moment was *right*, that Isabel had wanted the kiss as much as I did. Apparently, though, I was completely delusional, because I never expected the fear that radiated in her eyes when she pulled away.

After standing there in a stupor for what had to be a good five minutes, Ty brought me out of my thoughts. "You okay, mate?"

I threw a glance at him over my shoulder. "No." *Fuck no.*

"What did you do?"

"Nothing. I...I kissed her," I replied.

When I turned around, Ty's face was positively comical. "Really?"

"Apparently, I fucking suck at kissing."

Ty scowled at me. "Doubtful."

"You wanna snog me and see?" I asked, throwing the Britishism for kissing at him.

He chuckled. "Hell no."

Shrugging, I replied, "Then I guess I'll never know."

"Find out right now. Go see what's wrong," Ty suggested.

"Considering how quickly she jetted out of here, I doubt she wants to be around me."

"Just go."

I held up my hands. "Fine, fine, I'm going."

"Good."

Any bravado I had about busting down Isabel's door waned on the long walk back to the residence. Instead of going to her room, I went to mine, and Conan practically knocked me down the moment I came through the door. "It's okay, buddy. I'm back." His response was to shoot me a *Don't bullshit me* look. "Yeah, okay, I had a moment outside, but it's all good now." He cocked his head and once again gave me a look.

After I stripped off my suit jacket, I tossed it onto the chair. More than anything, I wanted to sleep, to escape the emotional overload of the day. I threw a T-shirt on and exchanged my briefs for a pair of boxers. Too restless to sleep, I prowled around the room. I checked my phone, flipped on the TV, and grabbed a beer out of the mini-fridge.

Chugging the beer didn't help. Instead, I felt even more fidgety. I couldn't stay in the room one more second. After hopping into a pair of jeans, I headed back out into the hallway. At first, I didn't know where I was going, but it seemed the minute I got outside, I had a purpose, and that purpose was talking to Isabel. I needed to know how I had possibly read her so wrong. Kissing her had been so much better than I'd even imagined it would be. It was several months of passion condensed into moments with her delicious mouth, and I wanted more —much, much more. However, I'd have to put those thoughts behind me if she didn't want me. I just didn't know what she wanted me to do.

When I got to her room, my knuckles rapped against the wood. A few seconds passed before the door swung wide, and Isabel's shocked face appeared before me. *Okay, Callahan, get it together.* After jerking a hand through my hair, I exhaled a ragged breath. "Listen, I felt like I should come in person and apologize for what happened earlier. I'm sorry if I offended you with the kiss. You know better than anyone I'm not one for spontaneity. What I felt in that moment has been building over time. However, regardless of my feelings, I didn't stop to take yours into consideration. I'm terribly sorry."

Isabel blinked at me. We stood there in an awkward silence for a few moments. The next thing I knew, she launched herself at me. Talk about climbing me like a spider monkey. After jumping into my arms, she wrapped her legs around my waist before her arms encircled my neck. When her lips slammed against mine, my heart threatened to burst right out of my chest.

"I'msorryI'msorryI'msorry," Isabel murmured against my mouth.

"You're forgiven," I replied.

She pulled away to stare intently into my eyes. "I was so stupid to run away from you. I wanted you to kiss me. I swear on everything that is holy I did."

I couldn't help chuckling. "I believe you."

"I've wanted you to kiss me for a really long time."

"And I've wanted to kiss you." Tilting my head, I added, "I'm glad we're finally on the same page."

"More than just a kiss, I want you." Isabel then ground her pelvis against mine, causing me to groan as my cock jumped. This woman was going to be the death of me, and we hadn't even gotten naked yet.

After we burst through the bedroom door, I staggered over to the bed. I was having trouble concentrating on walking with Isabel's tongue swirling in my mouth while she rubbed her fabulous tits against my chest, not to mention the fact that she was riding my hardened dick over my jeans.

When we got over to the bed, Isabel slid down my body onto her feet. Her hands then came to my belt buckle, and although my cock wanted nothing more than to have her hands on it, I knew it was the last thing I needed if I wasn't going to embarrass myself in front of Isabel. "We need to slow down," I panted.

Her head shook feverishly from side to side. "I want you inside me—now."

I took her hands in mine and moved them away from my belt buckle. "There's a reason I need to slow things down."

Isabel turned her wild gaze on mine. "What? Why?"

"If I fuck you now, I'm not going to last longer than about two seconds." When she blinked at me in confusion, I squeezed her hands. "I haven't been with anyone but my hand in a year. Because of that fact, I know I'll be shooting off like a teenage boy the moment I get inside you. I don't want that for our first time."

"Oh," she murmured.

"So let's slow it down, okay? I mean, we've got all night."

Isabel licked her lips. "Let me take care of you. Then you can build back up to be ready to fuck me for hours."

When I got her meaning, I happily released her hands. After she unbuttoned and unzipped my pants, she pushed them over my hips and down my thighs before getting settled on her knees before me. In my exhilaration about getting head, I hadn't stopped to think about the fact that she was about to feel my scars. Not only was she going to feel my scars, she was going to see them, like be up close and personal with them. An icy panic pricked its way down my back to settle in my stomach, and I fought the urge to pull her up off her knees before she'd even gotten started.

She raked her nails up my calves and over my knees. When she got below my hip where my skin became puckered and pitted, I shuttered my eyes. I couldn't bring myself to read the pity or revulsion in her eyes. I hated myself for being so vain. I should've been glad to be alive and not so fucking shallow. I'd dreaded this moment with any woman, but for some reason, I loathed it with Isabel. Maybe it was because I already felt damaged emotionally in her eyes and I wanted to appear physically perfect, to be the Adonis she thought I was.

At the feel of her soft lips on one of my scars, my eyes shot open and I jerked my head down.

Isabel's gaze flickered to mine as she pressed a trail of tender kisses down my skin. If there was ever a moment I knew I was in love with her, it was then.

I bit down on my lip to keep from blurting it out. Since we weren't remotely close to voicing that sentiment, I knew now was not the time, especially not with her on her knees about to give me a blow job.

After tenderly attending to my scars, her fingers came up to grip the waistband of my boxers. Slowly, she slid them down, sending my cock springing forward. At the look that flared in Isabel's eyes, I could tell she was impressed, which once again made me feel like a god among men.

After she gripped my cock in her hand, Isabel dipped her head. When she flicked her tongue against the tip, I threw my head back and groaned. She continued mercilessly teasing me by licking my dick like it was a fucking popsicle. She'd flatten her tongue against the root and then lick up to the top, and it was glorious torture.

Pressing my erection against my stomach, she then nipped and sucked at my balls before alternating sucking them into her mouth. Damn, this woman was good. My hips were already bucking, and she'd yet to even take me into her mouth yet. Of course, at the rate I was going, I might just blow my load the moment that happened.

Thankfully, when she slid her lips over me, I managed not to come immediately. Instead, I focused on the warmth of Isabel's mouth. Slowly, she took me as far as she could before she slid me out. Then she began to bob up and down on my cock while working me with her hand.

"Oh fuck, Isabel," I grunted. When she glanced up at me, the gleam in her eyes told me she was loving torturing me. After a few more pumps of her hand and mouth, I felt my balls tightening. "I'm going to come," I muttered through gritted teeth. I tried to push her away, but she remained firm. "You've got to stop."

She gave a quick jerk of her head, signaling she was going to see this through. The fact that she was willing to take all of me was my undoing.

"Isabel!" I groaned before I came.

Just like with everything in her life, Isabel gave one hundred and ten percent. After I'd come down from the fucking mountaintop, I glanced down to see her licking me clean. When she finished, she rocked back on her knees.

"That was…" I shook my head as the words escaped me. "Fan-fucking-tastic."

"You're welcome," she said with a laugh.

"You weren't worried to do all that?"

She flashed me a wicked grin. "Your life insurance file came to my office—I know you passed your STD tests with flying colors."

I snorted. "Thank God for insurance file mishaps."

"For the record, I'm clean as well." Just as I was about to do a victory dance at the thought of riding bareback, Isabel killed my dreams. "But I'm not on any birth control right now."

"Okay, I can deal with that." The mention of birth control had me thinking of being inside her, which I wanted more than anything in the world. Gripping her arms, I pulled her up off the floor. Now it was her turn to be worshipped. "Take your hair down," I commanded.

Without a word, Isabel undid the knot at the back of her neck, sending her long red hair cascading over her shoulders.

"Beautiful." A smile curved on her lips at my compliment, and my hands then swept around her back to unzip her dress. My thumbs lingered a bit at the zipper, brushing across her silky skin. Once her dress was unzipped, I pushed it off her shoulders. It slid to pool on the floor like a whisper, leaving Isabel in a sexy white bustier and panties. "You're so fucking sexy," I murmured as I took her in.

A flush bloomed on Isabel's pale skin. "Really?"

"Surely you know that."

"I like hearing it." She licked her lips. "Especially from you."

"Then I'll say it again." One of my hands came to cup her cheek while the other slid slowly down her neck. "You. Are. So Fucking. Sexy."

"Thank you, Thorn," she whispered.

As my hands came to take her breasts out of the bustier, I grinned. "Of course, these I'm familiar with."

Isabel giggled. "How well I remember."

"It's me who remembers. Every day for the last few months, I've recalled exactly how they felt and what they looked like."

"You have?" Isabel asked as her brows shot up.

"Yes, and I realize I'm a dirty bastard for thinking about your tits." When my thumb circled one of her nipples, Isabel gasped.

"I like that you thought about me."

"Even though I knew what they looked like and felt like, I didn't know what they tasted like."

Isabel's eyes flared as I dipped my head to suck one of the hardened points into my mouth. Her hands came to my hair as she sighed with pleasure. After flicking my tongue over her nipple, I brushed my teeth across it, causing her to jerk at the strands of my hair. If she was this responsive with her breasts, I couldn't wait to see what it was like when I touched her pussy.

After kissing a wet trail over to her other breast, I teased and tasted the nipple, causing it to pucker beneath my lips. One of my free hands dipped between Isabel's legs, and at the contact of my fingers to her clit, she cried out and swiveled her hips against my hand. When I slipped one finger inside, I found her drenched for me.

Once I added another finger, I began to pump them inside of her. Isabel's breaths came in harsh pants as her hips moved against my hand for friction. Considering how wet she was, I knew it wouldn't be long before I sent her over the edge. As my thumb rubbed against her clit, I thrust my fingers harder and faster inside her.

Isabel's hands moved from my hair to grip my shoulders. She pumped her hips furiously against my fingers before throwing her head back and a shriek of pleasure escaped her lips as her walls convulsed around my fingers. "Yes, Thorn!" she cried as she rode the wave of her orgasm.

As she started to come down, I pulled my fingers out of her and brought them to my lips. Damn, she tasted good. I wanted nothing more than to bury my mouth in her pussy, but with my cock already painfully erect, I knew I would have to save that for next time.

I eased Isabel back onto the bed. "Don't move," I instructed.

"Are you kidding? After that orgasm, I couldn't walk if I tried."

With a chuckle, I grabbed my wallet out of my jeans and fished a condom out. After ripping open the wrapper, I slid it on before joining Isabel on the bed. When I positioned myself between her thighs, I rubbed the ridge of my erection against her clit, causing her to moan. I dipped my head to kiss her mouth and her neck.

"Please, Thorn," Isabel murmured.

Her begging was my undoing. After guiding my cock to her core, my eyes locked with hers. Since I knew it had been a while for her, I didn't just drive right into her. Instead, I slowly slid inside, inch by inch. Isabel bit down on her lip as her slick, tight walls took my dick in.

"Are you okay?"

A lazy, almost satisfied smile lit up her face. "I'm wonderful."

I returned her smile. "You feel fucking wonderful."

"I could say the same thing to you."

As I rocked slowly back out of her, I said, "Just tell me how you want me to take you."

"I'll take anything you give me."

I groaned. "Now there's an invitation." Withdrawing my cock, I then thrust it back inside her, causing us both to hiss with pleasure. As I set up a slow, languid rhythm, Isabel's hands came to slide up and down my back. Our tongues tangled together the same way our arms and legs did.

Once I knew she was ready to take all of me, I pulled out. After arranging her legs flush against my chest, I plunged back into her. "Oh God, Thorn!" she cried as she twisted the sheets with her fingers.

The position was fucking amazing since I was able to go deeper than before. I began to slam in and out of Isabel, her hands moving from the sheets to grip my forearms. Her cries of pleasure fueled me on to pump faster and harder.

When her walls began tightening around my cock, I pulled out again. Isabel mewled in frustration, her frantic gaze meeting mine. Rolling her over, I brought her up onto all fours, and my palm reached to smack her ass before I slammed back inside of her. As I began to manically thrust into her, I dipped one of my hands to tease her clit. Isabel moaned and buried her face in the mattress.

This time when she started to come, I let her go over the edge, and the sounds of her orgasm sent a rush of pleasure through me. With Isabel's walls clenching my dick like a vise, I let myself go over the edge as well. Barking a string of curses, I came, completing the best sexual experience of my life.

CHAPTER TWENTY-SIX

Thorn

Post-fucking bliss was the only phrase I could think of to sum up my current mood. Talk about being rewarded for going without. Sex with Isabel was everything I had imagined it would be and more. I couldn't remember when I'd come so hard. If I'd been a smoker, I would have lit up not one but two cigarettes.

Flipping over on my side, I stared at Isabel. She was on her back with her gaze on the ceiling, and she appeared just as ravaged as I was. "Hey," I murmured.

Her head turned on the pillow to look at me. "Hey," she replied.

I smiled. "Can I be honest with you for a minute?"

Isabel's eyes widened as a horrified expression came over her face. "Oh God, you hate the way I give head?"

I blinked at her. "What? No."

"I'm too vocal."

"God, no."

"I'm—"

I brought my hand over her mouth to quiet her. "Would you stop?"

"Not until I know what I'm doing wrong."

"Nothing. There's not one damn thing you're doing wrong. Pretty much everything you do is fucking amazing."

"It is?"

"Uh, yeah. I thought I was pretty vocal in my appreciation."

"You were."

"Then why did you think you'd done something wrong?"

She fiddled with the spread. "You got all serious and said you wanted to be honest with me."

"So you automatically assumed I thought you were lacking in bed?"

"Maybe."

"Seriously, Isabel?"

"Haaaaa," she muttered while breathing into her hand.

"What the hell are you doing now?"

"Checking my breath."

"What for?"

"To make sure it doesn't smell bad."

"Isabel!" I growled.

She held up her hands. "Okay, okay, I'm sorry for being neurotic."

Shaking my head, I mused, "I don't think I've ever seen you so unhinged."

"I'm much more comfortable in the boardroom than in the bedroom." *What the fuck?* How did this beautiful woman before me think she wasn't a goddess in the bedroom?

"You have no reason to be." I placed my hands on either side of her beautiful face. "Believe me when I say you are a master in both the boardroom and the bedroom."

Disbelief flickered in her eyes. "I am?"

"Yes, you are. That was what I had planned to say before you went on your neurotic rant."

After nibbling on her bottom lip, she countered, "Maybe it's been so long for you that you don't remember what really good sex is?"

With a roll of my eyes, I said, "Please tell me you're not insinuating that after going so long without sex, your pussy could have blinded me from the truth?"

She laughed. "Maybe."

"Babe, I might've gone almost a year without sex, but I know good when I experience it." I pushed a strand of hair out of her face. "Man, I'd like to get a hold of the douchebag who did a number on your head.

"I wouldn't necessarily say it was the work of one specific man, more like my own neuroses trying to determine why things haven't worked out long term for me when it comes to relationships."

"It's their loss, not yours."

"Thank you," she murmured.

When she tried to stifle a yawn, I laughed. "Am I boring you?"

"Never, it's just been a big day."

"It has." I stared her in the eyes. "A fucking wonderful day."

"Are you going to stay the night?" she questioned, almost in a whisper.

"Do you want me to?"

"Part of me says you should leave so no one discovers us, but the other part of me wants to wake up with you in the morning."

"I feel the same way—well, except for the part about us being discovered. I only care about that because you do. I'd be happy to walk out of here naked right now."

Isabel's eyes widened in horror. "You wouldn't actually do that, would you?"

I laughed. "No. I wouldn't want to run the risk of my mother or sister seeing me naked."

"Just when I think you can't get any more infuriating, you go and say something like that," Isabel huffed before she turned away from me.

"Fine, I wouldn't do it because I know it would upset you —how's that?"

She glanced over her shoulder at me. "Much better."

"Does that mean I can stay?"

"Yes, but only if you promise to spoon me."

"You drive a hard bargain, Ms. Flannery."

"And I always win, Mr. Callahan."

"Is that a challenge?"

She grinned at me. "Maybe."

"Then I accept."

I slid in behind her, and between the wedding and our nocturnal exertions, I fell asleep almost immediately. Of course, I also think the warmth of Isabel's body against mine helped a bit.

Holy shit. There was a man on top of me, but it wasn't just any man— it was Thorn. *HOLY SHIT!* flashed in my mind again. *Thorn and I had sex. Thorn and I had* really *good sex—like exceptional, off-the charts sex...mind-blowing, life-changing sex.*

As I reminisced about what had transpired after the wedding, a flush entered my cheeks and between my legs, but it wasn't just the sex I remembered. When my fingers came to touch my swollen lips, I remembered our beautiful first kiss under the trees. While fireworks had gone off above us, we'd experienced some fireworks of our own.

I gazed down at Thorn's blond head resting on my chest. His warm breath fanned across my skin, causing goose bumps to pop up along my skin. I could've stayed in that moment forever, but my bladder screamed in agony for release. Gently, I eased out from under him and rolled over to the edge of the mattress.

When I flicked on the light in the bathroom, I jumped back at my appearance. Thank God I'd woken up before Thorn. The last thing I wanted him seeing was me looking like a crazed raccoon with my left-over eye makeup, not to mention the fact that I had some serious sex hair.

After relieving my bladder, I washed my face and then brushed the morning breath out of my mouth. I sprayed some product in my hair to try to tame my mane, and when I was finished, I looked infinitely better.

When I opened the door, Thorn was standing before me in all his naked glory, and I shrieked in surprise. *Dammit.* I had hoped to slink back into bed unnoticed—you know, give Thorn the impression I woke up looking like I did at the moment.

"I thought you were asleep," I croaked as I rubbed my chest.

"I was, then some buzzing sound woke me up." He grinned as he ran a hand through his own bed hair. "I had hopes it was a sex toy."

I laughed. "It was my electric toothbrush."

"Bummer." He reached over to pull me toward him. "I was going to offer my services in its place."

"Just because I wasn't using a vibrator doesn't mean you can't service me." A wicked look flashed in Thorn's eyes before he dropped to his knees in front of me. "Oh my," I murmured as he pushed open my robe's lapels. When I'd mentioned him servicing me, I hadn't expected this kind of service. At the same time, I wasn't going to protest.

Gripping my thighs, Thorn pushed them apart for better access. When he licked his lips, a shudder went through me. He then dipped his head to tongue my center.

With a gasp of pleasure, my fingers went to the strands of his hair. As he began lapping my now slickened core, I threw my head back and moaned with pleasure. His oral skills were exceptionally good. He wasn't one of those men who did a few licks and sucks before moving on. No, Thorn went for the gold by using his tongue and even his teeth. He made quick work of making me come.

"Oh God, oh Thorn!" I shrieked as I practically saw stars in front of me from the pleasure.

Thorn pulled me down beside him on the rug. "Don't move," he instructed.

Still blissed out from my orgasm, I nodded slightly. With lazy eyes, I watched as he walked back over to the nightstand where his wallet was. As he took out another condom, I snorted. "What?" he asked as he walked back over to me.

"For a guy who hasn't gotten any in the last year, you're awfully prepared."

He shocked the hell out of me when an almost shy grin curved on his lips. "I picked up a pack just in case."

Cocking my head, I asked, "Why do you seem embarrassed by that? Being safe is the right thing to do."

"I picked them up after we started hanging out together," he replied as he eased back down in front of me.

Oh my. That was an interesting development. "You thought we might have sex someday?"

As he slid the condom on, he appeared to be weighing his words. "You could say I did a lot of thinking about us having sex." He glanced up from his erection to pin me with an intense look. "I fantasized about us having sex a lot. I got off to the thought of us having sex...a lot."

A shudder went through me at his words as well as at the image of him pleasuring himself. "I thought about us having sex too," I admitted.

Thorn's brows shot up in surprise. "You did?"

"Mainly I had a fantasy of you going down on me like you just did, though we were in my office when it happened."

Stroking his cock, Thorn said, "Did you come when you fantasized about it?'"

"I wasn't touching myself when I thought about it." I licked my lips. "But I did get wet."

"Not as wet as I actually made you."

I shook my head. "No. Only your hands, mouth, and dick make me that wet."

"I like how wet I make you."

"You're doing a pretty good job making me wet while touching yourself."

He grinned. "Would you rather I be touching you?"

"Yes, but I'd also like you inside me."

"I want to be inside you too." He jerked his chin at me. "Get on your knees," he commanded.

"You sure do like to bark orders, don't you?"

A dark look flared in his eyes. "You don't know how to show respect."

"Hmm, are you going to punish me?"

"Maybe."

"How?"

"By making you scream my name."

I grinned. "That doesn't seem like much of a punishment."

With a matching grin, Thorn replied, "Not getting to come and screaming my name in frustration is an extreme form of punishment, I'd say."

"You wouldn't really do that to me…would you?"

"If you do what I say, I won't."

Well, all right then. I wasn't one for a man telling me what to do, be it in the bedroom or the boardroom, but for some reason, I wanted to see this through with Thorn, maybe because I knew he was used to giving commands in combat.

"Fine, okay," I begrudgingly grumbled. Once I was on all fours in front of Thorn, I glanced at him over my shoulder. "Is that good, *sir*?"

He rewarded my efforts with a panty-melting grin. "I'd say the view alone is pretty fantastic."

Thorn positioned his knees between mine, and at the feel of his cock nudging the entrance of my vagina, a shiver of anticipation rippled across my skin. Once he'd slid himself inside, his hands came to my hips, his fingers gripping my flesh. With one harsh thrust, he buried himself within me. My fingers raked against the antique rug as I cried out with pleasure.

As Thorn set up a punishing rhythm, I swiveled my hips against him. We just fit together so perfectly. Pleasure seemed to tingle all over my body, not just between my legs, though what was going on down there was pretty freaking amazing, especially when Thorn slid one of his hands off my hips to stroke my clit.

The combination of his thrusts and strokes sent me over the edge. "Thorn!" I cried, my walls convulsing around him. As I rode out my orgasm, Thorn's hips pumped furiously against me until he came with a loud shout.

We collapsed in a heap of arms and legs. After we had a chance to catch our breath, I turned my head to look at him. "I can't believe we just had sex on an antique rug in the Queens' Bedroom of the White House."

"What's wrong with that?"

I slapped my hand over my eyes. "Somehow I think I've disgraced the country."

Thorn chuckled. "I think the country will recover." Wagging his brows, he added, "The question is…will we?"

I laughed. "I think we have another round or two in us. After all, you've been saving up for a while."

"That is true." Thorn pulled himself up off the floor before offering me his hand. As he walked over to collapse on the bed, I grabbed my phone off the nightstand, and the headline on the locked screen caused me to gasp in horror: *Is America's most eligible bachelor off the market?* There was also a picture of Thorn and me dancing at the wedding.

My hand flew to my mouth. "Oh God," I groaned.

"What's wrong?" Thorn asked.

"The media has outed us."

"Excuse me?"

I thrust my phone at him. After glancing at the screen, he didn't exhibit the same horror I did. When he met my gaze, he shrugged. "It's just speculation. They don't know what's really going on between us."

"And what is that exactly?"

Thorn scratched the stubble on his cheek. "Scorching hot sex?"

I rolled my eyes. "Would you be serious?"

He flashed me a wicked grin. "I am."

"James Thornton Callahan," I warned.

"Ooh, I love it when you call me by my full name."

Shoving him back, I said, "Would you please be serious?"

"Fine. You want the truth? We're far more than just scorching hot sex. We're good friends, we're coworkers—"

"I think it's more boss and employee, or superior and subordinate."

With a roll of his eyes, he replied, "Semantics."

"Oh, I'm pretty sure if I read further, the article is going to bring up that salacious little fact."

"Isabel, you're getting your panties in a twist over nothing. We can be photographed together without facing any repercussions at work."

I swept my hands over my eyes. "God, can you imagine what

everyone at work is saying right now? Or what they will say when we go back tomorrow?"

"Considering most of our floor still thinks I'm a giant asshole, I'm sure it can't be worse than that," Thorn quipped.

"Once again, could you please take this seriously?"

"Okay, fine. Frankly, I couldn't give a shit less about what they might have to say about us. At the end of the day, it's nobody's business but our own."

"Don't you get it? Because of who you are, it will never just be our business. The media will always be splashing our private life across the screen."

"Once again, none of that matters to me."

"Well, it should, especially when they start digging up my less than desirable past."

Thorn cocked his brow at me. "Your past? Were you a hooker who did crack or something?"

"No, nothing like that."

"Then I think we're good."

"We come from two very different worlds. Your family has wealth and social prestige while I'm just the trailer trash girl from Georgia."

He shook his head. "That is not you, nor is it your family."

"But people are going to talk about our differences. They're going to assume I'm a social climber. They'll probably trot out a few of the undesirable relatives my family doesn't associate with but who will be more than happy to sell a few stories about us."

"Every prestigious family has black sheep or members who embarrass them. Jimmy Carter and Bill Clinton both had questionable brothers, and Ronald Reagan's daughter posed for *Playboy*."

I threw up my hands in frustration. "For Christ's sake, I come from a prejudiced town where my third cousin sells lawn jockeys and Confederate flags on the side of the road, and his isn't the only business like that. All of that can hurt more than just us—it can hurt your father. Political rivals would have a field day with it. Your father's administration is still young, and it can't withstand any scandal."

Thorn gave an exasperated shake of his head. "I hardly think you and I dating would be considered a scandal."

"Wait a minute—we're *dating*?"

"While it's been a while since I did it, I would think that's what we're doing."

Feeling slightly overwhelmed, I rubbed my forehead.

"Do you have a problem with that?" he asked.

"No, it's just…yesterday we were colleagues and friends, and now we've made the leap to dating in just a few hours?"

"I would think the fact that we slept together accelerated us to the next level." Thorn brushed a strand of my hair out of my face. "I'm probably going to sound like a giant pussy for this, but it kinda wounds my pride that you don't want anyone knowing we're together."

Oh God. Somehow in my neurotic rant, I'd hurt Thorn, which was the last thing I ever wanted to do. "No, that's not it at all."

"Well, it certainly sounds like that."

I placed my hands on his cheeks. "I'm honored someone like you would want to date me."

"And I feel the exact same way. So, what's the problem?" *He's honored to date me?* I didn't think he really understood. Maybe he'd been out in the desert and away from the world of social media for too long.

"It just seems fast."

"Isabel, I think it's safe to say what we've been doing the last two months could be considered a slow-burn romance. We're not leaping off a cliff into the unknown. We aren't two strangers who shared some bump and grind. I've gotten to know you, and you've gotten to know me." He waggled his brows. "Both in the personal and biblical sense."

I laughed in spite of myself. Thorn was right. We had turned into the quintessential friends to lovers. Our newly minted relationship had been building over time, and I had to admit that from the outside looking in, we had built a pretty solid foundation. I really liked him—he was intelligent, funny, sometimes crass while at the same time proper, and incredibly sexy. "You're totally right. We really have been taking it slow."

"Okay, so now that we've cleared that up, why does it appear there's still a problem?"

"Because there is."

"What is it now?"

"Oh, I don't know, maybe the repercussions of us having a relationship."

"With whom? My family adores you."

"I'm talking about the world—the company, the media."

Thorn stared at me intensely. "Fuck them all. You're the only thing that matters to me."

At that moment, I felt a little lightheaded. Here was a gorgeous, sexy, talented, and very naked man telling me I was the only thing that mattered to him. He didn't care what the media had to say about us. He didn't care if there were any work-related repercussions. He just wanted me. It was seriously mind-boggling.

As I stared at his handsome, determined face, I realized I wanted him just as much as he wanted me. Dipping my head, I placed a gentle kiss on his lips. "Thank you."

"For what?"

"Talking me down from the ledge and being the amazing man you are."

Thorn chuckled. "Maybe it's the line of work I've been in, but I know you can't sweat the small shit. Sometimes no matter how hard you try to alter it, what will be is just gonna be."

"You're so wise."

"It's called being an old fart."

I laughed. "You are not old—especially since you're only two years older than me, and I'm sure as hell not old."

Thorn ran his hand over my hip. "Your body sure as hell isn't old. It's fucking fantastic."

"I could say the same about yours."

His expression darkened. "Maybe everything but my leg."

I shook my head. "Don't you know how very manly your scars are? A warrior's body is marred and mangled. It bears the marks of battle."

I cupped his face in my hands. "You have a warrior's body, and it's the sexiest fucking thing I've ever seen."

At my declaration, words seemed to fail Thorn. Instead, he jerked me against him before crushing his mouth against mine. He poured everything into that kiss, and when he finally pulled away, I was completely breathless. "Thank you," he murmured.

"You're welcome," I replied as I panted.

"I'd really like to fuck you again, but I'm pretty sure if we don't start getting ready, our nocturnal activities are going to be made clear to everyone."

Although I totally wanted him to jump me again, his words were just what I needed to douse the fire. The last thing I wanted was for Thorn's parents to find out what had occurred between us. I didn't need the president and First Lady thinking I was a floozy.

Wriggling out of his grasp, I said, "You're so right. Time for you to go." I gave him a shove. "Now."

"I didn't necessarily mean right this very instant."

"Yeah, well, I do. I'm not going to be everyone's gossiping point."

"I think you already achieved that when you appeared in your robe Friday night."

With a frustrated growl, I scrambled past him off the bed. "Fine. If you won't go, I will."

"But this is your room."

Dammit. I'd forgotten that fact in my rage. "Then I'll go get in the shower." When it appeared that Thorn might follow me, I shook my head. "Oh no, that wasn't an invitation. I'm going into the bathroom alone, and when I come out, you better be gone."

Thorn chuckled as he held up his hands. "I'm going, I'm going."

"Good."

As he slid into his pants, I couldn't help admiring the view. "If you don't stop looking at me like that, you won't have a choice about me joining you in the shower."

I edged closer to the door. "I'll lock you out."

"And I'll break the door down."

My traitorous vagina stood up and cheered at his caveman attitude.

"You would actually break a priceless heirloom like a White House door?" I countered.

"If it meant fucking you, I would break it and burn the pieces," he countered with a wicked grin.

"You're impossible."

"Impossibly enamored by you."

I rolled my eyes. "Please. It's the area between my legs you're enamored with."

"True, but I also like what's attached to it," he joked.

I pointed to the door. "Enough yammering. It's time to go."

He shrugged his dress shirt on. "You do realize I'm about to do a walk of shame, right?"

He did have a point, and this was the White House we were talking about. There would be no sneaking back to his room unseen. Forget the cameras—he would come face to face with a Secret Service agent or part of the cleaning crew. There would be no hiding the fact that we'd slept together.

"The only saving grace is that it's you doing the walk and not me."

"Ouch, that's cold."

I grinned. "I'll make it up to you later."

"Considering we leave after breakfast, I'm going to be making good on that promise in the jet."

"Since I've never joined the mile-high club, I'll happily oblige you."

"That makes me very happy."

"Good. Now go."

"Yes, ma'am," he replied with a salute.

Once he was out the door, I exhaled a ragged breath. I had been in trouble when I'd been attracted to Thorn, but now I faced an even bigger dilemma. I really liked him...like maybe loved him. He had just fought against every perceived barrier I put up. I had never known a man like him, but it did baffle me that he was so intent on keeping me. He hadn't had to come apologize the previous night. He hadn't even questioned why I ran, which was good because I still wasn't completely sure. He simply accepted me. When I launched myself at him, his arms willingly opened. It had been a little like that right from the beginning...since we got past all the stupid shit anyway.

And his family—they were the same. He was right: his family loved me, and the feeling was mutual. So, the possibility that I might love him?

Terrifying.

CHAPTER TWENTY-EIGHT
Thorn

As we flew through the cornflower blue sky, Isabel's hands gripped my shoulders and the tight walls of her pussy held my cock in a viselike grip. Her hips rose up and down in a frenzy as she rode me like a crazed cowgirl. I lifted my hips up to meet hers as our pants and groans of pleasure filled the jet's cabin.

I'd held Isabel to my promise of taking her in the air. By the time we'd reached cruising altitude, I'd not only stripped Isabel down, I had her crying out my name as her walls convulsed around three of my fingers. Before she could fully come down, I was sliding on a condom.

After collapsing on the couch, I'd pulled her over onto my lap and onto my dick. I loved this position with her. I loved letting her take control as she set the pace and the depth. More than anything, I loved watching the pleasure wash over her. She was always so together in the office and in life that it was amazing watching her be so uninhibited.

As Isabel's tits bounced in my face, I couldn't help remembering that first day I'd come in contact with them. After touching them and seeing them, I'd fantasized about this very moment. Of course, the reality was better than anything I could have ever imagined. If I were honest, everything was better than I could have imagined with Isabel.

When I felt her getting close, I slipped one of my hands between us to stroke her clit. Almost immediately, it set her off. "Oh Thorn!" she cried as she buried her face in my neck. As she came down, I gripped her hips and began to pump furiously into her until I came so fucking hard.

In the now silent cabin, I ran my hands up Isabel's bare back. I loved the feel of her soft skin beneath my fingers, so creamy and smooth. There wasn't much I didn't like. She was pretty much the perfect package, everything I could ever want in a woman.

Isabel raised her head to stare into my eyes. "I don't think I'm going to be able to walk tomorrow."

The caveman in me beat his chest in pride. "You can lead everyone to believe you injured yourself dancing at the wedding rather than by having my massive cock pummel your pussy."

Isabel snorted. "I can't believe you just said that."

"It's the truth, isn't it?"

"Maybe for a frat boy bragging to his friends."

I grinned. "I'm sorry. Should I have found a way to say it in more dignified terms?"

"While I'm not sure that's possible, yes, I would have."

"You have my deepest apologies and utmost concern if my penis injured your vagina." Tilting my head, I asked, "Was that better?"

"A little."

I ran my thumb over her bottom lip. "All joking aside, I want to thank you for this weekend."

"For you reclaiming your manhood?" she teased.

"I said I wasn't joking."

Isabel's expression grew serious. "I know. I was just trying to deflect some of the emotion."

"Why would you want to do that?"

She shrugged. "Maybe because it still seems fast."

"Slow build, remember?"

A shy smile curved on her lips. "I remember."

"Are you still afraid of the world and the media?"

She shook her head. "No...just you."

"Me? Why are you afraid of me?"

"I'm afraid you might hurt me, and in turn, I'm afraid I could hurt you."

"The Isabel Flannery I know isn't afraid of anything. She has balls of steel."

Isabel laughed. "Maybe you don't know me that well."

"I know you would never willingly hurt me, just like I would never willingly hurt you. Life is all about taking chances, and it's our time to take a chance—together."

"You're right." She placed her hand on my mine. "I'm sorry I'm such a worrywart."

"It's okay. I happen to find your neurotic side endearing."

She cocked her brows. "You do?"

"No, not really."

Isabel playfully smacked my arm. "Just for that comment, here's a little more of my neurotic side—what happens tomorrow?"

"Well, we get up at an insanely early hour, I go for a run while you go on in to work—"

"That's not what I meant."

I pushed a strand of red hair out of Isabel's face. "You want to know how we're supposed to act?"

"Exactly."

I shrugged. "We act like we always did. We don't owe anyone an explanation."

"Except maybe the executives."

I shook my head. "We only owe them an explanation if they ask for one. We don't have to volunteer anything. Once again, it's nobody's business but our own."

"I hope you're right."

"I'm always right."

She rolled her eyes. "You're feeling awfully cocky."

Taking her hand, I brought it to my lap. "You can feel just how cocky I really am."

She grinned. "I think I've created a monster."

With a laugh, I brought my lips to hers and prepared to show Isabel just how much of a pleasure monster I could be.

CHAPTER TWENTY-NINE

Isabel

After we got home from the White House, Thorn and I finally parted ways, although it was done reluctantly on both of our parts. Of course, I crashed out on the couch the minute I made it through the door of my apartment then slept straight through until eleven when Mila got home and demanded a play-by-play of the weekend—well, at least of the PG parts.

The next morning I found an unfamiliar bounce in my step as I got ready for work. It was the same one I'd experienced when I thought I was about to land my promotion, but this time, I was pumped to get to the office to see Thorn again. We'd already spoken when he'd texted me good morning, but it wasn't enough. I couldn't wait to see his handsome face in person, to smell the masculine scent of his cologne, to feel his hands on me again, even if it was in the most innocent of ways.

When I got to the office, it was still a relative ghost town. I was partially grateful for that because I didn't want to endure the looks of my colleagues on the floor. Unless they lived under a rock, there was no way they hadn't seen pictures of Thorn and me at the wedding, not to mention the gossip mill had to have been churning overnight.

By the time Thorn arrived with Conan half an hour later, the floor had filled up, so he simply gave me his usual good morning wave on the way to his office. He knew me well enough to know I wouldn't want him to make a big deal this morning—the first morning of our changed relationship at work. His gesture wasn't overly romantic or even different than before, but it still sent warmth echoing through my chest.

Focusing on the tasks at hand, I spent the next few hours bogged down by numbers. From time to time, I would find my thoughts on Thorn, but then I would quickly refocus on my files. My head was buried in my computer when a knock came at my door.

"Yes?" I questioned. With it being Cheryl's lunchtime, I knew I had to deal with whoever it was.

As the door opened, I glanced over my shoulder. At the sight of Thorn, my heart started beating furiously. "Good afternoon, Isabel," he said, the deep timbre of his voice shooting straight between my legs.

"Good afternoon. Was there something you needed to see me about?"

"As a matter of fact, there is."

He stepped inside my office and closed the door. As he crossed the room, he didn't take his gaze off of mine, an almost predatory gleam shining in his eyes. After walking around my desk, he knelt down in front of me.

My eyes bulged at the gesture. "What are you doing?"

"I want to taste you."

Oh Jesus. Is he for real? "It's eleven-thirty in the morning."

"I'm aware of what time it is," he replied as he started to push my skirt up.

I swatted his hand. "Thorn, we're at work," I hissed.

"So?"

"*So?* That's all you can say at the moment?"

"I'm sorry if I'm too horny to form coherent thoughts at the moment."

With a roll of my eyes, I replied, "Would you get a grip?"

"I'd love to," he replied as his fingers gripped my inner thighs.

After sucking in a breath, I replied, "You managed to wait a year to have sex—you don't think you could possibly wait until tonight?"

"Nope. I have to have you now."

"You're ridiculous," I muttered.

"Yes, ridiculously horny." He tilted his head up at me. "Are you going to say you're not even remotely turned on at the moment?"

Dammit. He had me there. Although my mouth and brain were protesting, the rest of my body was totally on board with Thorn going down on me. I mean, it was one of my office fantasies come to life—who says no to that?

"Regardless of whether or not I'm turned on, we shouldn't be doing this."

"I disagree." He gave me a crooked grin. "And based on the wetness of your panties, I'd say your pussy disagrees as well."

"Yes, I'm turned on. Are you happy now?"

"Thrilled." Thorn dipped his head to kiss the tops of my thigh-highs. "You and these fucking stockings drive me wild."

Gripping my thighs, he spread them apart. At the sight of him licking his lips, I grew even wetter. I imagined I might be soaking the chair. When I finally felt the warmth of his mouth against my core, I cried out and shifted my hips against him. "God, you have the most amazing mouth," I moaned.

Thorn's response was to thrust his tongue inside me. Spreading my legs farther, I gave him easier access. I grabbed at the strands of Thorn's hair while swiveling my hips. Cursing and panting, I climbed higher and higher from the feel of his tongue swirling inside me. The man was seriously good.

A knock came at my door. Not only did I freeze, Thorn did too, which meant his tongue was still buried deep inside me. "Shit." Minutes ago, it had been appealing that Cheryl was gone to lunch, but now I was silently cursing her break. "What do I do?" I hissed.

Although he slid his tongue out of me, Thorn's head remained between my thighs. "Get rid of them."

"You're joking."

He stared up at me defiantly. "I'm not leaving until you come."

Okay then. After shoving my chair and Thorn farther under my desk, I croaked, "Yes?"

The door swung open and Murray rushed inside. After glancing around the office, he frowned. "I thought Thorn was in here."

Well, he is, but you see, he's indisposed at the moment because his face is buried in my pussy.

"He stepped out," I lied.

"Oh, I wanted to go over the new figures with the two of you."

"I'm sorry."

Murray glanced at his watch. "I have a lunch meeting across town in half an hour. Would you mind if I went over them with you really quick?"

Not just no, but fuuuuuuck no! How in the hell could I possibly concentrate on figures when I was strung out from almost orgasming and having a sexy man's warm breath on my inner thighs? Unable to tell my boss no, I merely nodded.

As Murray took a seat, I waited for Thorn to pull away from me, but he didn't. Instead, his tongue began to swirl around my clit, which caused me to jump in my chair. Instead of stopping, Thorn continued tonguing me. Raising my leg, I kicked his shin, causing him to grunt in pain. Murray paused and glanced up at me. "Sorry—leg cramp."

Nodding, he went back to reading from the spreadsheet. If I thought the kick had deterred Thorn, I was wrong. He began flicking my clit with his tongue, which caused me to squirm in my seat. After a few moments passed, he flattened his tongue and began lapping at my center. I bit down on my lip to keep from moaning.

Desperately, I tried focusing on Murray's face as a way to detach from the pleasurable assault below my waist, but it didn't help. I just got hotter and wetter with each stroke of Thorn's tongue. I began to slowly swivel my hips against Thorn's face while simultaneously fighting not to let my eyes roll back in my head.

When he sucked my clit into his mouth, I whimpered, and Murray once again paused. "Isabel, are you all right? You're all flushed."

It took me a moment to find my voice, or at least the voice I wanted to use with Murray. I didn't want to reply in a pant or with a shriek of pleasure. "No, actually I'm not all right. I don't feel like myself this morning." That wasn't a total lie. My usual self didn't let my boss go down on me in my office. My usual self had never had a man between my legs creating ecstasy while I listened to facts and figures.

Murray nodded. "I should have realized. You seemed off when I first came in."

Thorn's muffled chuckle reverberated against my thighs. I knew he was thinking the same thing I was—I seemed off because I was getting off. Actually, I was *almost* getting off, and if Murray didn't leave the room in the next twenty seconds or so, I was going to lose it. I was wired. "I truly am sorry."

"Look, we don't have to go over these figures now. We can work on them later."

Yea, much later—hopefully after Thorn has finished working me over. "Okay. Thanks, Murray."

He nodded as he rose out of the chair. Once my office door shut, I pushed my chair away from Thorn. As I indignantly glanced down at him, he had the audacity to smile up at me. "I can't believe you kept going down on me with Murray in here!"

Thorn licked his lips, or I guess I should say licked me off his lips. "Admit it—you got off on the fact that I was eating you out while our boss was sitting there."

I wrinkled my nose. "Ugh, I hate that term."

"Eating out?"

"Yes."

With a wicked grin, Thorn asked, "You don't like being eaten out?"

"You just had to say it again, didn't you?"

"You didn't answer my question about if you like being eaten out."

I rolled my eyes. "I love the act but hate the term, okay? Not to mention it makes no sense. If anything, you're eating in when your tongue is inside me."

"But I'm taking out all the sweetness in your center when I eat you out," he countered.

"Stop saying that."

"Isabel, I wanna eat your pussy out. I wanna eat you out until you come, screaming my name and clawing my hair."

I knew Thorn was getting off on getting me riled up, and I decided it was time to call his bluff. Sliding around in the chair, I brought one leg up and propped it on my desk. Thorn's eyes flared at the sight of my pussy. "Are you all talk and no action?"

"No, ma'am. I always finish a job," he replied before he dipped his head.

After being teased for the last few minutes, Thorn barely had to do any work this time before I reaped my reward of a shrieking orgasm. Of course, it was a shrieking orgasm with my arm draped over my mouth so no one outside could hear me. I'd never had any man go down on me with such...zeal. It was as if Thorn wasn't happy unless I was a writhing mess, completely and utterly sated. *Who is this man? And how did I get so lucky as to have him?*

As Thorn rose up from the floor, I glanced at his tented pants. "What are you going to do about that?"

His brows shot up. "What am *I* going to do? It's more like what's *your pussy* going to do."

"My pussy and not my mouth?"

He grinned. "I'll take either one as long as I come."

"Is it selfish of me to want you deep inside me instead of my mouth?"

"Even though you give amazing head, I can't imagine anything better."

"What about a condom?"

"Please, I'm a businessman—I'm always prepared."

As Thorn fished a condom out of his wallet, I jerked my head at the door. "Go lock it—I don't want a repeat of Murray." After he locked the door, Thorn began to unbutton and unzip his pants. "How do you want me?" I asked in a hoarse voice.

"Bend over the desk," he commanded.

Heat shot straight through my core. On shaky legs, I stood up. With my skirt already up over my hips, I placed both of my palms flat on the top of the desk before I leaned over.

Thorn groaned. "Do you know how many fucking fantasies I've had with you just like this?"

"Maybe as many as I have."

He smacked one of my ass cheeks before running his hand over it. "God, you have the most amazing ass." As he slid a hand between my legs, he paused at my anus. His fingers circled my hole, causing me to shiver. "Maybe one day you'll let me go here?"

"Maybe."

"Really? I didn't take you for the ass play type of woman."

I laughed. "Is that some kind of dig about me being uptight?"

Thorn grinned. "No, I just thought you were too ladylike or something."

"Even ladies like it kinky from time to time."

"Mm, I like to hear that."

The next thing I knew his cock was pushing against my vagina. Gripping the desk, I said, "Take me hard, Thorn."

He obliged me by slamming himself inside me. We both groaned, and he waited a moment before pulling out and then plunging hard again. Our pants and rushed breaths filled the room, and God, it felt so good. *He* felt so good. We fit together perfectly.

I wasn't used to experiencing two orgasms by noon, but apparently, it was my new reality with Thorn. After I came, he did a few more feverish pumps before burying his face in my neck and coming with a muffled shout. When he pulled out of me, I lay with my cheek against the desk, completely satiated.

Thorn kissed the back of my head. "Are you okay?"

"Oh yeah. I'm A-OK," I mused as I raised my head to look at him.

He laughed. "I'm glad to hear it."

"I'm sure I look a mess."

"You're always beautiful to me."

I pulled myself up onto my feet. "You always know just what to say." Although, with the way he looked at me, I actually felt beautiful.

"It's not a line—I really mean it."

"I know, and that's what makes it even better." I cupped his face. "You're always sincere." I leaned in and kissed him. When I pulled back, I smiled. "Thank you for the two orgasms before noon."

"You're very welcome. I'm pretty sure I can deliver those every day."

With a laugh, I replied, "That's awfully tempting."

"But the spontaneity is part of the allure?"

"Yeah, pretty much."

"How about after we get cleaned up, we grab a sandwich from the food truck."

"Sex and sandwiches—a winning combination," I mused.

Thorn rewarded my sassy comment by smacking one of my ass cheeks—because he wanted to, because he could, because he knew me well enough to know I'd love it. He was a man very comfortable with power and authority, yet I knew I'd never fear him or feel anything but respect for him. His touch, his affection, his focus...I wanted it all, especially when he smacked me one more time for good measure.

It was at that very ridiculous moment that I realized I loved him.

CHAPTER THIRTY

Isabel

The week following my office sexathon with Thorn flew by in a blur. After initially having trouble getting my head back into my work, I decided it was probably a good idea if I set some parameters about how we interacted at work, i.e. no more midday quickies—well, actually, no naughty trysts period during work hours, no matter the time. Trust me, it was hard not to jump Thorn every five minutes, but I found the sex was even more explosive after a day of abstaining with a constant state of foreplay made up of longing looks and brushes against each other.

Our days were spent together in the office, and our nights were spent at one of our apartments. For two people who had gone without sex for a while, we were certainly making up for lost time, but it wasn't just the sex—I was falling harder and faster for Thorn every moment. It was the small things he did that made me adore him, like the way he would absently run his fingers over my hand while we watched a movie, or how one morning he brought me back coffee and breakfast from my favorite little diner. My apartment was starting to resemble a florist's shop with all the flowers he sent me.

Most of all, I loved waking up next to him, being wrapped in his strong embrace. I loved feeling his rock-hard erection pressed into my ass and the gentle touch of his callused hands.

One day after our usual morning quickie, Thorn and Conan went for their morning run, and I got ready for work. Since I wanted to get a jump on a new account, I decided to head in early.

When I got there, Cheryl motioned me over. "Mr. Moskowtiz asked to see you at your earliest convenience."

"With Murray, my earliest convenience means ASAP."

Cheryl grinned. "I'll man the fort while you're gone."

"I appreciate that."

After I made my way upstairs to Murray's office, his secretary waved me right on in. As I opened the door, I asked, "You wanted to see me?"

Appearing all business-like, Murray nodded as he motioned to the chairs in front of his desk. "Have a seat."

Unease pricked its way up my spine. "I can't help but get the funny feeling I'm about to get some bad news."

When Murray gave me a tight smile, my stomach twisted into a knot, and my breath hitched as I eased down into one of the leather chairs in front of his desk.

Fuuuuck. Had Murray called me in here because he realized what had been going on in my office? At that prospect, mortification rocketed through me so quickly I shuddered. My lips had run dry, and I had to lick them before I could speak. "This must be about the no fraternization policy among executives. I know it might seem like there's something going on between us, but Thorn and I are just good friends."

Murray crossed his arms over his chest. "Don't bullshit me, Isabel." He was right. I'd never done that before, and I wasn't about to start now.

"Fine. There is something going on between us. We're dating." *And for once, everything feels right.*

"I thought as much, but my concern isn't specifically about the fraternization policy."

"It's not?"

He shook his head. "I'm more concerned about your career right now. You've worked so hard and come so far since you first started here as an intern. Until Thorn needed a job, I was fully prepared to give you the vice president position." Murray surprised me by popping out of his chair, his expression suddenly turning remorseful. "You know I see you as one of my own children."

"Yes," I said tentatively.

"After talking with some of the higher-ups, I don't like the vibe I'm getting."

"The executives were discussing me?"

"Yes. More precisely, they were discussing your relationship with Thorn."

I swallowed hard. "What about it?" We'd only been a couple for a week; how was it possible for the executives to be concerned about it? We'd been working together for months.

Murray exhaled painfully. "They don't think it bodes well for any future promotions for you."

"Excuse me?"

"They worry if you continue this relationship with Thorn, it will appear you're only being promoted out of nepotism."

I clenched my hands into fists as I saw red. "That's bullshit." I shook my head. "I mean, that's ridiculous."

"No, you were correct the first time. It's positively absurd, but they fear it will cause contention among the other vice presidents in this department."

"None of my prior work experience counts? The countless hours I've put in here, the money I've made for this place?"

"In their eyes, no, it doesn't. It's unfortunate that it's an unprecedented issue. No executive has ever had the opportunity to date the president's son, not to mention the grandson of the starter of the company. While this is a family-owned company, it's still a publically traded one with shareholders to answer to."

"Lucky me that I get to break the mold," I mumbled.

Murray exhaled a pained sigh. "I'm sorry, Isabel. I could have kept this silent, but I felt you had the right to know."

"No, I'm glad you told me."

"But my words have left you with a very difficult decision to make."

Tears burned behind my lids, but I wouldn't allow myself to cry—not now, not in front of Murray. On shaky knees, I rose to my feet. "If that's all, I need to get back to work."

"That is all."

"Thanks for meeting with me."

"You're welcome."

With unsteady feet, I turned and made my way to the door. Murray's voice stopped me. "Isabel?"

I slowly turned around. "Yes, Mr. Moskowitz?"

He gave me a tight smile. "For the record, I think the two of you look wonderful together."

Fearing I would come apart right then and there, I merely nodded before hurrying out the door. With a shroud of uncertainty hanging over me, I trudged down the hallway. When I got onto the elevator, the tears I'd been holding back began to flow. I realized there was no way I could go back to work in the shape I was in. Most of all, I couldn't face Thorn.

Not now. Not yet.

Seeing him would distract me from the decision I had to make. Instead of getting off on my floor, I took the elevator down to the lobby. With a determined stride, I made my way outside the building. If my life were a movie, this would be the part where I did some soul-searching as I walked purposefully around the city with a melancholy song playing in the background—but this wasn't the movies. This was real life.

I still walked around the city as I did my soul-searching. Feeling emotionally bereft at the choice before me, I picked up Dani and took her to Central Park. As we walked around, my mind spun frantically.

I thought of my parents and all they had sacrificed to get me where I was today. I thought about how I'd been able to better their lives with my job. I thought how I'd scraped by while getting my undergrad degree, the countless containers of Ramen noodles I'd dined on. I thought of the epically long days and sometimes long nights in my first days at the company.

I'd come too far and fought too hard to throw it all away. The solution before me was agonizing. Thorn had been wrong. Perhaps *he* could simply think *fuck them all*, but I couldn't, because as Murray said, the higher-ups had already made their decision.

"They don't think it bodes well for any future promotions for you."

Despite *my* efforts, despite *my* time there, despite *my* sacrifices, it wasn't enough, and it would never be enough. It wasn't enough for *me* and *my* future, which left me without any comeback, without any future, unless I did the one thing I was loathe to do. We were so new, and I had no idea where we were going to go, but I couldn't throw everything away.

I had to break things off with Thorn.

After Isabel's radio silence the rest of the afternoon and evening, I barely slept Monday night, and Conan didn't either since he could tell my emotional grid was all fucked up. When she didn't come back to work or answer my calls or texts, I decided on an ambush approach and went to her apartment, but she still wasn't there.

Next I stopped by the doggy daycare to see if she might be there, and they told me she'd picked Dani up around three. I couldn't imagine what could have possibly happened to cause her to flee work and then give me the silent treatment. It wasn't something I was accustomed to after making a woman orgasm twice in the middle of the day.

All joking aside, it sure as hell wasn't something I was accustomed to with a woman I had such an emotional connection with. After the last week we'd had together since the wedding, I couldn't imagine Isabel giving me the cold shoulder. I couldn't help thinking that as loveably neurotic as she was, there had to be something she was freaking out about.

Considering how much I cared for her, I wasn't about to let go without a fight. I'd finally found the woman I wanted to spend the rest of my life with, someone who proudly supported me and unselfishly gave her whole self to me. She challenged me to be the best man I could possibly be—the type of man I'd been when I was leading my men.

When I finally said *fuck it* to sleeping and got up to run at five instead of my usual six o'clock, I didn't bother texting Ty. Instead, I hit the predawn streets with Conan along with the jumbled voices in my head. Of course, it didn't take Ty's spidey senses long to find me. After exiting the car he'd used to catch up, he fell in step at my side. He didn't question me during the run. Instead, he just lent me his silent strength, which I appreciated the hell out of.

Once I got back to my apartment, I called Isabel two more times before I got ready for work. Frustratingly, she didn't answer or text me back. I debated going by her apartment once again, but instead, I decided to try work first.

Upon arriving on our floor, I power walked down the hall to Isabel's office. Without even stopping to ask Cheryl if it was a good time, I burst in. Startled by my appearance, she shrieked and clutched her chest. "Thorn, what are you doing here?"

"Cut the bullshit. You know exactly why I'm here."

Her eyes widened. "I do?"

I jabbed a finger at her as I started around the desk. "You're avoiding me, and I want to know what the hell is going on."

"I'm just busy with work."

"Bullshit. You've got the same workload as before, yet you can't seem to text or call me back. You ran out of here yesterday and didn't even tell me you were leaving."

"I just needed to take some time away from work."

Shaking my head, I replied, "You just had a weekend away a week ago. It would seem to me that you suddenly wanted time away from *me*."

Isabel paled slightly. "Fine. You want me to be honest?"

"Yeah, as a matter of fact, I do. I think it's past time you were honest with me."

She exhaled what appeared to be a pained breath. "I don't think we should see each other anymore."

What the hell? "Excuse me?" I demanded.

"You heard me."

"Yes, but excuse me for being fucking floored that after the week we've had you would all of a sudden say you don't want to see me." I tapped my finger on the desk. "Not to mention what happened right here."

"In spite of what happened over the weekend and in here, I think it's just the best thing for both of us if we don't continue anything but a friendship."

"That's bullshit because I know the best thing for me is being with you." I placed my hands on her shoulders. "While Conan has made a big difference, it's *you* who has made the biggest difference. Being with you these last few months has saved me."

Isabel's eyes shuttered in pain. "I can't," she whispered.

"What happened to make you change your mind? Did you read some bullshit article on the internet, or did someone say something?" When she bit down on her lip, I shook my head. "Honesty, remember?"

"If you must know, it appears we have already been the subject of discussion among some of the higher-level executives."

"You're throwing away a chance at happiness because of a few gossipy execs?"

"It's not about gossip. Apparently, word has gotten out that if I pursue a relationship with you, I will never be promoted without it causing contention or appearing to be nepotism."

"That's just stupid. No one who has worked with you would ever think you got a promotion just because you were sleeping with me."

"It isn't stupid. Murray thought it was important enough to warn me." Tears shimmered in her eyes. "I care about you very much, Thorn, but I've come too far and worked too hard to throw everything away for a relationship that might not work out."

"You know there are other jobs and other companies you could work for."

"But this one is like home to me. Besides, who's to say I wouldn't get blackballed by the executives when it came to references?"

Panic rose in my throat when it appeared I wasn't going to be able to change her mind. I couldn't let her go, not when we had finally come together and things were so perfect.

"To continue with this relationship, one of us would need to no longer work here for the executives not to bitch, right?"

She furrowed her brows. "I guess so."

"Fine." I whirled around and started for the door.

"Where are you going?"

I threw a glance at her over my shoulder. "To Murray's office to quit." If I hadn't been a fucking mess, I would have found the expression on Isabel's face hilarious. It was apparent she hadn't seen that one coming.

Rising from her chair, she sputtered, "B-But y-you can't q-quit!"

"I'm a grown fucking man—I can do whatever I want."

As I left her office, she was right on my heels. "Thorn, have you lost your mind? You cannot quit over me."

"If the only way we can stay together is for me to quit, that's the only option I have."

"And what if we don't work out?"

"We will."

"How can you be so sure?"

I brought my feet to a halt, which caused Isabel to run into me. Taking her by the shoulders, I stared intently into her eyes. "I know because I love you."

Isabel's eyelids fluttered in disbelief. "You love me?"

"I sure as hell do. I think I've loved you since the first moment I saw you outside the building."

"But haven't you been in love before and it hasn't worked out?"

"You're right. I thought was in love lots of times over the years, but it's nothing like what I've experienced with you over the last few months. You've given me a purpose I didn't know I had. I have never, ever connected with a woman the way I have with you." I slid my hands up her neck to run my thumbs along her jawline. "I love you in a way I've never loved any other woman."

Tears pooled in Isabel's blue eyes. "You really mean that, don't you?"

"Yes, I do, with all my heart."

"I love you, too," she murmured.

My heart threatened to beat out of my chest at her words. "You do?"

Smiling, she nodded. "Yes, I do. Unlike you, it came on gradually once I got to see the real Thorn. That Thorn is the best man I've ever met."

With my heart threatening to explode at any moment, I crushed my lips to hers. Her arms came around me, her fingers twisting into the fabric of my suit. I don't know how long we were kissing before applause broke out around us. When I jerked back, I saw the analysts around us had risen up from their desks and were clapping for us.

While she flushed under their attention, I laughed. "I guess that means we have their blessing?"

"Or they're elated because they think I'm going to get fired and they'll be able to move up to the next level," Isabel replied with a wry smile.

Winking at her, I said, "There is going to be one position open."

Her eyes widened. "You're actually going to quit?"

"Yes, I am."

"Just for me?"

I shook my head. "No—for *us*." When tears shimmered in Isabel's eyes, I reached up to cup her cheek. "Don't cry."

"These are angry tears."

"You're still angry I'm going to quit to enable us to have a relationship?" I demanded incredulously.

"I'm angry because you keep insisting on doing it without a second thought about how it might affect your life or your family's life." Gesturing around, Isabel said, "What do you think your Dad is going to say when his firstborn quits the family business?"

I shrugged. "I guess the same thing he said when I refused it at eighteen years old to go into the Army."

"That was then, but what about now?"

"For him, it won't change. All he's ever wanted for his kids is for them to be happy."

"There's being happy, and then there's him thinking some woman barreled into your life and screwed everything up." She tapped her chest. "The last thing I want is for your dad—or, for that matter, your mom—to hate me."

"That's not going to happen."

"How do you know?"

"Well, first of all, both my parents know I'm my own person and no one influences what I do, not even a woman." Before she could protest again, I said, "Dad knows I've struggled in this job because my heart wasn't in it so he'll support this, and my mom will feel the same way. Besides, Barrett isn't going anywhere, so Callahan still has a family connection with him. Not only that, Isabel, if I have my way, you will become a Callahan. *You* are the best person for this job, and I believe my parents will completely agree. They'll be glad to know the company is still very much in the family."

As she took my words in, the wheels in Isabel's head seemed to be spinning in overdrive. Finally, she seemed to have reached a conclusion. "As long as you're sure they won't hate me."

I grinned. "I'm not sure it would be possible for them to hate you considering how happy you've made me."

"I want to believe that."

"They already like you, and I highly doubt their feelings are going to go south once I tell them we're dating."

A slow smile curved on her lips. "It still seems so weird to be using that word with you."

"I think the d-word you associated with me most was dick."

"Or douchebag."

I chuckled. "Yeah, that one, too."

She slid her arms around my neck. "I guess from now on I should associate *darling* or *dearest* with you."

"I can hardly imagine you ever calling me either of those two words."

Tilting her head, Isabel retorted, "My dearest darling, you should have learned by now to never underestimate me."

As I laughed, I couldn't resist planting another kiss on that sassy mouth of hers. If we were together fifty years, I would never tire of her mouth. Most of all, I would never tire of the woman attached to it—the one who believed in me and challenged me to understand I still had value, even though I wasn't in the military anymore. My dad was who he was because of Mom's unrelenting and unshakable love, and I knew I could be a man of value and valor because of Isabel's love.

SIX MONTHS LATER

As I stood at the bathroom mirror on the Callahan Corporation jet, I smacked Thorn's hand away from the hem of my dress for the millionth time. "Would you stop it, you horndog? We're landing at the White House in ten minutes."

Dipping his head, Thorn licked a trail up my neck while caressing my buttocks. "I can make us both come in ten minutes. Maybe even twice for you."

"You just had me on my office couch before we left New York," I protested.

He met my gaze in the mirror. "I can never get enough of you."

I know, I know. Having a sweet, sexy, and good looking man desire me was a real hardship. Especially after going so long without someone wonderful in my life. Normally, I was just as up for sex as Thorn was, but today was different. We were on our way to the White House for the National Tree Lighting ceremony. Since it was the first one for the Callahan administration, I didn't want to do anything to mess it up. Arriving smelling like sex and looking bedraggled, as Thorn would say, wasn't part of my plan. The whole reason I was in the bathroom in the first place was to do a quick touch-up of my hair and makeup.

It was hard to believe six months had passed since Thorn had professed his love for me in front of most of our department. While the neurotic side of me had originally worried about us not making it as a couple, it had been smooth sailing these past months. In fact, last month we'd taken the plunge and moved in together. We'd found an apartment not far from my old one. Just when I'd worried about leaving Mila, she'd fallen for one of the producers of the show she was working on.

Thorn and I moving in together also made two certain furry friends incredibly happy. Now that he was doing better emotionally, Thorn didn't need Conan on a support level. Instead, he was there in a regular doggy capacity. Since Thorn worried about wasting Conan's talents, he had started making weekend visits to Walter Reed Hospital. Conan was able to lead the civilian life while also lending support to struggling soldiers.

Speaking of the civilian life, Thorn had been true to his word about quitting the Callahan Corporation. I knew his decision wasn't just about making me stay. His heart would always be with the military, and he desperately needed to find a job where he could incorporate that love. Not wanting to be accused of nepotism, he'd taken a lower-level positon in the Veteran's Administration back in August. He wasn't making the salary he had as an investment banker, but I'd never seen him so happy.

Thorn pushed the hem of my dress up over my hips. His finger ran along the top of my thigh high. "You and these fucking stockings drive me wild."

"I guess I'm going to have to stop wearing them."

Sliding his hand around the top of my thigh, Thorn's masterful fingers found their way to my core. I sucked in a breath as his thumb encircled my clit. "If I promise to make them circle the airport for five minutes, will you let me fuck you?" he asked, his breath scorching against my earlobe.

"Ty's just outside," I protested. Of course, the prospect of having an audience was oddly thrilling.

Thorn flicked his tongue against my ear. "He's got his noise canceling headphones on."

"I see you've thought of everything," I mused.

With a chuckle, Thorn replied, "That was just dumb luck since he's watching a movie on his tablet."

As I became wet and achy from Thorn's fingers, I let my head fall back against his chest. "Is that a yes?" Thorn asked.

I bit down on my lip as I felt myself growing close to orgasming. I don't know what it was about Thorn's touch that made me practically come within seconds. Where it used to take me forever to get off, it was almost instantaneously with Thorn.

Just when I was about to go over the edge, Thorn spun me around to face him. I scowled at him. "Bastard."

He had the nerve to chuckle. "I want you to come with me inside you."

As I brought my hands to his belt buckle, I shook my head. "I could have come twice, you know."

"I'll make it up to you tonight with some extra-long oral attention."

I pushed his pants and briefs over his delectable ass and down his thick thighs. "I'm going to hold you to that."

He waggled his brows. "I look forward to it." Placing his hands on my waist, Thorn hoisted me up on the sink. After he widened my legs, he settled between them. Guiding his cock to my core, I didn't need any more foreplay—I was dripping wet for him. With one harsh thrust, he buried himself deep inside me. As he began pounding in and out, he brought his lips to mine. I loved sex with this man. I loved everything with this man. I'd never had such an attentive lover. But the same could have been said for Thorn outside of the bedroom. He'd become my best friend. We laughed, fought, made up all in the same way. With love. With passion. Hot damn with passion. We got each other.

Just as the jet touched down, I gripped the sink as I went over the edge with a shrieking orgasm.

"Yes, Thorn! Oh God!" I cried.

After a couple of harsh thrusts, Thorn spilled himself inside me. As I came down from my high, I shot him a pointed look. "I thought you were going to have them circle the airport."

He gave me a sheepish grin. "I kinda got occupied." He gave me a quick kiss before pulling out of me. "Don't worry. You'll still have your five minutes to get ready."

"Try ten minutes."

"Fine. Ten minutes."

"You need to get cleaned up yourself." I motioned to his face. "My lipstick is all over your face."

"And you're all over my hands."

I flushed at his insinuation. "Just clean up."

"Yes, ma'am."

After he helped me down off the sink, Thorn started scrubbing his hands, and I went about cleaning up downstairs. Silently, I wished we were still using condoms because it would have made things easier. I ended up taking fifteen minutes, rather than ten, to make sure I was not only camera ready for the media, but I was also President and Mrs. Callahan ready.

When we walked off the jet, a car was waiting on the tarmac to pick up our party of four. Besides Ty, we also had Conan in attendance. He had become a celebrity in his own right with Thorn's campaign to help soldiers. Conan would be appearing at the tree lighting along with us.

Since Barrett and Addison's wedding, I'd become a constant figure at the White House. I'd munched on popcorn in the theater and swam a few laps in the pool. Of course, I'd donned a swimsuit instead of the formal wear I had before.

As we drove up to the VIP entrance, I couldn't help marveling at how festive everything looked. It was a true transformation into a Christmas Wonderland. Once we arrived, we headed up to the residence to meet with Thorn's parents, along with Barrett and Addison. Caroline was home from Oxford, and Thorn was thrilled to see his baby sister.

When it was time to leave for the Ellipse for the tree lighting, we piled into several SUV's. My jangled emotions ranged from excitement to happiness to anxiousness. Mostly, I feared making a mistake in front of the cameras.

"You look beautiful," Thorn murmured in my ear.

Just like always, he was so good at reading me. "Thanks," I replied as I glanced down at my attire. With Mila's help, I'd picked out an emerald green cocktail dress and paired it with a winter white dress coat.

We arrived to a flurry of flashbulbs going off. Thorn took my hand as we exited the car. From time to time, he would squeeze it. While I'd watched a few tree lightings on TV, it was nothing like being there in the moment. The gorgeous music, the celebrity singers, and the As I stood on the podium with the rest of the Callahan family, I couldn't help feeling extremely blessed. Most of all, I felt blessed I'd managed to find a man like Thorn.

After the tree lighting and festivities, Thorn and I arrived back at the White House. Instead of heading inside to thaw out like the rest of the family, Thorn took my hand. "Let's go look at the tree from up here."

"Sounds good."

As we strolled down the South Lawn, Thorn released my hand to point to one of the trees. "Do you remember what happened under there?"

A vivid memory replayed in my mind of fireworks exploding over our heads as Thorn's lips met mine. "Our first kiss."

He smiled. "One of the best days of my life."

"Mine too."

"There's been a hell of a lot of good days since then, but that was the best."

My heartbeat accelerated at his words as well as the tone in which he delivered them. Even though I was freezing my ass off, I could have stayed there with him in that moment forever. That was what love did to you.

When I turned around to check on Thorn's silence, he was no longer at my side. Instead, he was knelt down on one knee before me. My hands flew to my mouth. "Oh my God," I murmured as I fought the urge to pinch myself. Was this really happening? Was I going to wake up and find myself back in my bed in Manhattan and that all of this was a dream.

Unfazed by my outburst, Thorn grinned up at me. "Isabel Flannery, will continue giving me wonderful days for the rest of my life?"

"Oh my God," I muttered again. Even though we'd moved in together, I hadn't actually seen this coming. We'd only been dating for six months. Yes, they'd been the happiest six months of my life, but I never imagined getting engaged so quick.

"That doesn't sound like a yes," Thorn mused.

As I stared into his handsome face, his expression was one of absolute assurance. There was no doubt in Thorn's mind he wanted to be my husband and spend the rest of his life with me. His strength was what I needed in that moment.

"It wasn't. But yes, I would be honored to marry you, Thorn. Nothing in the world would make me happier than to be your wife." I then preceded to launch myself at him just like I had that night when he'd come to my room after kissing me.

Thorn welcomed me into his arms before bringing his mouth to mine. I'd have to say our first kiss as an engaged couple was pretty damn amazing.

After Thorn pulled away, an impish gleam burned in his eyes. "I guess you're wondering where your ring is."

I laughed. "It is kinda customary to propose with one. Considering you shocked the hell out of me with the proposal, I really hadn't stopped to think about it. Let me guess. You're afraid of disappointing me, so you're going to let me pick one out?"

With a shake of his head, he brought his fingers to his lips to whistle. My brows furrowed as I wondered why he would be summoning someone to such a private moment. But when I saw who came trotting down the steps, tears stung my eyes.

At the sight of us, Conan yipped before breaking into a run. When he reached us, Thorn commanded Conan to sit. In place of his normal collar was a beautiful red and green holiday bow. Thorn reached over to pluck a string off the bow. Tied to the string was a glittering diamond.

I furrowed my brows as I glanced from the ring to Thorn. "But how did you—"

Thorn motioned to the portico where his parents and Ty stood. "I had a little help from them."

This time I didn't fight the tears when they pooled in my eyes. I let them flow freely down my cheeks. "Does that mean we have their blessing?" I asked.

With a nod, Thorn replied, "Not only do we have their blessing, but they're already talking about another Rose Garden wedding this summer."

"Oh wow," I murmured as my head spun with the overwhelming thoughts of a celebrity wedding of my own. Addison had a past in the theater, so she didn't care about the harsh glare of the cameras. For me, it was a totally different ballgame.

Thorn tilted my chin up. "We can get married wherever you want to, Isabel. It can be here or back home in Georgia. Or we can go to the Justice of the Peace tomorrow." He drew me into his arms. "All I care about is that we get married."

"You don't think your parents would mind if we did something a little more low-key?"

"They don't care. They just wanted to make sure it was available if you wanted it."

"That's awfully sweet of them, and I really do appreciate it. But it's—"

"Not you."

"Exactly."

"Then we'll find what is you."

"Even if it's a small church off the beaten path in Rome or on one of the beaches in Hawaii?"

Thorn nodded. "Whatever it is you want, you'll have it."

My heartbeat fluttered like a hummingbird's wings at his words. It was hard not to feel overwhelmed by the sentiment. "You spoil me."

"And I love doing it."

I slid my hands up the lapels of his suit. "And I love you, Thorn Callahan."

A beaming grin lit up his face. "I love you, Isabel Flannery."

As Thorn brought his lips to mine, I thought about how incredibly lucky I was. I didn't care that he was the president's son. I didn't care that he had internal and external scars, some that might never heal. He was a hero for my country and for my heart. But I cared that the amazing man in my arms had chosen me. In his eyes, I wasn't a nobody from some Podunk town in the South. I was simply his. And our future together would be spectacular, because we would face everything together.

And okay, because Thorn was the orgasm-giving god . . . in bed . . . in the bathroom . . . kitchen . . . back seat . . . any surface really.

A year ago, I raced into a man's arms on my way to the office believing the only way I'd feel successful would be from a vice president's role. Now, I raced into that man's arms because there was no other place I wanted to be.

Success was now measured in ensuring this man knew he was loved, esteemed, and valued. Success was in creating our unimaginably happy home, two slobbering dogs and all.

Who knew that an unwanted officemate could turn into a mate for life?

NOW AVAILABLE: ROOMMATE

FROM THE TIME I was a kid, I knew I wanted a job helping people. After serving in the Rifles regiment of the British Army, I focused my civilian career on becoming a bodyguard to the rich and famous. For a Cockney Brit, I never imagined a twist of fate landing me a position in the United States Secret Service and protecting the President's son. But then my boss made an unexpected request: leave my current placement to move in with his only daughter to give an added layer of protection against the threats she had been receiving. I'd never lived with a woman who was off-limits to me. It wasn't just that Caroline had a boyfriend. She was my best friend's sister, and my boss's daughter. But the longer we're in such close quarters together, the greater the temptation grows, but I know I'll lose everything if I pursue her.

Growing up as the only girl with two overbearing older brothers, I'm no stranger to being overprotected. Just as I finished up college and prepared to truly dip my toes into the adult world, my father was elected President of the United States, which added a whole new level of protection with the Secret Service team attached to me. Just when I thought I couldn't possibly be more smothered, I began receiving threats, and my family decided it wasn't enough to just have an agent living down the hall from me. Nope, I was to have one move in with me, and not just any agent, but Ty Frasier—my brother, Barrett's best friend, and my brother, Ty's, head agent. While most women would enjoy living with a sexy, buff Brit, having a roommate threw a wrench into all my plans. Especially when I began noticing Ty was so much more than a hot guy—he was someone I could fall for.

Stand-alone set in the world of Running Mate and Office Mate

ABOUT THE AUTHOR

KATIE ASHLEY IS a New York Times, USA Today, and Amazon Top Five Best-Selling author of both Indie and Traditionally published books. She's written rockers, bikers, manwhores with hearts of gold, New Adult, and Young Adult. She lives outside of Atlanta, Georgia with her daughter, Olivia, her rescue mutts, Belle and Elsa, and cat, Harry Potter . She has a slight obsession with Pinterest, The Golden Girls, Shakespeare, Harry Potter, and Star Wars.

With a BA in English, a BS in Secondary English Education, and a Masters in Adolescent English Education, she spent eleven years teaching both middle and high school English, as well as a few adjunct college English classes. As of January 2013, she became a full-time writer.

Although she is a life-long Georgia peach, she loves traveling the country and world meeting readers. Most days, you can find her being a hermit, styling leggings, and binging on Netflix whenever her toddler daughter isn't monopolizing the TV with Paw Patrol or Frozen.

CONNECT WITH KATIE

➜ NEWSLETTER: https://bit.ly/2BHeOyI. ➜ FACEBOOK: facebook.com/katie.ashleyromance

➜ FACEBOOK READER GROUP (ASHLEY'S ANGELS): facebook.com/groups/ashleyangels

➜ WEBSITE: www.katieashleybooks.com

➜INSTAGRAM: Instagram.com/katieashleyluv

➜ TWITTER: twitter.com/katieashleyluv

➜ PINTEREST: pinterest.com/katieashleyluv

Made in the USA
Columbia, SC
06 July 2019